The Forgotten House

Helen Goltz

Atlas Productions

For Albert Watson,
who served in the Air Force
in WW2 as a marine navigator and
in the occupation forces in Japan.
My grandfather.

Chapter 1

Today ...

Frank Theroux hanged himself in the front room of Autumn Manor. Rachael Price, along with everyone else in the town knew the story even though they didn't know his name. But that was a long time ago and the tale had become nothing more than an urban myth by the time Rachael was born.

Rachael felt her grandmother's slender hand upon her own wrist; weightless and bony.

'This is it, dear,' Carrie said pointing to the derelict mansion.

'The ghost house!' Rachael exclaimed. 'You want me to stop at the ghost house! Why?'

'I want to see something,' Carrie said. 'And I want to show you something.'

They were on their way to the Rose Café for lunch; it was a tradition. Every Sunday Rachael collected her eighty-nine-year-old grandmother from the aged persons' home, inaptly named Hope Town, and dressed in their Sunday best, they enjoyed a light lunch of sandwiches, a shared scone with strawberry jam and cream and a cup of tea at the quaint café with its chintz curtains and Wedgwood tea cups. Rachael would miss it one day; miss her grandmother, but it was best not to think about that day yet.

She pulled the car over to the side of the road.

'The ghost house,' she muttered.

Carrie chuckled. They sat in silence for a few moments staring at what was now just the shell of a house. Rambling: that was the best word to describe Autumn Manor as it slowly edged its way ever closer to the town or rather the town, as it developed, edged its way closer to the manor's former boundaries.

Rachael leaned toward her grandmother and looked at the house through the passenger window. She shuddered; the place still gave her the creeps even though she hadn't been near it for years. It was part of her developing neighbourhood as a child. The brand-new estate except for this large, locked up house on multiple blocks of land. It was imposing, scary, and fun to ride by really fast on a pushbike with her friends, while scaring each other with stories.

Rachael remembered crossing to the far side of the road to pass the house on her way to and from school, and all the dares from the neighbourhood kids to run up the front steps, look in the window and run back. Once, she ran as far as the huge oak tree in the front yard, tapped it and ran back to her waiting friends. That scored her a Curly Wurly chocolate bar and the respect of a lot of her peers; it was worth it. But Christopher Harris was the champion. Ten years old, sporty and cocky, he held the record for lasting longest at the window, until one winter's day when he swore that he saw something; someone was looking back at him through the window and after that no amount of calling him 'chicken' would make him take to those steps again.

'It must have been quite something in its day,' Rachael said lowering the car windows. She turned off the ignition; a warm, spring breeze drifted in.

While her grandmother stared at the dilapidated old mansion, Rachael tried to read Carrie's expression; whimsical, sad, melancholy?

Rachael returned to studying the house. It wasn't quite as scary as it had been when she was a child. But even on reduced land, Autumn Manor was enormous by today's standards: the sweeping terrace framed by chipped masonry, specks of the original paint still noticeable in less weathered areas; the stone steps, cracked and in some places, missing altogether; glass window panes held together with newspaper and masking tape. Only the imposing entrance doors still had their stained glass panels fully intact. The property was now surrounded by a large wire fence, sparing the kids of today the challenge of the 'chicken' game.

'Sad, really,' Rachael said.

'What's that, dear?' Carrie asked.

'It's sad that it's abandoned. That nobody has restored it or taken pride in ownership of it.'

'It is disappointing. How could anyone let such a grand dame just fall into ruin?'

'I wonder who owns it,' Rachael mused. 'There must be a family member who refuses to sell it, otherwise it would have been snapped up by now.'

'I understand that it belongs to a charity; some charity that obviously doesn't see the value in maintaining it,' Carrie sighed. She opened the car door.

'Where are you going?' Rachael asked, alarmed.

'Just to the fence,' Carrie said and began to get out of the car.

Rachael opened her door and ran around to help her grandmother out. They walked to the fence and Carrie laced her fingers through the wire.

'There's a lot less land …'

'They must be selling it off piece-by-piece,' Rachael suggested.

'It was once so grand, the gardens and parks … acres and acres of it and inside …,' Carrie waved her hand around.

'You've been in the house?' Rachael's eyes widened. 'You mean to tell me that this is the house you are always talking about when you tell me about going to the balls … this house, the ghost house?'

'Oh yes. I spent a lot of time at this house,' Carrie confirmed.

'But you always talk about a grand house; you never said it was the ghost house.'

'But it wasn't the ghost house then. You probably only remember it being like this, well, in slightly better condition when you were a child than it is now, I imagine. But in my day, it was indeed grand. This road wasn't here of course; you would drive for a mile to reach the house. Autumn Manor once seemed such a long way from the town, but now it is practically on its doorstep.' She sighed. 'We often saw deer wandering on the estate; the grounds were always so well kept. Where this road is now was a fish pond.' Carrie laughed at the memory. 'Not a fish pond like you see these days, but a lake that was stocked with trout if I remember correctly … well, some kind of fish.'

'You mean like in the old days when they hunted on the country estates, but in this case they came to fish?'

'Yes, like those old days.' Carrie smiled at her granddaughter. 'They came to fish and to shoot.'

'Shoot for what?'

'Pheasant.'

'Pheasant? Sounds horrible, those poor pheasants.' Rachael wrinkled her nose and then instinctively rubbed it—conscious of not contributing any new wrinkles to her face; she was turning twenty-nine this year, too close to thirty for her liking.

'We always ate what was shot; it wasn't just sport,' Carrie continued, 'but I guess these days it does sound frivolous. But the grounds, they were breathtaking. And inside, oh the inside Rachael my dear was grand indeed. Autumn had such good taste.'

'Is that a name or a season?' Rachael fidgeted and turned her back on the house.

'Autumn was the former lady of the house; her real name was Audrey, I believe.' Carrie looked skywards as she thought. 'Yes, Audrey. 'But everyone called her Autumn. Of course, she was Mrs. Theroux to us. She was a lovely lady and knew how to keep a house. But she died when I was about thirteen or fourteen. In retrospect, she must have been quite young herself, but then, when I was young, everyone over thirty seemed old,' Carrie shrugged. 'I can remember her passing, it was quite a shock, she had been ill as I recall. The house was named in her honour.'

Carrie paused, and then continued, painting pictures in the air with her hands. 'Oh and the house was grand. Inside, there was a polished timber staircase that seemed to rise forever and some of the most beautiful furnishings you have ever seen: ornate gilt mirrors, Georgian cabinets and Empire chaises with the most intricate carved detail. Not that we appreciated that at the time my dear, that's all we ever knew. But now I am of an age where I can appreciate the beauty of those pieces.'

'I get that,' Rachael agreed. 'I appreciate any furniture that doesn't come in a box with instructions.'

Carrie laughed. She continued to stare at the house. 'Oh, and the fireplaces …,' she began again, 'the fireplaces were so ornate. They were rumoured to have been brought in from France especially for the estate. They had little gilt cherubs on each side.' Carrie smiled. 'Funny I should remember that. Lexie and I had too many champagnes here on several occasions.'

'Grandma, you were a wild child!' Rachael teased.

Carrie laughed. 'I don't think so. We were fairly conservative really; it was a different time.' Carrie looked at her granddaughter. 'In those days, women did what their fathers or husbands told them to do; we were somewhat reliant on men, not like you independent young things today.'

Rachael scoffed. 'There's a price for independence … it's called a mortgage and a car loan. As for being young, I barely remember it,' she said, her hand instinctively touching her neck.

'Twenty-eight is not old my dear, not when you are nearing ninety!' Carrie touched Rachael's face and then dropped her hand and returned her gaze to Autumn Manor. 'Your Aunty Lexie was an independent one though. She took on Father all the time and often got her way. Very brave really. In fact, if it hadn't been for the war, Lexie would have been the lady of this manor—I wanted that as well, but it wasn't to be. We both loved coming here.'

'What? How?' Rachael exclaimed, wheeling around to face the house again. 'What was our family's connection to it?'

'Our connection to it was such a long time ago, heavens, all those years. A long story for another time perhaps,' she said. 'I wonder sometimes if I imagined it.'

Rachael smiled. 'I can imagine it. I can picture it in its heyday.' She twirled around, swishing an imaginary skirt. 'Beautiful people lounging on the terrace balancing cocktail glasses, girls with fashionable hair, silk dresses and furs, men in black tie, dapper and charming. A bit like *The Great Gatsby*.'

'Yes, yes, it was a little like that …' Carrie smiled as she watched Rachael. 'We're not in a hurry today are we?'

'We've got all day, Gran. What did you want to show me?' Rachael turned to go back to the car.

'No, it's here, dear.' Carrie's voice betrayed her excitement. 'What I want to show you is here.' Carrie walked around the fence towards the side of the house. Rachael hurried to join her.

'Gran, you're not going in are you?'

Carrie turned. 'Why yes. Are you coming?'

Rachael looked at her grandmother, the house, the car and back to her grandmother.

'But, Gran, it's … haunted!'

Carrie laughed. 'Rachael, you don't believe that do you?'

'But, it's fenced off. We're not supposed to go in.'

'I'm surprised an intrepid reporter like yourself hasn't already been in.' Carrie turned and continued to walk along the fence. 'Come on, we can get through that opening there.' Carrie pointed to a break between two fence structures. 'I'm game if you are.'

'It can't be safe.' Rachael continued doing her best to avoid going near the house.

'So? A bit of danger is good for you. I survived the war, my dear, so I should be fine in this house.' She squeezed through the opening in the fence and turned to look at Rachael. 'Don't make me call you chicken,' she called back.

'Gran, you're wicked sometimes,' Rachael chuckled.

'If your mother was here, she would have beaten me to the front steps. She was such an adventurer. God bless her soul.'

Rachael went through the fence and followed her grandmother.

'And I'm nothing like her?' Rachael asked.

'On the contrary. I see her in you all the time. Sometimes, it takes my breath away.' Carrie waited for Rachael and took her hand. 'Come on, I want to show you something.'

'Inside the house?' Rachael looked up at it in dread.

'No. Behind it.'

*****

Rachael went ahead of her grandmother to knock back the weeds and hanging branches as they made their way towards the back of the house.

Her heart was beating fast. She shuddered and turned to see Carrie's face was lit with excitement. Rachael shook her head.

'What if we see a ghost hanging in the front window?' Rachael asked.

'Well we'll get a fright, dear, I imagine.'

Rachael laughed and watched as her grandmother went past her, down the side of the house. As they neared the back, Carrie stopped and clapped her hands together.

'What?' Rachael came quickly to her side. She turned her eyes to see what her grandmother was staring at and saw them. Hundreds of bluebells; a bluebell carpet covering the remaining half-acre of the property behind the house.

'The bluebells,' Carrie whispered. 'I remember them so well. Every spring, for just a few weeks. I can't believe they are still here.'

'Breathtaking,' Rachael agreed. She followed her grandmother as she waded through them, her hands touching the delicate bells.

Carrie turned to Rachael. 'Thank you, dear, I really wanted to see them again.'

'I can understand why,' Rachael said taking in the sea of blue and violet. As they walked around them and through them, touching the petals and admiring the carpet of blue flowers. Rachael turned back to look at the house. A large black crow was perched on the roof.

'You have to tell me the real story of this house, Gran, and don't say it's just a place you went to for a few dances and parties. Now that you've let the cat out of the bag and told me that I could have been living here, that this might have been my inheritance.'

Carrie laughed. 'True, but if Lexie had had children, then you would have been in a queue to own Autumn Manor.'

'It means more to you than you're letting on, doesn't it?'

Carrie shrugged. 'When you are my age, you get sentimental about the past. There's not much remaining of the property and I had been dreaming of the bluebells … wondering if they were still here.'

'But who's planting them? Why is the garden blooming and the house falling down?' Rachael frowned.

'You didn't inherit a green thumb my dear, don't worry, neither did I. They're perennials. If they get water and the right conditions, they'll just keep coming up year after year. They spread even if you don't maintain them, which is what has happened here. But I can't believe they are still so profuse. It's truly magical, perhaps the charity group did maintain them for a while,' she sighed.

Rachael looked around; despite the beauty of the bluebells, the lawns were long, weeds had overrun the path, and two of the windows on the top floor were broken.

'It's still creepy, Gran,' Rachael shuddered. She held up her arm. 'See, it gives me goose bumps.' She tugged her sleeves down over her arms. "Well, we're dressed for lunch, Gran, so I think we should go and you should tell me everything, and I mean everything, over a cup of tea. Shall we?'

'Indeed, we shall.' Carrie allowed Rachael to lead her back towards the side of the house and through the weeds and branches to the front.

Stopping for a moment to stare at the house, Rachael said, 'You know the rumour is that the rope that the old man used to hang himself is still tied to the beam in the front room.'

Carrie scoffed, 'Oh Rachael, how old are you?'

Rachael shrugged. 'Ten again. That's what they used to say when we were kids and I still remember it to this day, Christopher Harris in prep school swore on a stack of bibles that he saw the rope and saw someone—maybe the man who hanged himself.'

'Frank,' Carrie said.

'Frank. Frank who?' Rachael's interest was piqued. 'Was he the one who held the dances? Must have had some money; why would you hang yourself if you owned this?'

Rachael saw Carrie flinch.

'Sorry, Gran, I don't mean to disrespect the past.'

'Thank you, my dear. Come on then, we'll have a look for ourselves.' Carrie started towards the front steps and the window.

Rachael gasped. 'No, I'm not going up there.'

Carrie turned back, exasperated. 'Chicken!'

Rachael's mouth dropped open and then she laughed. 'Right then.' She marched past her grandmother and up the front steps and then she stopped.

She heard Carrie coming up the steps behind her.

'Go on, put an end to that rumour forever,' her grandmother encouraged.

Rachael looked at the front window to her left – one of the few that was still intact. She couldn't see in; the glass was reflecting a tree in the front yard. She took a step towards it and then turned back to Carrie who waited at the top step.

'You're not coming with me?'

'I know that there's no rope there and I know it's not haunted,' Carrie smiled.

'Hmm,' Rachael all but snorted. She turned back to the window and took another few steps towards it. Standing directly in front of it now, she could hear her heart beating. With an apprehensive glance around her, Rachael stepped forward, cupped her hands and looked inside before quickly stepping back.

'I did it!'

Carrie laughed. 'And?'

'No rope. No ghost. Let's go.' She hurried towards the front steps and past her grandmother, hearing Carrie's soft laughter behind her.

Ducking back through the fence and reaching the car first, Rachael unlocked it and held the passenger door open for her grandmother. As she waited for Carrie to lower herself into the car, Rachael asked, 'So did Frank really hang himself in that room?'

'Yes, Frank was the man who hanged himself in that very room. It was a sad, sad day,' Carrie said.

'Really? Why did he do it? I thought it was a myth.'

Carrie tucked her dress by her side, looked up at Rachael and nodded, giving her permission to close the car door. Rachael walked around the back of the car to the other side, slid into the driver's seat and fastened her seat belt.

'So did you personally know Frank?' Rachael asked.

'Yes and I knew his son, James.'

'Why did he do it?' Rachael continued to rattle off questions. 'What happened to James then?'

'James … James was in love with Lexie, they got married."

'Ah-ha! So this house belonged to your … brother-in-law! Why did he give it to charity? How come you never told me this before? How come Mum didn't mention it? I think you should start from the beginning, Gran, and tell me everything.' Rachael started the car and leaned over one last time to look at the house with a new interest.

Carrie sighed. 'My dear your imagination runs away with you. Yes, James was my brother-in-law ever so fleetingly.'

'Why fleetingly? Did Aunty Lexie ever live here then? Am I wearing you out?' Rachael smiled.

Carrie laughed. 'Questions, questions and more questions.'

Rachael drove away from Autumn Manor.

'You need to understand that it was a different time and I was a different person when Autumn Manor was in its heyday,' Carrie sighed. 'I was selfish, conceited, young and full of my own importance. I didn't realise the value of my sister and what she meant to me.'

Rachael nodded. 'Does anyone really value their family until they are grown up? When you're a kid, it's all about fun and games, mealtimes and who your best friend is that day—that's about it.'

'That's very true,' Carrie agreed. 'And in those days it was still very important for a woman to find a suitor and to get married too. Well, that was before the war changed everything and Autumn Manor began her decline.'

Chapter 2

1939 ...

Frank Theroux and his son, James, stood on the terrace, looking out over Autumn Manor's manicured grounds. Soon hundreds of guests would be arriving through the imposing iron gates, traipsing across the gardens, dancing by the fountain and possibly even swimming in it. For now, it was peaceful.

Frank Theroux closed his eyes and breathed in deeply—the air offered a heady mix of freshly cut grass and pungent roses, carried by the slightest breeze—it was promising to be a perfect evening. The only sounds that could be heard were the splash of water fowl on the lake and the occasional stray musical note floating across the grounds as a ten-piece band set up their instruments.

The house was ready for the evening's party; champagne flutes were lined up on tables adorned with well-pressed white tablecloths and small lights decorated the pillars and trees, ready to sparkle as night encroached. Inside, through the French doors and across the waxed floors, the kitchen buzzed with staff busily preparing food.

Frank Theroux opened his eyes and greeted the groundskeeper

as he walked towards them, his arms laden with long-stemmed white roses.

'Everything looks perfect, Kenneth; I don't think the grounds have ever looked as good,' Frank leaned against the balustrade and surveyed his domain.

'Thank you, Mr. Theroux. We're ready for tonight … everything that should be trimmed is trimmed and the lake is full of trout in case you want to invite a few guests to stay on and fish tomorrow.' He looked down at the roses. 'I promised Mrs. Atkinson that I would bring some roses up for the entrance vases.' As he spoke, the housekeeper, Mrs. Atkinson, bustled out and clapped her hands.

James smiled. 'White roses, Mum's favourite.'

'Ay,' Kenneth nodded. 'A hybrid tea rose … I named this one *Autumn Rose* in your mother's honour. Beautiful scent, the perfect rose.'

'Beautiful.' James agreed.

'Come on, come on, I have a party to organise.' Mrs. Atkinson took the roses from Kenneth's hands and shushed him along. 'Get off my terrace, Kenneth, you're trailing dirt.'

'Yes ma'am,' he barked with a salute and back tracked down the steps.

Frank Theroux laughed. 'That's why you are in charge Mrs. Atkinson! Thank goodness for you and Kenneth, what would we do without you, hey James?'

'Oh go on.' Mrs. Atkinson blushed with delight and disappeared back into the house, her arms full of roses.

Frank Theroux lowered himself into a chair. He wanted to put his feet up, but with a glance at Mrs. Atkinson arranging roses in the hallway, he thought better of it. James dropped down into the chair beside him.

There was a striking similarity between the men; shared angular faces, towering height and dark hair, although Frank's hair was more grey these days. There was equally as much of Autumn in James; his mother's features reflected in his fuller mouth, light blue eyes and compassionate nature.

'Suppose we should dress soon,' Frank said.

'Suppose so.'

They sat in silence. Eventually, Frank spoke.

'So, son, are you still intending to do it tonight?'

James smiled and turned to his father. 'Yes, I am.'

Frank nodded, a slow smile crossing his weathered face. He had aged since Autumn's passing, almost six years ago now, and loss of weight had contributed to his gaunt look. Still, the church auxiliary ladies persisted in dropping off casseroles for him, much to Mrs. Atkinson's chagrin. 'As if I'm not feeding you enough', she would exclaim, seeing right through their actions. 'They're looking for a husband, Mr. Theroux, mark my words, you be careful.' He would laugh and promise not to marry anyone without running it by her first.

Frank studied his son.

'Does Alexandra know?'

James nodded. 'Lexie and I have spoken. She knows I'm going to propose, she just doesn't know when. She knows I asked her father and he said no. But … I want her and she wants to marry me. What do we do?'

Frank looked at his son. 'Good question, what do you do? Well, you have my support, you know that and I hear Alexandra has a mind of her own, so I suspect she'll decide not her father.'

James laughed. 'Yes, thank God she does and thanks Dad, thanks for supporting us.'

Frank continued. 'I personally don't care if we offend Taylor.

It's a long life without love, James, and yes, you can grow to love someone or at least learn to happily co-habitate with someone, but why? Why not marry for love if you can?'

'It may mean she'll be disinherited,' James said.

Frank shrugged. 'I don't think you two will want for anything.' He glanced around at the estate. 'Alexandra is a lovely girl; she has her mother's charm and manners. Shame that Taylor's so set on pushing her towards Howell's son—he's a nice lad, Anson, but a bit of a peacock. I wouldn't have thought he had enough up top for Alexandra.'

'Unlike me.' James agreed.

Father and son laughed.

'Yes, you intellectual giant.' Frank teased him. 'At least you have a profession and some ambition, even though I would have liked you to have gone into the family business instead of journalism,' he said with a wink. It was an old discussion that Frank Theroux liked to thread into the conversation every now and then.

'I never thought about the family business …' James teased.

'Hmm! Regardless, I'm sure if your mother was alive, she'd have something to say to Alexandra's mother about the proposed forced marriage. They were good friends.'

James agreed. 'Lexie doesn't see herself as Mrs. Anson Howell but I think her mother wants to keep the peace and just wants Lexie to do what she's told and make all their lives easier!'

Frank nodded again. 'Taylor can't be easy to live with.'

The men, both the silent type, sat and looked out over the grounds.

Mrs. Atkinson's young housekeeping assistant, Miss Evelyn, stepped onto the terrace balancing a tray of iced tea and biscuits.

'Excuse me, sir, um, sirs, tea?'

Frank Theroux accepted the glass. 'Thank you, Evelyn, how thoughtful when you are so busy.'

'Pleasure, sir.' She reddened.

He raised his voice slightly. 'I hope you'll manage to sneak a glass of champagne or two for yourself tonight, Evelyn. You can blame me if Mrs. Atkinson catches you in the act,' he said with a glance inside towards Mrs. Atkinson.

'I heard that, Mr. Theroux,' Mrs. Atkinson called out.

Evelyn giggled. 'Thank you, sir, I would love to. Everyone's so pleased you're holding the ball again, sir.' Leaving a tray of biscuits, she hurried back inside.

James grinned at his father.

'What?' Frank asked.

'Nice one. You have them all wrapped around your little finger.'

Frank sipped his iced tea and sighed with satisfaction. 'I wasn't always so … pleasant. I learned from your mother that you catch more flies with honey than with vinegar.'

'What does that mean?' James picked a mint leaf out of his glass and cast it into the garden.

'It means I want to keep our staff happy and praising their efforts is a small thing. I'd hate to lose Kenneth or Mrs. Atkinson or any of their entourage. I know they get offers from other families. Besides, I can't imagine Autumn Manor without either of them. They've been here for as long as I have, we've all become part of the furniture.'

'That's why you've kept the same men in the manufacturing plant too, because you treat them well.'

'I've got a good foreman. He's fair and a good listener.' Frank jiggled the ice in his glass. 'Besides, everything is about to change … the next few months are going to be very interesting.'

'I know. Working at the paper, you can see it looming, but everyone seems to be in denial. The rumour is that Chamberlain is about to declare war.'

Frank nodded. 'Inevitable, I'd say; you can only negotiate with and appease a bully for so long before the time for action kicks in.'

James lowered his voice as Evelyn passed with drinks for the musicians. 'They say Poland will be the trigger and that may be sooner than we think. Hitler won't be able to help himself; he'll invade and then it will be war.'

'Maybe,' Frank agreed. 'Although no one lifted a hand to help Czechoslovakia, will they help Poland? Anyway, let the ladies go on believing the world is safe for a little while longer and let's just enjoy tonight. It's the end of the season, our last few warm days and this may well be our last ball here, ever.'

Both men sat in silence again. The prospect of James going to war hung in the air like a pressing weight.

James cleared his throat. 'So, how did you do it?'

'What?' Frank asked.

'Propose to Mum?'

Frank Theroux smiled, took a mouthful of iced tea and leaned back in his chair. He brushed a mark off his grey, pleated pants. 'I was just lucky. I don't know why she looked twice at me. Your mother was the life of the party; I swear at her debutante ball, every man in town was lining up to take her out. For some strange reason she decided on me. I could offer her a good life, but I was so quiet, I was never going to be much for company. But she used to laugh and say she could talk enough for both of us. Indeed she could.'

'So did you go down on bended knee?'

'Of course. As soon as I was sure that she was interested in me and there wasn't a better looking gent behind me whom she was smiling at, I marched over to her father's house, asked permission, then went out and bought the biggest diamond ring I could find.'

'Ah, doing all the right things,' James smiled.

'My mother, your grandmother, insisted I do it right. I got dressed up in my best suit—my only suit actually—and went back over there that evening with the ring in my pocket. I presented her with a huge bunch of flowers and asked for the honour of her hand in marriage. I promised her everything I could think of to persuade her to say yes.' Frank chuckled at the memory. He swallowed. 'I just hope I delivered. I hope she was happy, even though it was a shorter life than either of us imagined we'd have together.'

Frank looked away, swirling the remaining ice in his glass in an agitated manner. He finished his drink and leaned forward in his chair.

'I tell you what though, son, you were the pride and joy of her life. She would be so thrilled with your choice of Alexandra. This house needs a woman's touch again and I can't think of a better choice.'

'Thanks, Dad.'

'Be wary. Your proposal is going to cause a war—and I'm not talking about the one that's already brewing—a war between the Taylor and Theroux families and between father and daughter,' Frank said.

'I know. I'm ready for that; we both are.' James assured his father.

Frank frowned. 'Don't underestimate Samuel Taylor, James; that would be a big mistake.' He rose, stretched and tapped his son on the shoulder. 'Let's get dressed or the guests will be here while we're still sipping iced tea. Besides, I suspect you want to practise asking the big question?'

'No, I'm ready.' James rose.

Frank watched his son stride confidently into the house and then followed.

Chapter 3

'You look stunning, both of you.' Moira Taylor clapped her hands together as she watched her daughters preen in front of the large gilt mirror in Carrie's bedroom. The curtains moved slightly and Moira lifted her head to enjoy the faint scent of jasmine on the breeze as she sat in the bay window admiring her two daughters.

'Ah to be young and beautiful again with your whole future before you.' A look of sadness passed over her face.

Lexie looked at her mother. 'Mother you are one of the most stunning women I have ever seen! I bet with that tiny waist, you can still fit into your wedding dress.'

'And you snatched one of the most eligible men in the country,' Carrie laughed. 'Even if it was a hundred years ago!'

'Yes, well thank you Carrie, it wasn't that long ago but yes, I guess it was a well-matched marriage.' Moira Taylor added under her breath. She changed the subject. 'Noella has done a beautiful job with your hair; very elegant.'

'Thank you, ma'am.' Noella stood back. 'I think that might be it.' She took a mirror and held it behind Carrie, who turned sideways, and front again.

'Lovely,' Carrie admired her pinned-up, gold-toned hair and the loose ringlets that enhanced her neck. 'Thank you, Noella.'

'Pleasure, ma'am.' Noella gathered the brushes to clean them and left the room.

'You have lovely hair.' Lexie admired Carrie. 'It does what you tell it to do; you are lucky. Mine is so unruly.'

'You have my hair, Lexie,' Moira Taylor said. 'Thick and a little hard to manage, but it looks lovely tonight.' She studied her brunette daughter. 'Now Alexandra, tell me you don't intend to do anything rash tonight?'

'You're in trouble, Alexandra!' Carrie laughed, emphasising her mother's use of Lexie's full name.

'What would you consider as rash?' Lexie asked. She lowered herself next to her mother on the window seat of the bay window, fanning her dress out before her.

'You know what I'm talking about.' Moira Taylor remained serious.

'Like eloping!' Carrie exclaimed, continuing to preen in front of the mirror.

'Good Lord, no! Nothing like that. For heaven's sake, tell me you are not thinking of eloping?' Moira began to fan herself.

Lexie gave Carrie a wry look. 'Of course I'm not intending to elope. The thought never crossed my mind.'

'Well that's a relief. Carrie, stop giving your sister ideas.' Moira stood and moved to face both of her daughters. 'I know that James Theroux came to see your father and asked for your hand in marriage. I also know that your father refused.'

Lexie clenched her jaw.

'If he should propose to you tonight, Alexandra, it is your family duty to say no.'

Lexie scoffed. 'Family duty? It's not Victorian times for goodness sake. It's 1939! Aren't arranged marriages just a little bit old hat? I'm sorry to tell you Mother, but people marry for love nowadays.'

'It's not just an arranged marriage, it's a forced marriage,' Carrie chipped in.

Moira shook her head. 'Anyone would think that you might be a little excited about the prospect of being betrothed to one of the most eligible and handsome bachelors in the land.'

'I am excited about that prospect. I just have a different bachelor in mind.' Lexie shot back. She turned and looked defiantly out of the bay window.

Moira continued. 'Anson is a good young man, you will grow to love him and …'

'I don't want to grow to love him.' Lexie wheeled around, her eyes filling with tears. 'Mother, I don't wish to defy you or Father, but surely you can understand that I am in love with someone else; someone who is perfectly suitable.' Lexie moved closer to her mother. She held her hands. 'Please talk to Father.'

The two women looked like mirror images of each other.

Moira Taylor shook her head. 'I'm sorry but I can't. He is adamant about this. The future is uncertain and he considers this arrangement to be the best thing for both of our families. You could do a lot worse than Anson.'

'I agree with Mother,' Carrie said.

Lexie looked at her sister's reflection in the mirror. 'Of course you do, Carrie. Then why don't you marry Anson? He's not a great intellect and he likes a bit of preening, you would go well together.'

'Girls, please.' Moria shook her head.

Lexie turned back to face her mother. 'But that's a solution to the problem, Mother, Carrie and Anson can marry and that will protect both families' interests just as well.'

'You know that's not what your father wants.'

'I don't want that either!' Carrie exclaimed.

'But it achieves the same purpose,' Lexie stated.

'Your father wants his elder daughter to marry Anson, as agreed.'

'Agreed by whom?' Lexie asked.

'Let's face it,' Carrie cut in. 'Father wants his business-minded daughter to marry the heir apparent so both fortunes are protected. He thinks I'm flighty,' she turned around in a huff. 'Do you think this pink-coloured dress makes me look too young? Lexie's dress is a much more sophisticated colour … maybe I should change.'

'What would give him the impression that you are flighty I wonder, Carrie?' Moira Taylor rolled her eyes. 'Perhaps a lack of concentration in regard to the subject at hand or running away from boarding school for a week in order to discover who you really are, or the phase when you were going to be a poet and never marry or …'

'All right, all right, I was young,' Carrie shot back, finally turning away from the mirror.

'You were seventeen. It was only last year.' Lexie reminded her. 'But still, Carrie has a point. We all have big dreams for a while and if Carrie shows a keen interest in the business, then maybe…'

'Oh but the business is so boring.' Carrie rolled her eyes.

'Hmm.' Moira gave Lexie a knowing look.

'You're not helping yourself.' Lexie frowned at Carrie.

'I'm not helping you, don't you mean? I don't want to marry Anson. He's going to be twenty-one in four months' time and then he's proposing to you. He's nearer your age. I want you to stop looking at James and hurry up and marry Anson so that James notices me—we discussed all this.'

'Don't tell me you want James Theroux too?' Moira snapped.

Lexie glared at Carrie.

'Yes,' Carrie piped in. 'He was my friend first.'

'You know only too well, Mother, that if Anson wasn't on the scene, Father would be pushing me towards James and would be over at Autumn Manor doing business deals with Mr. Theroux,' Lexie said.

'Well, maybe, but it's not the case. So resign yourself to the fact that in a few months' time, you will be engaged to Anson Howell,' Moira said.

Lexie leapt up from the bay window. 'Resign myself to marrying a man I don't love and don't want to be with to keep you and Father happy?'

'For the sake of your family,' Moira added. 'For your family's future.'

'You know very well, Mother, our family fortune would be just as safe if I married James. This is all about deals done and Father giving his word.' Lexie's voice wavered. 'It's a shame he doesn't care a little more for my happiness than he does for his friendships.'

'That's not true, Alexandra, he loves you.'

'Did you marry for love, Mother? Were you truly in love with Father or did you do your duty?' Lexie asked.

'What a silly question.' Moira said and looked away.

Chapter 4

Dressed in full evening attire, James and Frank Theroux cut impressive figures as they stood framed in the doorway of Autumn Manor. One after the other, a fine collection of automobiles made their way up the long driveway. The air was buzzing with the excitement of another ball at Autumn Manor in the last days of Summer. Standing beside his father, where his mother had once stood to greet their guests, James scanned every arrival for the only face he was interested in, that of Alexandra Taylor. He caught his father's amused look every now and then and frowned in return.

'She'll be here, she's a lady. You can't rush a lady,' his father said between greetings.

James sighed. 'What do they do in that dressing room? How long does it take to put on a dress and shoes?'

'It'll be worth it, mark my words,' Frank Theroux answered as he reached out to welcome the pastor making his way up the entrance steps.

'Grand evening for a gathering, Frank,' the pastor nodded.

'We couldn't have chosen better,' Frank agreed looking at how the colours of the estate were bathed in a golden glow as the evening light dimmed. He shook the pastor's hand and pointed out a few of his parishioners who had already arrived and were mingling inside. Frank returned to his post.

'Watch out,' James muttered as Millie Ashcroft, thin, lively and loud, alighted from a grand Alvis sports coupé.

'You watch out,' his father whispered. 'She's had her eye on you since you were five years old.'

James turned on the charm. 'What a lovely automobile, Millie.'

'How kind of you to say so,' she retorted with a smirk, 'but I don't like those cars with no top, it messes my hair,' she flattened down her red wavy hair to no avail. 'I don't see the need for fresh air while you are driving.'

'You look lovely, Millie, just splendid.' Frank greeted her, picking up the compliment that James had failed to give.

Millie's face softened. 'Thank you, Mr. Theroux, as do you. You both look splendid.' Her eyes lingered on James as she passed between the two gentlemen and headed in to the party.

James exhaled.

'Really, James, save the compliments for the ladies not the cars,' his father teased. 'Have I taught you nothing?'

James chuckled. 'Evidently not. Anyway, I can't get into any trouble if I compliment the cars. It is swish though.'

'Beautiful piece of machinery,' his father agreed. 'We'd better join the party now. We've been out here long enough and door duty is mostly done. No doubt you'll spot Alexandra when she arrives.' Frank turned to move inside.

Begrudgingly, James followed.

*****

Moira Taylor rose from her dressing table, satisfied with the results of her grooming. She glanced at an old timber jewellery box on the dresser, stopped and ran her hand over it. Opening the lid, she could smell the muskiness of the red velvet interior. She caught her reflection broken in three frames of mirror inside the lid. She ran a finger over a royal blue pouch and then gently lifted it. Untying the ribbon, she slid a large silver locket out onto her palm. It had been a while since she had opened the locket, but she was always conscious of it in the room.

She pried apart the two sides to find her own faded photo on one side. Years old now—I was a beauty, she conceded. On the other side was a handsome man in his early twenties with a charming smile that could still stop her heart. The man, this man, whom she had watched marry someone else was never far from her thoughts. The pain was still raw, even after all the years that had flown by since they spoke words of love to each other. But she had done her duty and her children would benefit from that.

*****

'Let's go!' Carrie exclaimed with impatience. 'You look lovely,' she told Lexie for the hundredth time.

'I'm coming.' Lexie turned one more time in front of the mirror. 'Go and hurry Mother up and stop bothering me. And order the car,' she called after her.

Lexie checked her appearance for the last time, left the room and descended the stairs. Her father paced at the bottom of the staircase.

Lexie braced, anticipating a lecture. 'Are you sure you won't come, Father?' she asked.

'I'm very sure, thank you. And Alexandra, I don't want your company monopolised tonight by that Theroux boy. Anson will be there and I expect you to be civil and to treat him with the respect that is due to a future husband. I want you back by …'

Lexie cut him off. 'Mother is with us. I'm sure we will be fine.'

He grunted a reply and strode off to his office.

Lexie sighed and called one more time to her sister and mother.

*****

James found himself wedged between Agnes Blake and Alice Wheatley, both single, and attractive young ladies. Agnes was flirting outrageously and was onto her third champagne by James' count while Alice was playing cool and aloof, which suited him fine. His eyes kept darting to the terrace, where he expected to see Lexie any minute.

'And so, James, will you enlist?' Alice asked.

'Alice how morbid you are,' her friend scolded. 'No talk of that tonight. Tonight is just for fun, don't you agree James?'

'Oh come, Agnes, we can't talk of balls and gowns all night. How very dull,' Alice sighed.

'Ladies, please excuse me,' James cut in. He saw Moira Taylor making her entrance through the open doorway, which meant Lexie should be right behind. 'Enjoy yourself tonight won't you?' he said not taking his eyes from the terrace.

Lexie was not with her mother. He went out across the terrace and down the front steps. He strode past the group at the fountain, avoiding a play fight with Edward Mann who did his best to dunk him, straightened his jacket and kept walking. He still could not see Lexie, so he turned back towards the house. His father had already ensconced Moira Taylor into a group and then James spotted Carrie as she wandered onto the terrace to

29

join a younger group trying the punch fruit mix and covertly adding a little champagne that they were not allowed to have.

He increased his pace and then he saw her; she entered the house alone, turned to laugh at a comment from the group Carrie was with and turned back, her eyes seemed to be seeking him out. His heart raced.

*****

The music began to swell—*Ain't We Got Fun*—Carrie hummed the tune as she sipped her drink on the terrace. A shrill of laughter distracted her; Carrie recognised the exaggerated attention-seeking laugh of its owner, Anna Howell.

Anna waved and Carrie returned the salutation. Surrounded by suitors, Anna, with her fashionable dark, wavy hair trailing over her shoulder and wearing a fitted, chiffon cream dress was riding it out as always, continuing to move in the right circles as if nothing had happened since the Great War. Her family was recession-proof, as was Carrie's. They would be sisters-in-law within the next year if Lexie did as she was told and married Anna's brother, Anson; it had been planned since their birth, although no one had foreseen the Great War would change everything. The family estates were being divided up and sold off with so many resultant smaller holdings appearing in their place.

Carrie thought about her future brother-in-law—Anson was charming, ambitious and wealthy. *Why couldn't Lexie be happy marrying Anson and keep her mitts off James!* Carrie stewed.

As a waiter passed, she reached for a glass of orange juice in a flute with a wedge of orange and mint perched on the rim. Carrie turned to look over the expansive gardens and saw him, James Theroux, at home in his grounds. He was walking towards her, smiling, aloof and striking: his bow tie already undone and loose around his neck, his dark unkempt hair falling over his eyes. Carrie sighed, struck by his handsomeness. *Mrs. Carrie Theroux, Mrs. James Theroux,* she rolled the words over her tongue and then she realised he wasn't smiling at her. Behind her Lexie had walked out onto the terrace. A light breeze lifted Lexie's dress and she smoothed it down with one hand and walked towards James, as he came quickly up the front steps.

He reached for her hand, leaned towards her and kissed her cheek, stopping only to take two glasses of champagne from a passing waiter and to hand one to Lexie.

'Alexandra', James raised his glass.

'James', she smiled and touched his glass with her own.

'I thought you would never arrive', James said. 'I thought your father might have forbidden it.'

Lexie smiled. 'I did get a departing lecture. But I saw on my arrival that you were in good hands', she nodded towards Agnes and Alice. 'So, I stopped to have a quick word with the Pastor. I'm sure you wouldn't have been short of company.'

'Ah, but you are wrong. I was wasting away, distracted, of no social value to the poor ladies at all.'

James turned noticing Carrie for the first time.

'Hello there, Carrie', he smiled. 'Well, well, the two beautiful Taylor girls, how lucky can a man be?'

'How lucky indeed', Lexie teased him.

'And beautiful in … what colour is that?' James admired Lexie's dress.

'Champagne.' Lexie twirled for his benefit. 'Mother says it is the fashionable colour of the season.'

'Well if it wasn't before, it is now', James assured her.

Carrie rolled her eyes and turned towards the sound of a

scream followed by a splash, the party had moved to the fountain. Turning back, she saw James still staring at Lexie.

'Now James,' Carrie attempted to distract him. 'You know my sister is forbidden fruit.'

Lexie laughed. 'Am I? Who told you that?'

'Your fiancé,' Carrie smirked.

Lexie looked at her unadorned hand. 'Mm, last time I looked, I was unattached.' She raised her eyes, challenging James. He smiled, took her hand and pressed it to his lips.

'We must do something about this naked hand.' He held her gaze with his intense blue eyes. 'What a vision you are.'

Lexie blushed and looked out across the lawn.

Carrie bristled. She wanted to scream, 'Lexie you have Anson. Go away, I want James. I knew him first, he was my friend first!'

Carrie knew she had lost him.

✳✳✳✳✳

James reached for Lexie's champagne glass and put it down on the table next to his own. 'Come for a walk with me? Carrie, please excuse us won't you?' He took Lexie's hand without waiting for a response from Carrie and led Lexie down the front steps.

Off to one side, James saw his father talking with one of the widows from their local church. He caught his eye and his father winked. She wouldn't be the only woman present at the party with the hope of becoming the next Mrs. Theroux and lady of the house.

They walked down the path, past the fountain where guests lolled in various stages of undress, past the rotunda where the band played *It's De-Lovely* and guests danced as if all was well in the world.

'Did I mention that you look stunning?' James cast a glance over Lexie's gown that moved fluidly around her with every step she took.

'I can't recall whether you said that to me or some other girl,' Lexie teased.

'Are there other girls here?' James looked around. 'I didn't notice.' He led Lexie off the path and through the green maze of Kenneth's trimmed hedges that dwarfed them. A timber bench overlooked the lake and the area was deserted; the party had not moved as far as the maze yet. James stopped, spun Lexie around and held her close to him.

He heard her gasp with surprise. James smiled and taking a loose strand of her hair between his fingers, moved the lock from her face. He touched her cheek and then cupped her petite face in his hands.

'Lexie, I can't see a future without you by my side.' He moved to kiss her. He could hear her short, sharp breaths but his eyes never left her lips until he felt the touch of them on his own; he closed his eyes and inhaled her scent, feeling the returned press of her lips on his.

James pulled away slowly, opening his eyes to look into hers. He dropped to one knee, took her small white hand and pressed it between his own. Looking up he smiled and spoke. 'Alexandra, you have my heart. Will you have all of me? Please do me the honour of being my wife? I offer you all I am and all I can be. I will do everything in my power to make you happy and for the rest of my days on this earth you will be loved and respected. Marry me?'

Lexie smiled as tears ran down her face.

'Yes,' she whispered, 'yes, I would be honoured to be your wife.'

James rose quickly and kissed her once again, holding her tightly before pulling away suddenly. He reached into his jacket pocket and pulled out a small red velvet box.

'I almost forgot,' he smiled. 'That naked hand needs to be adorned.'

Lexie laughed and watched as he turned the box towards her and opened it.

She gasped, her hands rushing to her cheeks.

'Oh James, it's stunning.'

'Then,' he said, taking out the ring and returning the empty box to his jacket pocket, 'it has found the perfect place to rest.' He reached for her left hand, and slipped the ring on to her engagement finger.

'Perfect,' he admired the large solitaire diamond that sparkled dramatically on her ring finger.

Lexie stared at the enormous ring and then returned her gaze to James. She leaned into him. 'I don't think I could be any happier than I am right now, ever.'

'Me neither, Mrs. Theroux-to-be.' He kissed her again.

Chapter 5

'I absolutely forbid it, do you hear me? I forbid it!' Samuel Taylor bellowed with such fury that the walls seemed to shake. His face flushed with anger, he grabbed Lexie by the shoulders and shook her.

Pulling away, Lexie put her hands behind her back, hiding the large engagement ring. She shuddered; her father was frightening when he was in a temper, but she refused to show him her fear. In the corner of the living room, she could see her mother hovering, ready to step in if needed but preferring not to share the wrath of her husband's tongue.

'I told Theroux that the answer was no.' Samuel Taylor stamped around the room stopping in front of his desk. 'But you, knowing full well my intentions, agree to marry him anyway.' He stopped yelling and standing within a few inches of her, his voice took on a threatening quality. 'Return the ring and tell him it is off.'

Lexie inhaled. 'I won't, Father. You will have to partner with Frank Theroux if you are so adamant about safeguarding our fortune. I don't want to anger or disobey you, but I can't just marry so that you will have a better bank balance.'

Samuel Taylor thudded his fist on his desk making Lexie and Moira jump. 'The needs of the family and my methods for securing our future are not for you to second guess. You are unaware of the humiliation you are causing me and this family. Howell is living up to our agreement, Anson is prepared to marry you and you treat this like a game. You should be proud to marry into that family. You will marry Anson Howell and you will return that ring to Theroux or else.'

Lexie cocked her head to the side. 'Or else what, Father?'

'Or else you will no longer be a member of this family!'

'No, Samuel.' Moira stepped forward. 'That will not happen.'

'Be quiet woman, did I ask for your opinion?'

'No, but you will have it.' Moira said.

Lexie saw her father bristle as he stood to full attention.

Moira Taylor moved between Lexie and her husband. She stood resolute at full height and spoke, her voice assertive.

'All these years I have been the dutiful wife to you, Samuel. I have supported your businesses, entertained your clients and raised your children, but need I remind you, that our wealth is largely from my side of the family and my daughters will not be disinherited from what rightfully belongs to them nor be sent away from their home. I'm sorry, but I am firm on that.'

Lexie could not believe what she was hearing. All this time, she thought her mother had married well when in fact it was her father who had secured a bright future for himself. She thought her father was going to explode; the colour of his face was bright red, his fists were clenched.

'I have worked hard since our marriage to ensure our financial future; it is my work, my contracts and my contacts that have maintained this lifestyle and increased the fortune we started with. Don't you ever forget that!'

'I agree,' Moira said. 'You are a fine businessman, you always were, which is why my father insisted I marry you.'

Samuel Taylor scoffed.

'Come Samuel, neither of us married for love,' Moira retorted. 'We did our duty.'

Lexie's eyes widened in surprise as she looked from her father to her mother. Samuel Taylor glared at Moira.

'Lexie has made a sensible choice, Samuel, and you know it. James is from a good family, he is worthy of her on many levels. The only issue here is your keeping face and that is not enough reason to force our daughter to live her life with a man she doesn't love. I could understand if James was penniless or …'

He turned and stomped from the room, slamming the door with such force that Lexie jumped.

Lexie and Moira did not move for a few seconds. Eventually, Lexie exhaled and sank into a large chair.

'Thank you,' she turned to her mother. She braced as she saw the door begin to open, but it was only Carrie hovering on the other side.

'Is it safe to come in?' Carrie looked around.

Lexie nodded.

Carrie opened the door and sidled in, dropping down on the couch next to her mother. She wrapped her feet inside her dress.

'You could hear that in town, I'm sure,' Carrie said in a hushed tone.

'It was never going to go well,' Lexie said. She looked down at her hand and saw the beautiful solitaire ring. 'But it was worth it. I'm sorry.'

Moira shrugged. 'It's done. It is something I should have done when I was your age.'

Lexie reached for her mother's hand.

'Oh yes. I was pressured to marry a family connection. Samuel's family were respectable and affluent, as was my own family. But not long after we married, Samuel's family lost all of their money in shipping. Our remaining fortune came from my side.'

'But why wouldn't you stand up for me before this?' Lexie exclaimed.

Moira rubbed her hands and placed them on her lap. 'Because, I wanted to keep the peace and I understand your father's motives even if I don't agree with them. From a purely business perspective it would have been ideal if you and Anson had willingly partnered.'

'I'm sorry,' Lexie said, 'but that was never going to happen. I think when we were about thirteen I might have been happy to be paired with Anson ... but not since then.'

Carrie rose and went and sat on the arm of Lexie's chair. Taking Lexie's hand, Carrie studied the ring.

'Beautiful.'

Lexie smiled up at her. 'Breathtaking isn't it? The happiest night of my life. Before I came home that is.'

'I'm surprised James didn't come with you. Not very heroic of him,' Carrie stated.

'Oh he wanted to, he insisted on it. Even his father was prepared to come, but I wouldn't allow it. It would have only have made matters worse.' Lexie rubbed her forehead.

'I think that was the right decision,' Moira agreed. 'But you know girls, let me share something with you. I'm old enough to know that there is no secret formula for success in relationships. Some of us marry for love, some for business reasons and some out of desperation. There's no guarantee that any couple will live happily ever after, but it is promising to start with a happy foundation.'

Moira Taylor dropped her voice. 'I was banned from marrying

the man I loved, Patrick. There, I've said it,' she whispered to herself. 'Patrick. He married eventually, but died in a hunting accident before his thirtieth birthday. Your father was handsome and a good man. He had great business acumen and as I said, it was what my father wanted.' Moira sighed. 'I had little choice.'

'Not much has changed,' Lexie muttered.

'No.' Moira rose and tightened her silk robe around herself as though warding off a chill ever present in her husband's presence. 'You might have won this round, Lexie, but I know your father only too well. We haven't heard the last of this matter.'

Chapter 6

Carrie flicked a stone across the stream. It skipped twice, breaking the glass-like surface of the water before sinking.

'Not bad.' Lexie settled herself on a flat rock that held the sun's warmth and was partly shaded by a canopy of trees. She closed her eyes and inhaled the sweet smell of the earth and trees.

'James taught me how to skip stones; he gets at least four skips. I'm not that good yet,' she waded through the ankle deep water, holding up her skirt.

Lexie studied Carrie as she spoke of James.

Perhaps she really does love him, more than I have given any consideration to, Lexie thought.

She watched Carrie swipe several leaves off a nearby rock and sit down, extending her legs in front of her and raising her skirt to feel the sun on her skin.

Lexie removed her shoes and put her feet into the cool water. Scooping some water up in her cupped hands, she took a sip before wiping her wet hands over the back of her neck. She sat and stared at the stream for a while before speaking.

'Carrie, about James …'

'Yes.' Carrie looked over at her, 'About James.'

Lexie cleared her throat. 'Are we both in love with him?'

Carrie squinted at her sister. 'Maybe. Can I ask you something?'

'Of course.' Lexie invited.

'Aren't you even remotely in love with Anson?'

Lexie sighed. 'You know I'm not. You should put yourself in my shoes, Carrie. If Father was forcing you to marry Anson and you had feelings for James, what would you do?'

'I do have feelings for James!' Carrie said.

'Fine. Then how would you feel if Father insisted that you marry Anson?'

'I guess, if I knew I was always meant to marry Anson, I wouldn't have developed feelings for James in the first place,' Carrie retorted.

'You can't turn your feelings on and off like a tap,' Lexie said. 'I love James. It's not a game, I love him. How could I wake up next to Anson every morning, aching for James and wondering where he is and who he is with?' Lexie put her hand on her chest, 'I couldn't bear it. Can't you at least support me? It's hard enough fighting the battle with Father without having to fight alone.'

'But this is about more than just you,' Carrie said. 'Besides, you liked Anson well enough before James came to your attention.'

Lexie sighed. 'I liked Anson in my younger years, yes, but so did every girl who was taken by a handsome face and a bit of charm, we were children! None of us was thinking long-term! The Theroux family is as well placed financially as the Howells. It's because Father's made a big man of himself and now he's being defied by his daughter.'

'Well, I've seen James as a potential husband for years, from when we used to come here to swim … my potential husband!'

'But that's my point. You had a crush on him because you were young, like I had a crush on Anson when I was young. But now, well, Anson is so very …'

'Anson?' Carrie added and smiled.

The sisters exchanged looks and laughed.

'Yes,' Lexie agreed, 'he's so very Anson. And yes, I know he's good looking and a good catch, so he should easily find someone else, shouldn't he?'

'Hmm, tell that to Father,' Carrie dared her. 'He is not going to let those Howell pounds out of his sight.'

Lexie sighed. 'He can't force me to marry Anson. When I marry James, I will have my financial independence from Father.'

'Just for argument's sake, what if James withdrew his offer—would you marry Anson?' Carrie asked.

'No. I don't love him. I'm not marrying for financial reasons. We don't have to anymore Carrie, that was our mother's era and our grandmother's before that. We can get jobs. I could work.'

'At what?" Carrie asked. 'Being a lady?'

'I could tutor. I can sew or work in a shop.'

'Father would have a heart attack,' Carrie added.

'Then problem solved. He won't disinherit me, will he, because he's too scared of losing face. That's his biggest problem,' Lexie said with a smirk. She put her head back and closed her eyes again, feeling the last of the season's warmth on her face. She felt a warm breeze touch her skin and listened; nothing but the sound of the leaves whispering and the occasional bird.

Lexie smiled and opened her eyes. 'I love this spot.'

'Me too,' Carrie agreed. 'I love swimming here, completely naked.'

'Carrie, that's indecent!'

'Well I don't do it when anyone is around.'

'How do you know someone is not going to show up?' Lexie reached for her straw hat as though another layer of clothing compensated for Carrie's behaviour.

'You can hear them coming through the hedge,' Carrie said.

'Unless you are underwater,' Lexie reminded her.

'Then I suppose I would have to rely on their honour to look away while I dressed,' Carrie said defiantly. 'But I haven't been caught yet. Want to go in?'

'Naked?'

'Well you can leave your undergarments on Miss Prude if you like,' Carrie teased.

Lexie shook her head. 'Maybe later. The water is cold and I'm not hot enough yet. I'm not sure I'll be hot enough until next summer.'

Carrie lowered herself further down the rock to immerse her legs up to her knees. Lexie saw her shudder.

'Told you … it's freezing.' Lexie grinned.

'It's invigorating, it'll wake you up!'

'Do you love him?' Lexie asked, watching Carrie's eyes widen with surprise. 'It's not that I want to hurt you, sis,' she continued not waiting for a response. 'I'm not doing this to spite you. Do you really love James or is it just a crush?'

Carrie frowned. 'What's the difference?'

'I guess love is about the long-term. Would you still love him if he wanted different things than you—say he wanted you to be a certain type of person, or if he came home from the war with a missing limb, or he was moody most of the time?'

'But he's not,' Carrie interrupted.

'How do you know? How does anyone know, really? A crush is how you imagine it is going to be with him; the romance element might not be realistic. But I would never love Anson, really love him. When I see James or I am near him, it's powerful. When I'm not with him, he is all I think about, constantly. Do you think about James all day and night?'

Carrie kicked her feet in the water.

Lexie continued. 'But aside from the physical attraction we have for each other, we share the same outlook. We want similar things and it is not all about empire building. It's about security and family and even creativity. Anson could never understand a desire to write or create. He doesn't understand why James would pursue a career in journalism when the family business is there for the taking and would make more money.'

Carrie smiled. 'That's true. But this decision is not ours to make. It's James' decision. And he has picked you.' She threw a stone into the water; it sank without skimming the surface. Carrie began to take off her outer layer of clothing.

'The men are going away,' she stammered. 'Everyone is talking about it. There will be no dances and by the time the war is over, I'll be an old maid!'

'That's not true. We don't know what's going to happen in the future.'

'Marry James then, Lexie. You'll be disinherited despite what Mother said. You will break her heart and give Father a heart attack.'

'And what about you, Carrie, will I break your heart or will you stand by me?'

Carrie stood and removed the outer layer of her dress. She stared down into the water.

'Tell me Carrie, what do I do, what do we do?' Lexie persisted.

Carrie scoffed. 'What can we do? We're female.'

Carrie dived into the water; Lexie watched her disappear below the surface. She sighed and looked to the heavens.

'Tell me what to do?' She whispered. 'Send me a sign. Do I break my family's heart or do I break my own heart and James' along with it?'

Chapter 7

Samuel Taylor cut an imposing figure; rugged, tall and domineering. Born into money, married into money, successful in his own right and at home in his London Gentlemen's Club with its air of superiority and exclusive membership. He was early for his meeting with the Editor of the *Daily News*, the same newspaper that had both a London and a county edition, the same newspaper that a young James Theroux worked on; the boy trying to court his already spoken-for daughter, Lexie.

Not for long, stewed Taylor. *A sizeable donation should provide for a new position of foreign correspondent for the up-and-coming young journalist. Maybe even a war correspondent position,* Taylor smiled; a lot could be done with a little persuasion.

He saw the newspaper editor, Charles Robson, at the entrance, handing over his hat to the porter. Taylor studied him; Robson was well groomed, but vain, his eyes flicked around to see who was there and in whose company he would be seen.

Taylor smiled. *This will be a piece of cake,* he thought. *The man is sufficiently venal to be easily manipulated.*

Extinguishing his cigar, Taylor rose and extended his hand to the newspaper editor. Despite the immaculate suit and well-trimmed features, Robson couldn't mask the roughness of an old news hound; an ink and cigarette man. He would never have been admitted as a member of the Club had he not held the position of editor; he was no gentleman.

'Charles, good of you to come.' Taylor shook his hand.

'It's been too long, the Christmas party wasn't it?' Robson asked.

'At least. Shall we go in?' Taylor gestured to the dining room. As they passed tables discreetly obscured by ornate posts and ornaments, Samuel Taylor nodded and waved cordially at other members and guests. They were seated at Taylor's usual table.

'Dare I ask a news hound "what's news"?' Taylor asked.

Robson chuckled. 'Politics and war-talk and a bit more of both. But it's still early; some of our best stories don't hit the fan until just before deadline.'

They were seated with napkins in readiness. Taylor reached for the wine list. 'Red?'

'Please.' Robson read the menu.

Taylor could sense his hesitation.

'The duck is excellent here. Such a delicate dish to do well.'

'Duck it is,' Robson agreed. The waiter was there in an instant and gone just as quickly.

Taylor offered the editor one of his expensive cigars; Robson declined, pulling out one of his own cigarettes.

'Your lad, is he all right?' Taylor asked after the editor's son.

Robson shook his head. 'As far as we know, but how can one ever know for sure? He wanted to report in Europe. I'm dead against it as you can imagine, but he's a chip off the old block. How could I stop him? I envy you with two daughters and no sons to risk if the worst should happen …'

Taylor nodded. 'There's been many a time I've envied you. What I wouldn't give to have a son to run the empire.'

'You've got two bright girls in Alexandra and Carrie.'

'I'm not as liberal-minded as you, Charles. I expect them to marry well to keep the business going.'

Both men stopped talking as the waiter approached with the wine. Taylor nodded at the label, sampled it and nodded again. The waiter poured and left them.

'To a prosperous future,' Taylor toasted. They clinked glasses, smoked and sipped in silence for a few minutes.

'So how is business?' Robson leaned back, alternating between sipping his wine and puffing on the cigarette.

'Well I hate to say I may prosper from the potential of war but the buzz has been remarkably profitable for us; people are stocking up, businesses are reviewing how they trade and are open to new alliances. Did you hear I'm going after Theroux's contract when it's up for renewal?'

Robson nodded. 'I did hear that—word travels fast. You're partnering with Howell?'

'That's right.' Taylor nodded impressed with Robson's inside knowledge.

'Good luck,' the Editor continued. 'It's a huge manufacturing contract from what I hear and if war breaks out …'

'Precisely. Between you and me.' Taylor looked around, 'Howell Snr and I are fairly confident we have that one in the bag.'

Robson looked impressed. 'Hmm, well luck may not be needed after all. However, I hear Theroux's very much in favour with the board and he's doing a brilliant job, even ahead of schedule on delivery. Still nothing ventured …'

'Exactly. Speaking of Theroux, Charles, I want to speak with you about Theroux's kid,' Taylor cut to the chase.

Robson nodded. 'James.'

'Yes, nice enough young lad but it seems James and my Lexie have formed an … an attachment.'

'I thought Lexie and Howell's son were engaged,' Robson said. 'What's his name?'

'Anson.'

'Anson, that's it.' Robson frowned. 'Given Theroux's assets, I would have thought you'd be pleased about an alliance between his son and your daughter?'

Taylor extinguished his cigar. 'Yes, James is a promising lad, as is Anson, but I would prefer if Theroux's lad formed an attachment to my second born. I have plans for Lexie and they involve her marrying Anson—I gave my word on that many years ago. Carrie hasn't got the concentration span or temperament for my business but Lexie will be an asset and good support for Anson when he runs it.' Taylor stopped as the waiter delivered their meals. He sipped his wine before continuing.

'The two young people are not formally engaged yet—Anson is waiting until his twenty-first birthday to propose. Howell and I have had those kids partnered since the day they were born. It's the best way to protect both estates and family names.'

Robson nodded. He cut into his duck with gusto.

'Good?' Taylor asked.

'Delicious,' Robson agreed. 'But as for protecting both estates, Theroux's got to be worth a bloody fortune … not that it's any of my business, but so what if Lexie marries his son … he'd be worth as much as Howell surely, maybe more?'

'It's not just about money, it's about the business and the historic merging of two old family estates, plus I gave my word and Howell's holding up his end of the bargain. James is a clever young man, but he's not cut out to run a business. He's a writer.'

'A damn good one at that, a great news sense,' Robson added.

'Well then I'm happy for him to fall for my second daughter, Carrie, and I'm happy to share in their fortune down the line. But Anson is the one to run my business eventually and I need that boy to come into the family. He's bright, ambitious and he's already studying the business. He'll do the right thing by his father and me, and Lexie will do the right thing by him.'

'I see.' Robson wiped his mouth with the white linen napkin and nodded as the waiter offered to refill his glass. He turned back to Taylor. 'So where do I come in?'

Samuel Taylor sat back. 'I was wondering if the *Daily News* might be interested in a fully-funded foreign or war correspondent position, albeit pre-war at this stage, and maybe the editor could also use a bonus for his own ... uh development.'

Robson smiled. 'You're good. I do have a few correspondents already overseas, including my son; there's not much happening there at the moment, but that could all change.'

'Yes, but this would be an exclusive, fully-funded position that would provide *Daily News* readers with the inside story—an exclusive view of the swelling of unrest that only *Daily News* readers would be privileged to read about,' Taylor added.

'It would be a bonus for circulation.' Robson nodded. 'We have well over a million readers a day you know?'

'I know,' Taylor said with growing impatience. 'I also know that if war was to be declared, car production may soon after be suspended. Could be a very good time to put in an order for some new wheels?' Taylor saw the interest spark in Robson's eyes. The deal was done. Taylor raised his glass again. 'This situation, the possibility of war that is, won't go on forever. Just long enough to be useful hopefully.'

'I think we have a deal,' Robson agreed. 'To the war.' He clinked glasses with Taylor.

Chapter 8

On Sunday, September 3, 1939, at 11.15 a.m., people gathered in the streets, huddled in their homes, and held hands around wireless sets all across the country tuned to the BBC as Neville Chamberlain, the Prime Minister, spoke to the nation from the Cabinet Room at 10 Downing Street.

He solemnly told the people of Great Britain that the German government had that morning, been given until 11 a.m. to confirm that they were prepared at once to withdraw their troops from Poland, otherwise a state of war would exist between the two countries. He went on to say that no such undertaking had been received and that consequently, the country was at war with Germany.

Frank Theroux grabbed the table to steady himself; he swayed on his feet. The announcement was not a shock; but now the inevitability that his son, James, would be sent to war, overwhelmed him. James—all that he had left and held dear in the world—was of age to bear arms. He straightened and moved slowly to the window overlooking Autumn Manor's grounds. Frank lowered himself into a seat and buried his head in his hands. From the doorway, Mrs. Atkinson dabbed her eyes and left to make him a pot of tea.

James Theroux felt alive; the buzz in the newspaper office was electric. The weekend editor had called all available staff in and was handing out assignments to everyone as they walked through the door. James was given the job of speaking to survivors of the Great War about their thoughts regarding the announcement. He grabbed his notebook and headed for the door, knowing that at some time he would have to face his father and pretend that neither of them was truly worried.

Samuel Taylor smiled; his plan was going to work well. That Theroux boy would be sent overseas sooner rather than later. Out of sight, out of mind. Then Anson could work on winning over Alexandra. Soon, the two families' business interests would be safely entwined. Meanwhile, he and Anson's father had to do some serious lobbying to get that manufacturing contract. The demand would now skyrocket and he knew just how to put Theroux out of the running.

Moira Taylor dropped to her knees and prayed. Her memories of the Great War were still fresh; she was sixteen when it broke out and she had married Samuel at the end of the war. In her heart, she would not have been devastated had he not returned, not that she would ever have admitted that to anyone, but she had secretly hoped he might not. Then she suffered from guilt and remorse for thinking such evil thoughts. Patrick returned and so did Samuel. Today, she gave thanks to the Lord that she had two daughters and no sons.

Lexie felt ill. She and Carrie had been window shopping in town when they came across a group of people, listening to the wireless outside Davies General Store. The Prime Minister was addressing the nation, declaring that Britain was now at war with Germany. Several women fainted around her but the younger men, naively, seemed happy.

Lexie grabbed Carrie's arm, the colour draining from her face.

'Let's go,' Carrie whispered. 'Mother might need us.'

Lexie stared at Carrie as though in shock. She couldn't hear what she was saying.

'Lexie, let's go.' Carrie pulled her away from the crowd.

'Yes,' Lexie agreed, hardly able to remember how to put one foot in front of the other. She needed to see James, she needed to hold him, now.

Chapter 9

John Gibson, the weekend editor at the *Daily News*—a bespectacled and balding man—opened his office door and glanced out across the room. Heads were down and everyone was frantically typing or dictating to secretaries who sat primly with their pads on their knees, taking shorthand. A haze of smoke hung over the room; nearly every journalist had a cigarette between his or her fingers.

Gibson was a well-liked editor, renowned for being tough but fair. The same could not be said of the top boss, Charles Robson—the very same who had met with Samuel Taylor—who was based in London, but managed nonetheless to put as much pressure on the paper's country edition as in the city.

Gibson cast an eye around the room and, spotting James Theroux, yelled out to him. 'James, got a minute?'

James looked up and nodded. He held up a finger begging for a few more minutes and typed furiously. At the end of his report, James yanked the sheet out of the typewriter, gathered the pages and headed to Gibson's office.

'Boss?'

'Come in, come in, take a seat.' Gibson indicated the tattered leather chair opposite him.

'I just wanted to say congratulations.' Gibson beamed.

James nodded. 'Thanks, boss. For what?'

Gibson slid a piece of paper across the table. 'You've been selected for the war correspondent position. Robson tells me there were a number of high quality applicants, but you were considered by the panel to have the most promise.'

James turned the piece of paper around to read it. He wiped his hand across his face, putting a thin shade of black newspaper ink across his cheek.

'You don't look that pleased,' Gibson remarked.

James looked up at him. 'I didn't apply; I don't know anything about this.'

Gibson looked surprised and shrugged. 'Maybe you were nominated. I don't think I'm letting the cat out of the bag to say you are highly regarded by the top brass.'

James frowned.

'It's a pretty big honour, James.' Gibson chuckled, sitting back at his desk. He slid open a drawer and pulled out a box of cigars. He opened the dark wood lid and pushed the box across the table. 'A celebratory cigar?'

James looked up from studying the paper.

'Um …no thank you.'

Gibson took one and leaned forward again. 'This is an honour, James, we don't want to lose you here, but you've been given a plum opportunity to report from all over Europe to our readers. We're lucky to even have our own reporter; usually we'd have to pick up bits from the London dailies.' Gibson clipped his cigar and reached for the lighter. 'If it wasn't for the scholarship …'

'Scholarship?'

'Yes, a benefactor put up a scholarship for us to have our own war correspondent.'

James nodded his head and smiled. 'He's good.'

Gibson puffed and exhaled.

'What's that?'

'Nothing.' James rose. 'Thank you, Mr. Gibson, thanks very much. Here's the story you wanted from the Great War vets. If it's okay with you, I'm going to go and tell my father about the … scholarship?'

'Of course, I knew you'd be excited.'

James nodded. 'That's one way of putting it.'

*****

The trip to London normally took Frank Theroux about twenty-five minutes travelling at a comfortable speed; today it took him half that time. He didn't enjoy the scenery or the thrill of driving his Mercedes Benz Barker Limousine; he was focused on getting there and on arrival he scanned the street for a suitable place to park. Frank Theroux had one thought in mind—his son James 'winning' that scholarship.

He parked his car and stormed into the offices of the *Daily News*. Passing through the marbled entrance foyer, decorated with framed photos of past headlines, Frank Theroux followed the signs to reception, taking a set of stairs two at a time. He arrived at reception and waited impatiently as the young receptionist finished a phone call. She hung up and looked at him with a smile.

He demanded to see the editor.

'I'm sorry sir, but he's in a meeting and can't be disturbed,' she informed him.

'Miss, get him out of the meeting or I will go into it.'

'Um,' she began to stammer and cast her eyes around to look for help.

'It's very, very important,' Frank Theroux said in a calmer voice.

'Can I tell him who wants to see him?' she asked rising and straightening her pencil-thin grey skirt.

'Theroux,' he pronounced. 'James Theroux's father.'

She repeated his name and wrote a phonetic version of it on her pad. Frank Theroux watched her slip into the back offices through the swinging doors. She glanced back once as though expecting him to do something extreme.

Frank Theroux turned and walked to the window. He looked down at the street and noticed several people circling his car with interest. He would gladly give it all away to protect James.

Someone to his right caught his attention; it was his own reflection in a mirror. He was surprised that he didn't recognise himself: his suit was too large now, he looked tired, gaunt and old. He stood straighter; he wasn't beaten yet. Hearing a noise he turned around as the *Daily News* Editor, Charles Robson, followed the receptionist through the glazed doors, at the same time struggling into his suit jacket. Robson extended his hand to Frank Theroux. 'Delighted to meet the father of James Theroux,' Robson began.

Theroux ignored it. 'A handshake would imply we are friends, Mr. Robson, or at least intending to be cordial to each other and I have no such intention.'

Charles Robson looked nervous. 'Would you like to come through to my office …'

'What I have to say won't take that long,' Theroux told him. He saw Robson's eyes flicker to the receptionist and a photographer who had just arrived at the top of the stairs.

'Miss Watson, perhaps you would like to have a tea break,' Mr. Robson suggested.

'That won't be necessary.' Theroux turned to her. 'I won't be using offensive language Miss Watson, or saying anything that you can't hear.' He returned to study Robson.

'I have heard on good authority that my son has won a scholarship that he never applied for and, as a consequence, has landed a plum position as a war correspondent for this paper.'

'Yes, he's one of our best …'

Frank Theroux talked over Robson. 'This so-called scholarship he won without applying for has less to do with the paper's need and more to do with Samuel Taylor I assume?'

'Ah, Mr. Theroux, I don't make it my business to disclose how I determine my staff's promotions and …'

'Is this true?' Theroux shut him down.

Charles Robson swallowed.

'Your son is an exceptional writer and this was a great opportunity for him and the paper …'

'Is it true?' Theroux thundered again.

'It is not quite that clear cut. As I'm trying to explain, we got offered a fully-funded correspondent position and it was a great opportunity for one of our best journalists …'

'So only your newspaper was offered this fully-funded position paid for by Samuel Taylor?'

'I can't be sure if any of the other newspapers were offered, um … you would need to speak with Mr. Taylor about that …'

'Oh I fully intend to speak with Taylor.' Theroux continued to cut him off. 'Did you offer the opportunity to all your staff to apply for this scholarship or did this fully-funded position have a name on it already?'

'James is one of our best …'

'Yes, I understand that, Mr. Robson.'

Both gentlemen stood in silence. Theroux glared at the editor who lowered his eyes. Behind him, the photographer shuffled nervously and the young receptionist looked relieved to have a phone call to answer.

Theroux sighed and continued in a low voice. 'Mr. Robson, I understand you have a son who is of fighting age and yet, you would take from me the only family member I have left for the price of a new automobile? I could have bought you twenty new cars if I had known you were a man so easily bought. I am a very wealthy man too, Mr. Robson, but I am a man of honour and so is my son, James. I won't pay you to not send James away, he would never forgive that. But be it forever on your conscience should anything happen to him.'

Charles Robson looked concerned. 'But he would have signed up regardless. I'm doing you a favour. He's going as a journalist not a soldier.'

Theroux reached into his jacket pocket; Robson flinched and stepped back.

'I'm not a violent man, Mr. Robson. What does that ever solve?' Instead Frank Theroux pulled out a small black bag, no larger than his palm and handed it to Robson.

Confused, the editor took it. 'What's this?'

'Thirty pieces of silver,' Theroux said. He turned and departed. Robson dropped the bag to the ground.

*****

Frank Theroux had one last trip to make. He knocked on the large timber door and stepped back.

Inside, he could hear a person approaching, feet tapping along a stone floor. An older lady, a housekeeper, opened the door.

Theroux removed his hat. 'Would Mr. Taylor be in please? Frank Theroux calling.'

He declined the offer of a seat and waited near the window in the large entranceway as the housekeeper went down the hall and knocked on a door, entering at the sound of Taylor's voice.

'Hello!'

Theroux swung around as Moira Taylor approached him. 'Mrs. Taylor.' He bowed.

'Please, Mr. Theroux, Moira, I insist. We weren't expecting you, this is a pleasant surprise.'

'Just business,' he smiled. 'A small matter between your husband and myself.'

'I hope everything is all right?' She frowned.

'Yes, yes, no need for concern. You look very well,' he commented, observing her rose-print frock and her hair tied up showing off her slim neck.

'Thank you.' Moira blushed. 'And you look thinner since last I saw you, if I may say.'

Frank Theroux laughed. 'Yes, I suppose it is a bit difficult to reciprocate my compliment. Mrs. Atkinson, my housekeeper, constantly tells me I look too thin.'

'Forgive me, I didn't mean to be rude.'

'Not at all.' Frank assured her. 'And your lovely daughters, Alexandra and Carrie, are they well?'

'Very well, thank you.'

Frank Theroux shuffled his hat from hand to hand. 'Moira, I know it is not what your husband wants, but we, that is, I am delighted to welcome Alexandra into our family.'

'Thank you, Frank.' Moira lowered her voice. 'Believe me, the feeling is mutual. I think James and Lexie are very well suited and I know Lexie is blissfully happy. What more could any mother want for her daughter?'

The conversation stopped as they heard Samuel Taylor's footsteps approaching. Holding himself to full height, Taylor's eyes narrowed at the sight of Theroux.

'Leave us dear,' Taylor said to his wife. He stopped in front of Theroux.

'Of course,' she said. 'Very nice to see you, Mr. Theroux.'

'Mrs. Taylor,' he smiled ignoring her earlier request to be informal.

They waited until Moira had left the entrance hall. Frank Theroux turned to face Samuel Taylor.

Samuel Taylor's lips narrowed and his jaw tightened, 'Frank,' he greeted Theroux.

'Samuel.' Theroux answered him in like fashion.

They were equally matched in height but Taylor had more of the look of a well-fed man.

'Please, this way.' Taylor indicated his office.

'That won't be necessary,' Theroux said. 'I don't intend to stay. I've just been to see Charles Robson.'

'Oh.' Taylor nodded. 'You heard then that I funded a war correspondent position for the *Daily News*?'

Theroux glared at him. 'Samuel, let's not play this game. We are both intelligent men. James is my only son, my only family. Sending him away just to honour an archaic family promise is unconscionable when you consider the danger you will be putting him in.'

'You mean James got the job? I had no idea James was going to get the job.'

'Stop it!' Theroux snapped. 'Repeat that lie often enough and you may convince yourself but we both know the truth. The car was a nice touch.'

Taylor's eyes widened.

'Yes, I know about that too. You can relax … I didn't match or increase your offer. My son would never want that.'

'Robson said he was one of the paper's best journalists. He would have been sent anyway, even if …'

'They would have taken the reports from the daily paper in London. Save it, Samuel. I'm not here to listen to your excuses. I hear you are now going for my manufacturing contract as well. Good luck to you. I am happy to compete with you, but only on a level playing field. Competition is good and healthy for our country. You've taken my son, if you have to take my livelihood, then at least do it because you're the better man and not dishonourably.'

'Spare me the sermon, Frank. This is business. If you can cut it, you'll keep it. If I'm savvier, then bad luck to you.'

Theroux returned his hat to his head. 'Sleep well, Samuel. This ignoble act is bound to catch up on you.' He turned and let himself out.

Samuel Taylor flinched as the door slammed.

Carrie emerged from the shadows of the staircase, shocked at what she overhead; shocked that her father could do such a thing to Lexie.

'Father, tell me you didn't pay to get James out of the way?'

Samuel Taylor walked past her, back to his study and slammed the door.

*****

They fell quiet as they sat on the bench, in the maze of hedges, only a few feet from where James had proposed only last weekend. Finished with the small talk, the silence enveloped them.

Lexie slipped her hand into James' hand.

She looked straight ahead and whispered, 'What if you get killed?'

James squeezed her hand.

'How do I go on ...' she continued whispering the words as though hiding them from fate.

James cleared his throat. 'Lexie, I'm going to be carrying a pen, not a gun. I'm reporting, not shooting.'

'That's just as bad,' she turned sharply to look at him. 'You will be close to the war zone with no protection. Couldn't you say no to the scholarship?'

James shrugged. 'I could have, but then I would have been conscripted anyway, I'm of age. At least this way I'm over there working rather than as a soldier. Don't you think that's a safer option?'

'I don't know,' Lexie answered truthfully. 'All I know is that you are going to war and we will be separated, maybe forever.'

'You can't think like that.' James played with the ring on her engagement finger, turning it back and forth. 'I'll be coming back as soon as I can so we can put another band behind this one.'

Lexie smiled and swallowed hard. 'We could get married before you leave, just a simple ceremony, the two of us ...'

James kissed her hand. 'No, I don't want that for you. I want you to have the big dress and the bridal shower. I want you to be excited about planning the invitations and table settings and I want to watch you walk down the aisle towards me, with our friends and family sharing the day.'

'All I want is you.'

'I'll be there too, at the end of the aisle,' James teased her.

Lexie smiled. 'Very funny.'

'Will you do something for me?' James asked.

'Of course, anything … well maybe; if you are going to ask me to knit socks and send them to you, we might have a problem.'

James laughed. 'Well there goes that idea. No, I was going to ask you to call in on my father every now and then.'

'I would love to, that will be my pleasure,' Lexie assured him.

'I know he's got a business to run and a house full of staff, but he's a bit of a loner and I don't want him sitting on that terrace, worrying himself to a skeleton.'

Lexie patted James' knee. 'Don't you worry, I'll adopt him.'

James grinned. 'I had better warn him.'

'You know all we'll do is talk about you anyway,' she rolled her eyes.

'Well that will be riveting. You'll have plenty to talk about.'

Lexie hit him playfully. He leaned in and kissed her.

'I'm going to miss that,' James sighed and looked away.

Lexie smoothed her dress, frowning as her hands travelled over the folds of fabric. She looked up to find James staring at her.

'What are you thinking?' he asked.

'I'm thinking how much the world can change in a week,' she answered.

'Yes,' James agreed. 'Although we knew trouble was brewing.'

Lexie nodded. 'Regardless, last week, my biggest concern was what colour dress to wear to your party and how to handle the inevitable blast from my father when I came home with an engagement ring.'

James sat forward and twisted on the seat.

'What do you mean? Did you know that I was going to propose to you at the party?'

Lexie tried to change the subject.

'Did you?' James insisted, not letting her get away with it.

'I might have heard on the grapevine ...'

James frowned. 'How? Dad wouldn't tell and none of the staff knew ...'

Lexie made a face at him. 'You're missing the obvious ... you did buy a big enough ring to set every tongue in town wagging! I just guessed that of all nights, that would be the night.'

James smiled. 'Oh yes, I forgot about that part. So much for discretion.'

They sat for a while, inhaling the fresh air and the sweet smell of the flowering jasmine. Their smiles faded.

Lexie spoke. 'It all seems so trivial—the dress, the party, the parading around in the latest fashion—when nothing is certain.'

'It was nice though wasn't it, to just have fun without anything threatening? Some things are still a certainty. My love for you won't change whether I am here or somewhere in Europe writing about the fighting.'

'But I saw our future; our house, your work, our family. Now there's no certainty ... we don't know if we will get married, if we will have a family, even if we will be the same people this time next year. Who is to say how this war might change us.'

James took her words in, and gave a small nod of agreement.

'You are right, I guess there's no certainty.' He moved closer and put his arm around Lexie.

They sat like that for a very long time.

Chapter 10

A veritable sea of soldiers covered the station platform from one end to the other—smartly attired in their clean, pressed uniforms. Draped on every arm was a loved one: a mother, wife, girlfriend, child, father, waiting to see their men off to war. Lexie stood beside James—she felt separated from him already; the crowds around them made her feel like he was no longer hers.

James held her tight. 'I have to go,' he said not releasing her.

'I know,' she held on.

'Lex, there are not enough words in the world to tell you how I am feeling …'

'Write as much as you can,' she begged, 'and please, James, don't be a hero, don't take risks, don't give up the pen and pick up a rifle, don't …'

James smiled, 'I've got it.' He patted his jacket pocket where her photograph and a strand of her hair sat next to his heart.

Lexie pulled away and blinked back tears. She swallowed and nodded.

The final call to board the train boomed above their heads. James turned and embraced his father. Frank Theroux patted him on the back and then stood back. James returned to Lexie and whispered his love to her once more.

'I'll miss you …' she whispered back, as he turned and joined the uniformed men boarding the carriages. Lexie reached for Frank Theroux's arm, threading her arm through his for support. They stood and watched as James jumped on board with the other young men and waved until he was out of sight.

*****

Carrie found Lexie at the stream, sitting with her feet in the water, staring down at the surface; her face puffy from crying. Carrie lowered herself beside her sister without speaking.

Eventually, Lexie spoke. 'Thank you.'

Carrie looked up. 'For what?'

'For just sitting. For not saying "he'll be back, don't worry" or any one of those dreadful things that don't make me feel any better.'

'I didn't know what to say, so thought I'd best say nothing,' Carrie admitted. 'For a change.'

Lexie smiled then laughed. Carrie joined in. 'Well, this time, you did the perfect thing.' Lexie squeezed Carrie's arm.

'You know, isn't it odd that everything looks the same?' Carrie looked around. 'Even though most of the men have gone and the women are trying to run businesses and trying not to cry; all of this, everything here looks the same.'

'It is funny, isn't it?' Lexie agreed. 'I bet over hundreds of years people have fought for our town, built houses, worked farms, married, had babies, even drowned here maybe and yet, everything looks the same; the stream looks the same.'

Carrie shuddered. 'I wonder if their spirits are still here.'

Lexie continued. 'It's like when something awful happens and you think the clocks should stop and everyone should be silent, but life just goes on and eventually you catch up with it again.'

Carrie circled her feet in the water creating a small whirlpool. 'I hope it will always go on. Kind of like somewhere that you can always come back to.'

'One day, I'll be coming home to Autumn Manor,' Lexie sighed.

'It's Father's fault,' Carrie blurted out.

'What is?' Lexie turned.

'I didn't know whether to tell you or not.' Carrie rubbed her sleeve over her face in an agitated manner. 'It's so warm …'

'Carrie, what are you telling me?' Lexie grabbed her sister's arm.

Carrie looked down at her skin going white around her sister's tight grip.

'Sorry.' Lexie released her grip. 'What is Father's fault?'

'I'm not completely sure, so please, please don't get me into trouble …'

'I won't, I promise,' Lexie assured her younger sister. 'Just tell me what has Father done now?'

'Mr. Theroux came over to see Father …'

'When?' Lexie cut in.

'About a week ago, before James left us.'

'And, what happened?' Lexie prodded, ignoring Carrie's joint possession of James.

'Mr. Theroux accused Father of creating the war correspondent position and paying the editor to send James to do the job.'

'No!' Lexie gasped. 'No. Surely not even Father would stoop that low.'

Carrie watched her sister absorb the information, processing in her head if it was possible.

'Mother told us we wouldn't have heard the last of it. She warned us Father would do whatever it took.'

Lexie shook her head. 'No, surely not. How desperate could he be to get rid of James? How could he do that to Mr. Theroux when he knows he's a widower and James is all the family he has left? I can't believe Father would be capable of doing that.'

'I challenged Father about it,' Carrie said proudly, 'when I overheard the conversation, I confronted him!'

'And?' Lexie asked.

Carrie sat upright, 'He just stormed off, but he didn't deny it. He didn't say anything which is as good as admitting it, I think.'

Lexie stared at Carrie dumbfounded.

'Why didn't you tell me sooner?'

'I didn't know … I wasn't sure and … it wouldn't have made any difference, you knowing I mean.'

Lexie looked away. 'No, I suppose not.' She stood abruptly and began to shake the water off her legs.

'Where are you going?' Carrie jumped up beside her. 'You promised not to tell Father I told you.'

'I won't.' Lexie grabbed Carrie and hugged her. 'Thank you.'

Lexie snatched up her shoes and stockings and began to climb back over the rocks.

'Where are you going?' Carrie called again, startling several birds that took to the air.

'I'm going to see Mr. Theroux. I'm going to ask him if it's true.'

Carrie watched her sister until she was out of sight. She turned back, picked up a stone and skimmed it four times, perfectly.

*****

Lexie walked the three miles to Autumn Manor, getting more upset by the minute and oblivious to all else around her. She arrived at the imposing white gates and pushed them open. There was still another half a mile to the front door but fuelled by anger at her father and concern for James and Frank Theroux, Lexie would barely have remembered walking the distance or the time it took to get there, if not for her feet reminding her with every step; blistered and aching, the skin rubbing raw on her heel.

As the house came into view, she was overwhelmed with missing James but at the same time, flushed with excitement that one day, soon, she would be living here. She would be the lady of the manor; this was her future home.

She looked down at her attire and straightened her crepe suit. She felt hot from the walk and her shoes were covered in dust. Lexie could feel her mother's rebuke for arriving at someone's house in such a state. It never occurred to her that after seeing James off at the train station, his father might have gone to work to keep himself busy or perhaps visited friends to console himself.

Then, she spotted him. He was chopping wood; a task normally reserved for his servants. She sighed with relief and continued walking up the driveway towards him. Frank Theroux's sleeves were rolled up, the back of his shirt was covered in sweat and he was chopping with gusto. Around him were piles of wood, cut and neatly stacked.

As Lexie approached, Frank lifted a piece of cut wood and as he moved to place it in the nearest pile, he saw her, a broad smile lit his face.

'Alexandra!' He put the axe down.

'I'm sorry to intrude unannounced.'

'Never,' he smiled, 'this is your home now too.'

Lexie attempted a half smile. 'I've just heard something terrible. I had to come right away. It's about Father,' she assured him hurriedly, 'not James,' and then Lexie burst into tears.

Frank Theroux dropped the wood and wiped his hands on his trousers. He looked uncomfortable. He didn't have any daughters and wasn't quite sure what to do. He glanced around and was relieved to see Mrs. Atkinson bustling out of the house and coming towards them.

'There, there, Miss Taylor,' she cocooned Lexie with her arms and ushered her towards the terrace. 'Mr. Theroux you go change that shirt and I'll organise some iced tea.'

'Right, yes, good idea.' Frank Theroux followed the two women to the terrace. He excused himself, and Lexie saw him disappear up the expansive staircase. He returned several minutes later wearing a clean shirt, with his hair stuck down and hands freshly washed.

Lexie rose from the cane terrace chair.

'No, please,' he indicated for her to sit and took the seat opposite. He sipped on the waiting iced tea.

'I'm sorry, Mr. Theroux,' she began. 'I'm such a … girl.'

Frank Theroux smiled. 'Please call me Frank. You are a lady and I'm fairly sure that's part of the reason my son is in love with you.'

Lexie smiled her thanks.

'But there's nothing to be sorry about,' he continued. 'We've both had a terrible day. Terrible. I'm only pleased that you feel you can come here. Did you walk all the way?'

'It didn't seem that far today.' She looked down at her scuffed shoes. 'It's my fault,' Lexie blurted out.

'What is?' Frank Theroux asked.

Lexie sat upright, wiped her face and regained her composure.

'My sister, Carrie, was in the hallway when you visited Father last weekend. She overheard your conversation … she just told me about it now …'

Frank nodded.

'I need to know if it's true. I can't believe that my Father could stoop to that level. I can't believe he would be so desperate for me to marry Anson at any cost. Tell me, please, is it true? Did he pay for the scholarship and insist it is given to James?'

Frank Theroux cleared his throat.

'It's really not my place to say, and I certainly don't wish to disparage your father to you,' he started.

'I know,' Lexie interrupted, 'which is why you are twice the man he will ever be if it is true. Is it?'

Frank licked his lips and stalled.

'Maybe it's something you should ask him …'

'It is,' Lexie concluded. She sat back and looked away, over the grounds.

Frank nodded. He reached for his drink and gulped a mouthful.

'It's true,' Lexie said to herself.

'It's done now, Alexandra, don't you go fretting about it. It's done and neither James nor I decided to change it. We talked about it of course, James could have resigned and I could have raised the stakes and offered a higher inducement than your father, but we decided not to do either of those things.'

'But don't you see,' Lexie said, 'it's my fault.'

Frank Theroux slowly shook his head. 'No, I don't see that.'

Lexie exhaled, trying to keep her composure.

'My mother warned me about the consequences of disobeying Father but it is you and James who have paid the price. If I had just done as he asked—if I had been obedient and accepted Anson as my future husband, James would not have the scholarship, he would be here and you would have your son at home.'

'I see,' Frank said, finishing his drink and sitting back.

Lexie felt fear rising in her; the bile coming from her stomach to her throat. *Now he knows it was my fault, my doing.* She waited for her future father-in-law's reaction.

'Alexandra ... Lexie, James and I both think your father has inadvertently done us a favour.'

'What?' she said surprised. 'How could that be?' Lexie turned to face Frank Theroux.

'Well, James was of recruitment age; it was only a matter of time until he was called up and then he would have been posted God-knows-where. At least this way, he starts off reporting, even if he does end up enlisting. He's not just going in blindly to fight.'

Lexie nodded and thought about it for a while. 'I will never forgive Father. His motives were anything but honourable. If I had done what I was told, even if James was recruited eventually, he would have been here for longer. Maybe six months, maybe a year ... who knows ...' Lexie's voice trailed off and tears flowed down her cheeks again.

'My dear, listen to me. Imagine if you had broken off with James to please your father, do you know what James would have done?'

Lexie shook her head.

'I can tell you. He would have been devastated, as would have you. He would have wanted to get as far away as possible and he would have hastily signed up. He would have got his orders and been sent overseas and then he'd have been reckless. Knowing there was no one waiting for him, he'd have thrown himself into every battle with no regard for his own life. He would have played the hero with no desire to return. You, my dear, have preserved him.'

Lexie studied Frank Theroux's face.

'I never thought about it like that,' she wiped her face. 'Do you really think he would have acted in that way?'

'I don't just think, I know. Wouldn't you act that way? Don't you agree?' Frank asked.

'Yes.' Lexie nodded. 'If I couldn't have James I would do anything in my power to get away.'

'Exactly.' Frank agreed. 'This way, he is over there, treading carefully because it is your photo and your lock of hair next to his heart.'

Lexie blushed to know that Frank had heard James speaking of his tokens of love.

'You have preserved him, Lexie. While you write to him, pray for him and want him home, he has every reason to want to come home safely. Promise me that you will do that for him and for his poor old father?'

Lexie grabbed Frank's hand. 'Thank you. Thank you for taking that burden of guilt from my shoulders. Believe me, if I could will your son, my fiancé, home I would. He is in my thoughts with every breath I take.'

'Then he'll be just fine.' Frank patted her hand. 'Just fine.'

Lexie nodded in relief.

Mrs. Atkinson bustled back out to the terrace. 'I'm sorry to interrupt,' she started, 'but will Miss Taylor be staying for lunch?'

'Oh no.' Lexie rose, 'I'm sorry I've intruded too much already, I'm on my way now.'

Frank rose beside her. 'Stay for lunch, please. I had no appetite before but you have changed that. Your company will be most welcome.' He nodded at Mrs. Atkinson. 'Have you had a tour of your future home yet?' Frank crooked his arm inviting Lexie's hand.

Chapter 11

James was torn by doubts; he appreciated that as a war correspondent he would be relatively safe reporting on the progress of the conflict from behind the front line, and he knew only too well how relieved his father and Lexie were. But the Military Training Act had come into force early that year, and all the men aged twenty to twenty-one were required to register for enlistment in one of the armed services. Did being a 'war correspondent' exempt him? Even if it did, could he live with himself knowing that his peers—these men in uniform sitting all around him on the train—were out there fighting on the front line while he observed?

No, it was unacceptable. James knew what he had to do, and he did it. He got off the train at the next station and lobbing on an old school friend in London, he secured a bed, dropped off his gear and went to enlist. He decided not to say anything to Lexie or his father yet.

Within a week he received orders to attend basic training at Chatham Barracks in Kent, and three months later found himself attached to a platoon in France. I'll still send in copy, he told himself, and it will be all the better being first-hand from the front.

*****

December 12, 1939

My dearest Lexie,

How I miss you. You are all I think about day and night—the only thing that keeps me going. No words can capture my yearning for you. Do you think of me? Can you believe I have now been gone a little over three months? It seems like a lifetime since we said goodbye at the station.

Lexie, I have to tell you something—you won't like it but my sense of honour left me no choice—I've enlisted in the army. I can't tell you exactly where I am, but I am allowed to say bonjour! Yes, somewhere in France. Even in my reports that I'm filing to the newspaper, I am only allowed to say France, for fear of putting the boys in danger. Have you seen any printed yet? If you can keep them for me that would be greatly appreciated; I want to see what gets through the censors—that being the war censors not our editor! We've been told we can't send postcards home or be too descriptive for fear of giving anything away to the Germans. Even the weather and descriptions of our surroundings are not allowed. So please don't feel that I'm purposely not telling you things or that I don't want you involved in my life (although I would rather not bore you or scare you), but protocol is protocol.

We have been made very welcome here especially by the children. They run beside our vehicles and cheer as if we are the rescue squad. I've even had flowers hurled at me! I can't wait for us to have our own children. A little angel just like you and a little devil to wear us out!

Given that my French language skills are so poor, well let's say they don't exist at all, and none of the others in my platoon is any better, we are trying sign language with the locals and are getting by. It's pretty easy to mime all the basics like food, drink, sleep and so on. I've added some words to my French vocabulary and will practise a few romantic phrases for my return so I can impress you. Please pretend you don't speak any French and just smile if I accidentally say 'I sock you' instead of 'I love you'.

At the moment, I am far from clean and I am sure you won't have any romantic thoughts about me when I tell you that I am sitting in a trench. Yes, Sandy, our Corporal, and I are in a trench both writing home. You should see us. We are filthy and infested, sitting in mud and scratching the lice. Not filthy like you get from gardening but dirty to the bone. I won't elaborate as I want you to think of me fondly not with disgust. Any chance of that now? Funny, the first week it bothered me; now, it's the last thing on my mind. I love lying at night thinking of you at home, safe, warm, clean, smelling of lavender and waiting for me.

How different our lives are from that day when we shared a glass of champagne by the pool at home. Was that for real or am I imagining it? How naive were we to think life would continue so. You, gorgeous in your flowing gown, champagne-coloured as I recall! Your sister madly in love with me (I'm teasing you). See, men can recall detail even if I did call it a dark cream dress on first guess. And there I was; clean, spruced up in a tux, surrounded by our friends as if we had all the time in the world.

If you're wondering how the reporting is going—well it's not really. I've filed a few stories, maybe four at the most, but there's not much happening. Hence the nickname that you may have read about or heard on the wireless—the Phoney War. But let's not jinx that by wishing for action. So most of the writing I am doing is letter writing. I have my rifle and it always has to take priority over the pen.

I'm also getting pretty handy with a shovel and very good at digging trenches. By the time I come home, Kenneth will have to fight me to keep his gardening job; I'll have those garden bed trenches dug in no time to six-foot depth!

At least I am in good company. You make friends quickly here. When someone is watching your back and you are living on top of each other, you soon form a close team. My platoon is about thirty-strong but then we were divided into squads and there are ten men in mine. So I'm shacking up with nine other chaps who are as different as you can be—Sandy, Gunna, Ham, Shorty, Misty and four young ones who I swear must have lied about their age to be here. They are all related and there's a set of twins amongst them. They stick together pretty tightly and I think they're a bit blown away by it all. We call them the four Stooges. I can't remember which one is which half the time because I met them all at once and two are identical, so, like the rest of the platoon, I just call them all Stooge! I hope they make it.

I guess I'm closer to the other five men. Our Corporal, Shaun Gibson, we call 'Sandy' because every part of him is sandy coloured. He'd be great in the desert, you'd never see him. He's about my age, just short of six foot and a maths teacher. How weird is that? A journalist and maths teacher fighting a war?

Then there's Private Albert Hassett who is a crack shot, so we call him Gunna. Do you know him or his family? Albert grew up in our area—small world, and he has a sister, Jane Hassett, a few years younger than you, probably about Carrie's age. Gunna's not the sharpest fellow, but he's loyal and will work until he drops. He was a farmer at home.

Private Harry Haines is a red-haired character who could make you die laughing. He wants to be an actor and he's got a loud enough presence to pull it off. We call him Ham, because he is a ham. He was studying law before he came to the war... a long way *from acting but his father insisted he study something sensible, you know how that is!*

Then there's Shorty who is great with a map and a compass. His real name is William Beaumont and he's six foot four. Yes, we're original with our nicknames aren't we? He's a big, black, boisterous fellow and you wouldn't want to take him on in a dark alley. I'm glad he's on our side. He's a mechanic by trade, so he can pretty much fix anything he puts his hands on.

Finally, there's Alastair Mistoff whom we call Misty. He's a baker. Nicest guy you will ever meet and a gentle soul. Misty can make your mouth water with talk of recipes that we don't really want to think of while we are all eating tinned food.

I'm amazed by these chaps. Here we are stuck together in this situation, making the best of it and looking out for each other. I guess it's the same on the other side too, the same for the enemy that is. And before you ask, yes, I have a nickname too—Scribbler. You know why.

I've picked up another skill too; I've learnt to sleep just about anywhere. Exhaustion helps. I swear I can sleep standing up now. So watch out … church, any boring parties we go to, our parents' dinners … I'll be asleep upright and no one will ever guess. Speaking of parents, how is my father? His letters give nothing away but he speaks highly of you. Thank you for seeing him and going over to dine with him. It means more to me than you will ever know. Since Mother died and I am over here, I don't think he is coping too well but having your company has lifted his spirits I'm sure. He praises you incessantly in his letters. I think Mrs. Atkinson is keen to get a lady back in the house as well.

Please pass on my regards to your family and let me finish this letter on a high.

I love you my Lexie. I see my ring on your finger and your face next to mine when I wake each morning. I want it so badly I can taste it.

This would have been our first Christmas together, if I was at home. We will make up for that in the years to come, many times over, with a grand tree and everyone around us in Autumn Manor.

Wait for me.
James x x

James folded the pages and tucked them along with his pencil into his uniform pocket. He picked up the shovel again and fell into rhythm with Sandy who had finished his letter too and got back to work only minutes earlier. They dug in silence emptying out another two feet or so of dirt.

James stopped and wiped his hand across his face, smearing dirt with the sweat. He looked around; the trench digging was advancing nicely. He suspected the idea was to keep them busy; idle men sometimes led to an outbreak of fighting. The need for the trench was probably secondary and unlikely to keep an enemy at bay for too long. He could feel the sweat running down his back.

'Not as cheerful now are you, Scribbler? Harder digging than writing?' Sandy ribbed him.

James winced more at the newly-coined nickname than the jab.

'Was I ever cheerful?' James reached for a cigarette and offered the packet to his trench-digging partner.

They leaned back against the dirt wall and lit up, neither speaking for some time. Then it started—the rain.

'For Christ's sake,' Sandy hissed.

James lifted his feet in the forming squelch. 'Mud bath,' he muttered.

'What I wouldn't give to sit and have a drink ...'

'Don't start.' James cut him off. 'Seriously, don't ...'

'You're right,' Sandy muttered. 'Best not to I guess.'

'Come on, we'll be freezing in a minute if we don't start working.' James flicked the cigarette into the pit, lowered his shovel into the wet mud and began to pile it out.

*****

December 23, 1939

Hello my James, or should I say Scribbler, and Merry Christmas my love.

It was a huge shock to me, and to your father, to learn that you had enlisted into the army, but we both understand and could not be more proud. Of course I now have much more to worry about, but I will try and bear it with grace to make you proud of me.

Anyway, it is so wonderful to hear from you. I read your letter over and over again, trying to feel closer to you and clinging to the hope that you are safe and well. I am so pleased it is a 'Phoney War'. I hope that doesn't change and that soon the whole thing is called off and you come walking up the driveway, home to us.

Despite your claim that it is a phoney war, I can't sleep for thinking about the danger you are in; and I pray to God every minute of every day for your continued safety. It must be a terrible job being God with all of these wives, girlfriends, fathers and mothers on both sides praying for the safety of their men. If I was God, I would wash my hands of it and leave us all to our own despair since we on earth were silly enough to start the war in the first place. But I'm digressing and I'm sure you would rather hear some news from home than my views of heaven and hell.

Please continue thinking of me as smelling of lavender and drinking champagne. However, the reality is far from that; I have become a war volunteer! Let me tell you what I did yesterday. Saturday morning, I rose at 6.30 a.m.—yes, unheard of—I dressed and went down and had breakfast with Father. He was the only one up at that time and then he gave me a lift into town (on his way to the office—yes, on a Saturday). We don't speak very much as you can imagine and I guess until I stop defying him, our conversations will remain stilted at best. He did however take the opportunity on the trip to suggest I move ahead with my life in your absence and marry Anson. Can you believe it? Now don't you worry, that will never, ever happen which is why I am telling you, knowing that you are secure in my love and can see the funny side of his relentless campaign.

Back to my story—Father dropped me at the train station to start my shift. I've joined The Women's Voluntary Service (WVS) and four days a week I do a shift in the canteen at the local railway station. They are open seven days, but Mother likes me to be home a few days; just for the company I suspect. There are a number of canteens in and around London, and they don't usually open them until ten in the morning, but they stay open until about ten that night. So, I get to the canteen soon after eight in the morning and then, with the other ladies who have the morning shift, we make sandwiches, cakes, biscuits, etc., and prepare a few simple meals like fried eggs and baked beans on toast.

There you go; your fiancée can now cook something—you won't starve to death if Mrs. Atkinson is away. We normally do a three-hour shift, but I do double shifts; three hours on, a one hour break and another three hours on. I go home exhausted and I love it— not only the company of the girls, but being busy, feeling useful and having several hours free from thinking too much. Carrie was keen to come with me but they prefer women over 18 years of age; probably because of all the young men that we are exposed to during our shifts. Luckily, I only have eyes for you. Anyway, in a few months' time, after her eighteenth birthday, she will be able to come along.

Do you remember Christopher Ingram? Last week, the Ingrams received a telegram telling them that he had been killed; he was a pilot. He wasn't in action, it was just a freak accident during manoeuvres. What a terrible waste of a life. I know his sister, Mary, quite well. She is also a volunteer and was at work today, but she was pale and did not look at all well. Mary said she could not stay home a minute longer with her parents. Their grief was overwhelming her. She has another brother—Gerald—somewhere in France as well. I remember him better than I remember Christopher. Gerald is awfully good at sport, and as I recall, Christopher was a good swimmer. What a terrible thing to get that telegram ... don't do that to me James, please.

On the social front, there are a lot of parties with a lot of visiting soldiers waiting to be sent here or there. Carrie does her part and attends, as do Anson and his sister, Anna. Can you believe he is claiming he can't sign up as his father needs him to assist with the business? What next?

I am sure Carrie still has feelings for you and I read her parts of your letter. Why can't she fall in love with Anson and then we could marry them off? But I won't begin on that subject again.

Mother is very concerned about her sister, my Aunt Josephine, in Australia, but Father says being over there is the best thing in the world for her. But it's not Aunt Jo's safety we are worried about. Uncle Will has been recruited and Aunt Jo is there alone, with no family. Mother wanted to sail to Australia to be with her, but of course Father forbade it. I doubt she could get passage anyway unless she offered to assist on one of those ships that are taking the children to safety … I've heard they have a few adult handlers on board. Not to worry, Father would never allow it.

Our Christmas decorations are up, but it doesn't seem right to be celebrating. Everyone is trying to carry on as normal. It is heartening to see the children so excited by Christmas; oblivious to what is going on. I love the festivity of it and I wish you could be here to share in it. I can't wait until next year when I'm sure the war will be over and we can spend Christmas together at Autumn Manor as husband and wife.

In closing, know that my love for you is a constant, as sure as the moon rises and the sun sets. In every soldier's face I search for you. I know you won't walk into my canteen, but still I am ever hopeful—silly I know. To bed now, as it is quite late. I will write again tomorrow, and the next day and the next day …

All my love and prayers
Lexie xxxx

Lexie put down the large teapot and rubbed her aching arm. She had poured her last cup for the day and the next shift of ladies was about to begin at the canteen. She took off her apron and hung it with the others on a nail near the entrance door.

'Busy one today,' she said to Marjorie Dawes, a woman twice her age and a mother to them all.

'Wonderful isn't it?' Marjorie smiled. 'To be able to offer so many of our boys a cup of tea and a place to rest between their travels. You look exhausted my love.'

'Nothing that a cup of tea won't fix.' Lexie smiled.

'Take a sandwich with you for the journey home. Eileen, will you wrap a sandwich for our Lexie? We can't have you fading away.'

Lexie pecked Marjorie on the cheek. 'You would never allow that, I'm sure. Besides, I've taste-tested every pudding you've brought in this past week.' Lexie rubbed her stomach.

'Perks of the job.' Marjorie winked. 'I hear rationing may come into effect soon, so we might be restricted to a sandwich and sugarless-biscuits made without butter! Heavens! See you tomorrow my dear.'

'See you then.' Lexie waved. 'Bye ladies.'

A chorus of goodbyes farewelled Lexie as Eileen, with a wink, pressed a sandwich into her hand at the door.

Outside Lexie noticed the chill for the first time; she had been busy working and had stayed warm up until now. She pulled her coat tighter around her body and moved away from the railway station to sit in the park opposite for a break before beginning her walk home. Collapsing onto a bench, Lexie put her feet up and began to indulge in one of Eileen's generous sandwiches, when she heard her name called. She looked around to see Carrie on the platform.

'Hello! Stay there.' Lexie ordered and crossed back over the road to the station. 'What are you doing here?' She gave Carrie a kiss on the cheek.

'I got a lift in with Kenneth. He had to pick up some fertiliser or something for the Theroux's garden and saw me as I was walking to the station,' Carrie said.

Lexie noticed Carrie was dressed impeccably and was drawing admiring glances from the soldiers. She self-consciously looked down at her dowdy uniform.

'Where's Kenneth now?' Lexie asked.

'He's coming back for us in about twenty minutes. He said to wait here and he'll drive us home in the lorry.'

'Oh, good, my feet are killing me.' Lexie dropped down onto a platform bench and raised her legs, moving her feet in a rotating motion. 'Want half a sandwich?'

Carrie looked at it hungrily. 'You've probably earned it …'

'I'm too tired to eat.' Lexie gave her half. 'So, did you just come down here to have a look around at the scenery?'

Carrie smiled before biting through the egg and lettuce. 'Mm, it is good—the sandwich and the scenery—but no, I have news.'

Lexie sat bolt upright. 'What?'

'Don't panic.' Carrie rolled her eyes. 'Not that kind of news.'

Lexie took her hand off her chest. 'Don't do that to me.'

Carrie continued. 'Kitty dropped in earlier to see you. She said she never gets to see you anymore.'

'Is that all?' Lexie sighed with relief and took another bite of her sandwich. 'I told her what days I work.'

'Well she forgot, but she said she would come back tonight.'

Lexie frowned again. 'Why, what's up?'

Carrie finished the last bite of the sandwich and pulled a handkerchief from her purse to wipe her hands. 'Well, I'm not supposed to tell, but Kitty was in town yesterday and she ran into Father Ranken.' Carrie stopped as a group of young soldiers went past.

'That's nice,' Lexie prompted her, 'and?'

Carrie smiled at a soldier as he dipped his cap to her.

'Father Ranken?' Lexie nudged her.

'Oh yes, sorry. Father Ranken said to Kitty that he looked forward to marrying you and Anson next month.'

Lexie's jaw dropped open. 'What?'

'Precisely, what indeed!' Carrie agreed. 'I raced here to tell you and to let you know that Kitty will be back later to give you more details.'

'I don't believe it.' Lexie stood up, pulling her volunteer uniform down and placing her hands on her hips. 'Father has gone too far this time, he really has. I wonder if Anson knows.'

'Kitty will be able to tell you tonight. She was going to drop in to say hello to his sister, Anna, this afternoon.'

'Bless Kitty,' Lexie mumbled. She reached for Carrie's hand and squeezed it. 'Thank you, sis. I owe you.'

'Yes you do. Can I have James?'

Lexie turned to find Carrie smiling. She sat back down and kissed Carrie's cheek. 'You can have him as a brother-in-law.'

'Phooey,' Carrie snorted.

'Look at all these gorgeous soldiers,' Lexie said in a hushed voice. 'Couldn't you fall for one of them? You're getting plenty of attention.'

'Am I? Maybe I could fall for another man ...' Carrie agreed playing modest and looking away as another soldier greeted her while passing.

'You know Carrie, this calls for drastic action.'

Carrie shrugged. 'I'll meet someone eventually.'

'What? No, not your love life! My love life—Father and the marriage situation. I have to get away from here before that date.' Lexie narrowed her eyes, plotting.

'How? Where will you go?' Carrie stared at her.

'Shh, there's Kenneth.' Lexie waved and grabbed Carrie's hand. 'Let's hear what Kitty has to say first.'

*****

Kitty barely had time to offer a greeting to Moira and Samuel Taylor before she was whisked away by Lexie and Carrie for a walk.

'But I don't feel like a walk,' Kitty complained. 'I just walked all the way here!'

'Shh,' Lexie shushed her. 'Let's just walk far enough so we can talk in private.'

'Oh.' Kitty nodded, 'I get it.'

Lexie led the way as Kitty and Carrie followed her down the front path and across the grounds. She stooped under a vine to enter the path to the stream that she and Carrie so often took. They walked for another five minutes.

Kitty glanced behind. 'We're about half a mile from the house now. How good is your parents' hearing?'

Lexie laughed. 'Fine, we'll stop then.' She pointed to a log at the top of the next rise. 'Can you get that far?'

Kitty frowned. 'I suppose so.'

The girls seated themselves. Lexie and Carrie stared at Kitty who spread out her skirt and adjusted some stray strands of her light brown hair back into the knot at the back of her neck.

'Well?' Lexie pounced.

Kitty smiled. 'It appears I am going to be a bridesmaid and you haven't told me.'

'So it is true then,' Lexie shook her head. 'Father is a tyrant, the most selfish man who will stop at nothing to get his own way.' She turned and spoke to Carrie. 'He is ruthless.'

Carrie nodded her agreement. 'What did Anna say? Does Anson know?' she asked.

'Yes he does. He spoke to Father Ranken about calling your marriage banns and then the Howells are planning to invite your family over for Sunday lunch on the last Sunday of the month when the wedding is to take place. Both parents will have everything ready from the cake to the priest,' Kitty announced.

'Imagine if I didn't know?' Lexie exclaimed. 'How mortifying. How embarrassing to have to storm out in front of Anson's parents.'

'I suspect you would have heard,' Carrie said. 'It's not much of a surprise if Anna and Father Ranken keep telling everyone.' Carrie turned to Kitty. 'I love your dress. That lilac colour is beautiful.'

'Thanks.' Kitty brightened. 'I heard that we won't be able to get much variety soon so I bought a few frocks now.'

'Kitty!' Lexie exclaimed, 'the frock is beautiful, but concentrate.

I can't believe Anson would go along with this knowing that I'm engaged to James. Didn't he think I would notice when the banns were called?'

'Well, according to Anna, Anson is excited and believes you will be delighted by the surprise,' Kitty said. 'Just the immediate two families on the grounds of Howells' estate.'

'And if I say no?' Lexie asked.

Carrie made a face. 'Could you say no under that kind of pressure?'

Lexie groaned. 'This is an ambush.'

Kitty rubbed Lexie's back. 'I'm sorry Lexie, it's not fair and it's an awful situation to put you in. I'm just so delighted that Father Ranken let the cat out of the bag. I don't think he realises that you don't know.'

'So, what is your plan?' Carrie prodded Lexie.

'Plan? You have a plan already?' Kitty looked impressed.

'Sort of, Carrie gave me a warning of what you were coming to see me about. So I've been playing around with some ideas.'

'And?' Kitty asked.

'What do you say to joining the Voluntary Aid Detachment and staying in London permanently with me?' Lexie asked eagerly.

Chapter 13

January 10, 1940

Hello my darling James,

Happy belated New Year to you, my love. I wish you were able to write to me more often, but of course I understand why you cannot. I have memorised your last letter almost word for word, sentence by sentence, inhaled it, kissed it and cried over it. I am so glad you have a group of friends and you all watch over each other; your Christmas wouldn't have been quite as bleak in such good company. I am happy to write to their families, their wives or girlfriends or visit them if they live near. Sharing news makes everything much more bearable. My Christmas was somewhat morose; luckily I had plenty of shifts at the canteen. Father fumed every time he saw me, Mother was over-animated trying to keep the peace and Carrie continues to sulk because she is not of an age to do anything useful.

James, how I miss you and pray for you to come home safely. I know I am supposed to be strong and supportive, but I can't bear the thought of continuing without you. Promise me you will do everything in your power to stay safe and come home to me?

Some nights I dream the telegram arrives at the door but I never open it. While it is unopened, then you are alive. Sometimes I dream of our wedding day and I awake missing you more than ever and ache for you.

But now, for some news from the home front; it's official … can you believe Anson won't be going to war? He has been given an exemption as a government contractor because his services are necessary for his father's business and their war-time contract. What next? His sister told Kitty. I had thought it was just a rumour; how dishonourable he is when it is not really true and his father could do perfectly well without him. I don't know how he holds his head up in society, but believe me he does. And Father thinks it is all perfectly acceptable. Anson and Anna are out every night socialising as if there is no war. She said she is doing her bit to keep the visiting soldiers happy! I want them to be happy too, but I assure you, I am home writing a letter to keep my away-soldier happy. I guess I shouldn't be so judgemental. Anna is my age and needs some company and socialisation.

Did you know that Father and Mr. Howell are working on a bid for a major government manufacturing contract? The very same contract that your father currently owns, and which is up for renewal soon. Father and Mr. Howell have spent months building up contacts and putting together their bid. I wouldn't put it past Father to pull some strings to get his way. I'm sorry my love, enough about my father and his fantasies.

As you know I'm doing a few days volunteering at the canteen; the uniform is very drab, but who cares. I have developed muscles in my arms from lifting huge teapots and I have learned to cook just about every kind of cake and pastry there is to cook from the Volunteer Matron, Marjorie Dawes. Marjorie is wonderful. She's about fifty, I think, a bit portly and motherly and we all love her.

So you can look forward to my chocolate slice and my lemon pie is dreamy—that is assuming we can get the ingredients. Rationing is not too bad at the moment, but it all depends on how long this war lasts doesn't it?

But let me tell you about last week. Father went to London for the week for business. He agreed to allow me to accompany him—I had a plan which he was oblivious to and I needed to be in London to put it into action. More on that later. We barely spoke the entire week but I am past worrying about that now. London was so different from home; the hotel we stayed in had all the windows covered as part of the blackout rules. I experienced my first blackout drill. We haven't been too vigilant at home about the blackout but the drill in London was quite frightening. The street lamps were turned off, sirens started to wail and because we were running late to get back to the hotel, we had to stay down in an underground tube station.

We were far from alone; everyone seemed to be there. They even handed out snacks and there was bedding and pillows. It was very odd. After what seemed like ages, but I'm sure it probably wasn't all that long, a different siren sounded the "all clear" and we went out. Father was in a hurry, as always, and I almost had to run to keep up with him.

We passed over a bridge and there was a crowd gathering, looking into the water. We didn't stop, but I read the next day that three people drowned during the drill. They became disorientated and fell into the water when all the lights went out. Isn't that a terrible thing? I was very shocked. I know my darling that after your dreadful experiences my story probably seems silly, but it is so very sad, I was really quite affected by it.

But back to my reason for wanting to be in London; Father has been undermining me again and has accelerated HIS plans for me to marry Anson. Kitty ran into Father Ranken in town and he said he was looking forward to marrying Anson and me next month! God bless him for being so indiscreet. Well that was news to me and the final straw. Well, I am learning from the best and I beat Father at his own game. Kitty and I had a plan. We joined the VADs! That's the Voluntary Aid Detachment Nurses in case you can't tell one nursing group from another and I begin training next week.

So Kitty and I are moving to London and have secured a room with a widow whose son has gone to war. She has a number of her rooms billeted and it is within walking distance of our headquarters. I am very excited. I love feeling useful; I'll be working non-stop and living full-time in London, so I won't be available to wed Anson. Isn't that unfortunate? I can't help smiling at the thought. After training we may get posted somewhere away from London. Kitty has a friend at a hospital in Aberdeen, but Scotland is a little too far. I would like to stay somewhere around London initially so I can instigate my next plan.

A few days ago I told Father that I was accepted into the VADs. He was furious, particularly given I spent my days planning and plotting all of this while he thought I was shopping and socialising in London. He yelled until he turned purple. But now he has turned full circle. He was dead against it until the Chairman of the Board on this big government contract he's after caught up with him at their Gentlemen's Club and congratulated him on my joining. It appears he has been encouraging women to do their bit. Now Father is boasting that his daughter is a member of the VADs, purely for his own gain of course. But I don't care, I have had a small victory! What can he do next? That must be the end of his attempts to marry me off, surely.

James darling, I know what you are going to say about me

joining the VADs especially since I just told you I was distressed about the three people drowning, but I'm sure I will become braver as I get used to the work. I much prefer to be moving around than being cooped up in a canteen all day, even though it was fun in the company of the ladies. At least now I will be busy as a trainee nurse and distracted from worrying myself sick over you! As for my next plan, well I want to get shipped abroad and stationed where you are! Wouldn't that be something?

James stopped reading and lowered the letter.

Lexie, you have no idea. It's no picnic here. You will have no luxuries, be overworked, hungry, and in danger. He groaned.

'What's up Scribbler?' Sandy stopped cleaning his weapon and looked over.

'Nothing.'

'Dog die?'

'No.'

'Cat die?' Sandy persisted.

'No, no one died.'

'Girl left you?'

'My girl has joined the VADs,' James replied, 'and she's going to be nursing soldiers.'

'Well good for her,' Sandy said.

'You might get to see her yet, hey? Get yourself shot in the big toe or something. Want me to do it?' Shorty piped up.

'You're just a bit too keen to do that for my liking,' James frowned at him.

Shorty laughed his booming laugh. 'Just offering to help.'

'She'll be all right, Scribbler,' Sandy continued. 'It's not like she's staying at home and going to dances with visiting soldiers is she? At least working as a nurse she's exposed to ugly mugs like this bunch.' Sandy nodded at some of the squad sitting around.

'That's lovely isn't it,' Shorty muttered back. 'We wouldn't be at war if the enemy had caught sight of your head before battle began. They'd be running, sir,' he added as an afterthought.

James laughed.

'Yeah, ha-ha.' Sandy grinned.

'It's a good point though, thanks. I'm feeling better already.' James looked around. 'I'm going to look pretty good to her after she sees the likes of you lot.' He carefully folded Lexie's letter and put it away.

'Good. Now make yourself useful.' Sandy tossed over a rag. 'Start cleaning.'

*****

Moira Taylor watched her daughter pack. She turned away to look out through the bay window at the grounds of her home. The world was changing and she felt powerless to stop it.

'There's no need to worry, Mother, really,' Lexie assured her.

'I think this is ridiculous.' She turned to confront Lexie. 'Your father should put a stop to it.'

'Why is it ridiculous?' Lexie folded a blouse without looking up at her mother. 'Everyone is being called on to help, why not me?'

Moira shook her head. 'Because we are not people who empty bed pans and clean rooms, that's why.'

Lexie sighed and looked at her mother. 'Really Mother, it is war. Do you think any of the boys fighting are the type of people who get dirty and kill people? Do you think the ladies working in the factories are the type of people who would normally pack goods? You heard Father, it is every woman's duty to volunteer for some form of service.'

Moira clucked her tongue. 'Don't quote your father at me. I know his motives have nothing to do with national service and he would agree with me if he wasn't trying to win that contract.'

Carrie entered the room and dropped onto the seat in the bay window. She folded her legs up around her chest.

'I think it's great you are volunteering, Lexie,' she said. 'I can't wait until I turn eighteen and I will be joining you!'

Moira Taylor looked upset.

'Thanks.' Lexie looked at Carrie suspiciously, knowing there would be some ulterior reason for her loyalty.

'And I know why you are doing it,' Carrie continued.

Lexie shot her a look. 'Well, keep your theory to yourself.'

'Well I think it's menial work that is below you and I think it's too dangerous,' Moira Taylor continued. 'London is being bombed all the time and there are a lot of men pouring into the cities at the moment, not all of them well-intentioned I'm sure. I am surprised Kitty's family has agreed.'

Lexie noted the worried tone in her mother's voice.

'I'm only going to London, not the front line,' she said.

'We're at war; London is dangerous too,' Moira said.

'I'll be fine. I'm going to be living in quarters near the hospital where we will be trained, so when we are not working, I will be in the company of women and probably too tired to do anything. We are going to get rooms in the hospital eventually. The billeting is just short-term until we all get settled and put into rosters. Then I'll be permanently in the safe environment of St Bartholomew's hospital.'

Moira did not look convinced.

Lexie continued. 'For the first month it will be just study; there are lectures about first aid training and then we get practical nurse training on the job. After that, I guess I'm going to be working in the wards. You could come and visit me.'

Moira ignored the invitation. 'Why couldn't you stay here and continue at the canteen a few days a week?'

'Because she would have to …' Carrie began to explain but Lexie cut her off.

'Because I will be of more value doing this, Mother, I want to do this. You should consider helping at the canteen. It would be good for you.'

Moira frowned but said nothing.

'Really Mother, you should. The ladies need you and it will give you a sense of worth. Carrie can take you down there and introduce you. She's met some of the ladies.'

'I can!' Carrie agreed. 'And maybe they'll let me start work prior to my eighteenth birthday if you are there.'

Moira Taylor said nothing.

Lexie closed her suitcase. 'Well, that's it.'

'It's not too late …' her mother started.

'It is Mother. I am going, I want to go. I can't stand being around the house feeling useless. At least I'll be busy and while I'm busy I don't have time to think too much.'

'About James,' Carrie added.

Lexie turned to face her. 'About all of our boys who are away fighting.'

Carrie snorted. 'And one in particular.'

*****

France, April 30, 1940

Hello my love,

I wonder what you are doing as I write this. Are you taking someone's temperature, rubbing your feet after a hard day's work or out with Kitty having a little bit of well deserved fun? How very admirable that you would do your bit but I am not surprised. You are such a compassionate person. I'm guessing since leaving the canteen you no longer have time to bake or do those knitting lessons. I was looking forward to wearing a pair of your knitted socks even if they are a beginner's pair; different lengths, different stitches or different colours. I would have you close to my skin the whole time I was wearing them.

Well the word is that the so-called 'Phoney War' is over. I met up with a journalist visiting our base who had just come from Norway. Apparently the Germans invaded it in April and there were hundreds and hundreds of casualties. I think British politics might also have been a casualty from what he said. We heard that Chamberlain has resigned and Winston Churchill is now PM. I am sure you know more than I do, being on the home front and all.

I have just filed a story during a break—yes I managed to do what I came here to do. It was good to write again. Coming back and resuming life as a journalist seems like a dream.

The air attacks have increased and the sound of bombing is so disorientating; you never know where it is coming from and whether one is going to land on top of you! I seem to be permanently flinching. I wanted to stay upbeat in this letter but I am so overwhelmed with loneliness for you. I am not sure how much of this letter you will get … whether it will be censored or not … it may arrive in ribbons.

The Germans have started attacking some of our positions, Lexie, and yesterday I killed one, a German man. My first. I can't believe I have killed someone. We are doing search and destroy at the moment and I literally stumbled on him. We both got a fright. He fell near me and just for a few seconds he looked at me. He was about my age and all I could think of was who he was leaving behind; that I had robbed his girl, his mother, father, brothers and sisters of ever seeing him again. It's a terrible, terrible thing, Lexie. Then I vomited with the grief of it. When I mentioned it to Sandy, he shrugged and said 'that's our job'. Guess I should just toughen up and shut up.

Yesterday there was another random attack and we waited and waited; all huddled for hours in this freezing hell-hole waiting for the signal to advance. When it did come, most of us couldn't move because our limbs were so frozen. I thought if speed was needed to save me, then I was a dead man. But it's amazing how fast you can move when the adrenalin kicks in. I once told you I was more of a poet than an athlete, well my love, I could have earned a place on the national sprint team with my effort yesterday.

So tell me, my lovely girl, what's happening there? The last letter I got from you seems a lifetime ago. I am overwhelmed with the battle you have fought to stay engaged to me and defy your father. I am sorry you have to do it alone, but knowing you are mine is the only thing that keeps me going day and night. Trust me, Lexie, after being here, the importance of family estates, wealth and a name has become non-existent to me. Not that it ever was a big deal before the war.

Do you still write to my father or are you too busy now? Are you finding it hard to get some items? Are you still forced to darn stockings in the absence of new ones?

I've heard about those soldiers who are charming girls with

'The whole front's collapsed, everyone's heading for the coast.' Sandy squatted down in front of his squad which had expanded in number as more soldiers drifted into camp, separated from their own units and waiting for instructions. 'They're evacuating now, so we need to get moving and catch up.' Sandy breathed out and looked around. A debris graveyard surrounded them— the result of days of work destroying everything left behind by their own soldiers so it would not be of use to the Germans: vans, lorries, motorbikes and field guns, even deceased livestock littered the area.

'I think we've destroyed everything that can be destroyed, Corporal.' Misty followed Sandy's gaze.

'But why?' one brave soldier's voice asked.

Sandy looked between the heads to where the question came from.

'Well, Private, I'm not usually in the habit of explaining why we have to follow orders …'

'Sorry, Corporal,' the young man said.

'But use your head, Private. If we can't take it with us, why would we leave all this equipment for the Germans to use against us?'

'Uh, yes Corporal, sorry Corporal.'

Sandy nodded. He glanced at the boys' faces. As well as his usual team of James, Shorty, Ham, Misty, Gunna and the Stooges, he counted an additional five fresh-faced kids who looked like the only action they had fought was in the playground.

'The order is to evacuate,' Sandy continued. 'Everyone's shipping out from Dunkirk Beach. We need to move it; the rest of our platoon has a few days start on us already. When you get to the beach, look for a lift home and get on anything seaworthy. Don't wait for your friends, me, or anyone else, just get moving. It's every man for himself. Questions?'

No one spoke.

'Let's go.' Sandy ordered the men into two vehicles. After ensuring everyone was accounted for, he leapt in beside James at the wheel.

'Move it out, Scribbler,' he ordered.

'Yes, Corporal.' James started the lorry's engine.

Chapter 14

'I always wanted to train to be a nurse.' Kitty exhaled smoke and offered Lexie the cigarette. 'Being a VAD is like a shortcut.'

Lexie declined and sipped her tea. 'Then why didn't you pursue it before now?'

Both girls jumped as a tin tray hit the floor of the cafeteria behind them. A couple of women giggled, realising they hadn't been bombed.

Kitty turned back to resume her conversation with Lexie. 'The same reason as you, I guess; my parents would never stand for that. I was supposed to get married, have children, manage the household, join the Women's Society, play tennis …'

Lexie nodded.

The cafeteria was filling up with an assortment of staff: nurses, doctors, volunteers, and carers pushing their patients in wheelchairs or leading them to chairs.

Kitty's eyes followed every handsome male that entered the room. She caught Lexie's eye and grinned. 'I may be tired, but I'm still red-blooded.'

'I'll worry when you are not, shall I?' Lexie said. She finished her cup of tea and sat back, groaning.

'I don't think I can get up. Did we go to bed last night?'

Kitty pursed her lips while she thought. 'Yes, I think we

finished near midnight … I remember lying down but not falling asleep.'

'I remember getting up but not going to bed,' Lexie added.

'I got called into an operation this morning,' Kitty added casually.

'Really?' Lexie's eyes widened.

'Really, straight into the deep end.'

'But how?'

'I was passing by and apparently there weren't enough hands on deck. The matron pulled me in, told me to scrub up and then next thing I'm pressing on some poor man's vein.'

Lexie grimaced. Kitty leant forward and whispered 'it was amazing. I felt like I could make a difference, I could keep him alive.'

'You are obviously cut out for this, you really are. I'm not sure I could do that,' Lexie said.

Kitty's face flushed with excitement. 'There's more … I stayed there for another two patients and then I had to mop some blood off the floor. That I could have done without, but the matron said she was pleased with my efforts. I wish I could do work in the operating theatre all the time.' Kitty stubbed out her cigarette and stacked her lunch dishes. 'Are you glad you volunteered though, even if you're not sure it's for you?'

Lexie nodded. 'I don't regret being here for a minute, I would do that again and again, and having you with me makes it so much better. But I wouldn't say it's my natural calling. I'm just pleased to be doing something useful and to not be sitting around home spending all day worrying about James. Speaking of which, Kit, you know I want to serve overseas as soon as I get enough skills to get transferred?'

'I know, I haven't forgotten.'

'Will you still come with me?' Lexie asked.

'If I haven't fallen madly in love with a doctor who works here at the hospital, who refuses to let me leave and can't live without me … if that doesn't happen, I'll come.'

Lexie began to laugh.

'What?' Kitty smiled. 'Do you think that's unlikely?'

'No, I think it's inevitable.' Lexie patted Kitty's hand. 'Let's go. Time's up and I've got bandages to change.'

*****

That evening, Lexie hungrily opened the letter from France that the landlady had left on her bed. She felt a rush of excitement seeing James' handwriting. Large black marks obliterated some of what he had written where parts of his letter had been censored. She read on regardless, filling in the blanks as best she could.

France, May 22, 1940

Dearest Lexie

We are on the move, that's all I can say. We destroy everything we come across; it seems crazy to ------------------------------------- --------------------------------- I hate destroying working machinery but we can't leave anything behind for the Germans to use.

We lost Gunna yesterday, one of our very own. He was taken out by a bullet. He was so pepped-up though that he thought it was sweat, not blood, running down his back. When I saw how blood-soaked he was, I made the mistake of telling him. He was fine before then but as soon as he knew he was hit, his body gave out on him and he collapsed. It's odd how the mind works.

Shorty carried him about a mile back to --------------------- --------------- Shorty's so big I swear he didn't even break into a sweat. Gunna hung on for a few hours and then passed away. I don't know when his family will be notified so don't spread the word, you know how it travels. His poor parents … he's the only son, and he was needed on the farm. It's going to be weird here without Gunna around. --- ----Can you believe it? Guess we'll have to break in someone new. I could write a book already about the things I've seen and done, but somehow I can't find the words to put down on paper. I wonder if I ever will be able to. I don't want you to worry though my love, I am doing my best to dodge bullets; self-preservation is an acquired skill and I will be coming home to you.

More soon … I'm sorry this is going to be short; it's madness here. Sometimes we only get a few minutes to write before being on the move again or falling asleep upright. I'll gather all my 'extracts' and send them together.

Love, James xxxx

*****

James heard the whistle; that warning sound just before the explosion.

'Christ,' he muttered, 'close.' Then he saw it—a live grenade. James looked left and right; there was no one around, no one near it. He could make it if he ran fast, but then Lexie appeared out of nowhere. She saw him and her face lit up. His face contorted.

James began to run towards her screaming.

'Get back, bomb, get back!'

He saw her face crumble, the look of confusion and then the flash and the heat. He yelled. Someone was grabbing him.

'Scribbler! Wake up for Christ's sake before you wake up everyone else.' Misty shoved James with his boot.

James sat bolt upright.

'You were dreaming.'

'What?' James looked around.

'You were dreaming. There's no bullet with your name on it tonight, go back to sleep.'

'Dreaming?' James ran his hands over his face.

No Lexie, no bomb, just the occasional stuttering of gunfire miles away, and miles and miles between him and Lexie.

*****

London, June 1, 1940

My darling James

We have heard stories of dreadful fighting in France, a place called Dunkirk. I hope and pray you receive this letter in a state of good health my beloved, and you are not involved at all. Be assured all is well here, although we have had some terrible casualties and every injury I see haunts me. I can't help but worry that you may be lying out there somewhere suffering the same fate. If that should ever happen, I hope some wonderful nurse will take pity on you and care for you. It would be good if she wasn't really attractive, though. I'm just teasing you of course.

I'm sure I talk about you way too much to anyone who will listen; I guess we all talk about our loved ones a lot. I'm surprised your ears don't burn around the clock, even that far away.

This is a tough role, I admire the women who do it and I am proud to be with them. But once the war is over, I am hanging up my uniform and dedicating myself completely to being Mrs. James Theroux and making chocolate slice!

Kitty, on the other hand, is truly in her element. She is a natural at nursing and has a strong stomach for the worst. She can do anything and has no real abhorrence for the wounds. Everyone loves her bubbly personality which just lifts the ward from gloomy to bright and of course she is always surrounded by eligible men from doctors to soldiers. Despite the war, I don't think I've ever seen her happier.

I had three days off last week and returned home. It was good to see Mother and Carrie again. Can you believe they are both working at the canteen? I never thought Mother would do that but she seems very happy and is in a position where she manages some of the younger ones. There is no way in the past Father would have agreed to them both working, but now he has no choice with these war contracts that he is pitching for, it serves him right!

I dropped in to see your father and received a most welcome reception. My apple slice was most welcome too—he seemed genuinely impressed with my baking skills, even if the pastry was a bit hard to achieve on our rations. I had some time with Mrs. Atkinson before your father joined us. She is lovely and we will get on very well. She said your father is doing fine but is lonely without you and your mother. He has been throwing himself into his work and has also taken up growing vegetables. Kenneth recommended a plot of earth on your property that would be ideal for growing anything and Mrs. Atkinson said he is down there watering those seeds religiously.

Your father told me it will soon be the anniversary of your mother's passing. I thought perhaps I should visit him that day as well, just to help him through it. I have asked for the day off, but don't mention it in your correspondence to him in case I can't get away from the hospital.

How are the lads? Shorty who is not short, Misty the baker and Sandy the boss? Have you got any new troops in your squad? Is that what you call it … a squad? I saw Gunna's parents, Mr. and Mrs. Hassett, at Church when I went home for the three days. I am so very, very sorry about his passing. His parents seemed to have aged a hundred years; I guess that's not surprising.

But enough, on to a brighter subject to keep your spirits up— my nursing skills are much improved. While the training was brief, it was well supported by a lot, and I mean a lot, of hands-on experience in the hospital. I am quite good at giving needles and bandaging. It's the cleaning wounds that I find difficult; all that blood, and the ways in which the human body can be injured are quite frightening really. Some days I am surprised that we survive at all given how vulnerable the human flesh is.

The matron at the hospital is very good to me. Some of the girls are terrified of her but she has a job to do and she does it efficiently. I try and stay out of her sight as much as possible. There are also several senior sisters who I work with that are very knowledgeable, although two of them are quite curt. Still, I tell myself that I am not there to socialise or make a career of it. I am there to help and be useful and to maybe get to you my love. Imagine!

I am sharing a room with three nurses—it's a tiny room with the four of us sharing a bathroom. There's Kitty, whom you know of course. She hasn't changed a bit; she still says exactly what she thinks and is full of life. She always tells me to send her regards to you when I write and to tell you to look out for handsome men for her, preferably at Captain level or above. See, she hasn't changed! It is so funny seeing her working in the wards; she's so tiny that sometimes she stands on a box to dress wounds or assist *the doctors. She has had her dark hair cropped very short, very boyish—but she did grow up with seven brothers, yes seven and no sisters, so she gives as good as she gets. Kitty is amazing; five of her brothers are now serving but she refuses to dwell on that and always thinks positively. I'm so glad she's here with me. Now don't worry, I haven't gone down the same path … my hair is still the same; long and unruly.*

The third lady we share a room with is Esther. She is nearly 25, a few years older than Kitty and I, and she seems so much more mature. She is married and her husband is fighting abroad in Italy. She is quiet, shy and a little homely but such a lovely girl. She spends all her spare time writing to her husband. They have been married for seven years and she is keen to start a family. If he gets any home leave she will be working on that. Esther is one of five: three girls and two boys, but they are all over the place and she has no family in London, so we are her family now.

Finally there's Frances, or Franny as we call her, who is beautiful. All the soldiers in our wards, and the doctors, propose to her all the time. She is twenty-one, a classic beauty and very polished. Before joining up as a VAD, she was at finishing school in Switzerland being groomed, I suspect for the right man, although she claims she was sent there as her father wanted to keep her out of harm's way until she was a little older. Oddly though, she shows no interest in any of the men here. She says she doesn't have anyone, but yet she gets packages all the time with silk stockings (impossible to get) and jewellery. We suspect she has a rich lover somewhere abroad … a taboo lover. You can see that we gossip too much when we are not busy, so it's a good thing we barely have time to breathe. She is very religious though, our Franny. I wish sometimes I had that strength of faith; it must be of great comfort.

I should also mention that Anson dropped into the hospital the other day and invited me for tea. I was a little suspicious, thinking surely he hasn't organised a surprise wedding ceremony at the tea house. But I went, of course; we are childhood friends and there is no need to offend him. He told me that he is still prepared to marry me if I 'drop this silly nursing charade and come home now.' Can you believe it? Obviously he was sent by the two fathers and this is their final ploy. Anson is not a bad person and I know many girls would be flattered by his attention, but I find him dull. I would be nothing more than a trophy in an advantageous marriage.

Still, it was nice to see a face from home and to get out of the hospital for a while. For just a brief moment, he seemed genuinely sad that I refused him; I don't know what I saw on his face, but he looked vulnerable. Then he bucked up again and that look was gone. Perhaps I imagined that he had some real feelings for me. But don't worry my love, I sent him back with a very clear message that there will be no marriage now or in the future and he has my blessing to find a more worthy girl.

Please keep writing to me my darling. When I get your letters telling me what you are up to I am so relieved because without your words, my imagination has you combat fighting, ducking and weaving to dodge bullets and facing the enemy at all hours of the day. I make myself sick worrying about it which is why I work so hard and try and keep distracted. I long to see you. Some days I ache for you so badly that I wonder how I will keep going. Other days it seems that you are so far away from me that I cannot feel your presence in the universe. To compensate, I dream of our future and dare to plan it in my head, waiting for you to come home so that we can begin to live it. I love you and you alone and I will wait for you. You have my word, and my heart.

Lexie xxxx

Chapter 15

Being called to Matron's office did not go unnoticed and Lexie's walk down the hallway seemed to her to echo throughout the hospital. The sympathetic smiles of other nurses said it all; she was in trouble. Lexie glanced over her uniform again; everything was clean and as it should be. She stopped outside Matron's office, took a deep breath and knocked on the door. No point being timid, let's face the music.

Matron called her in. Lexie felt the chill in the air which matched Matron's austere presence. The room was tiny with a small timber desk, three grey filing cabinets and two chairs squeezed into what remained of the room. The blind was pulled down but Lexie could see through a small tear that the view was equally bleak; the hospital building next door. Lexie hid a smile; if Matron were an army-issued bed, you could bounce a coin off her; her hair was pulled back tightly, her uniform was neatly pressed and the only jewellery she wore was a time piece Even her skin seemed clean and shiny.

'Good morning, Matron.' Lexie held her breath as she stood in front of her.

The matron looked up from her files and offered Lexie a stiff grimace resembling a smile.

'Good morning, Alexandra, please take a seat.'

Lexie lowered herself into the vinyl chair opposite.

The matron looked at Lexie, then to a piece of paper in front of her and back to Lexie.

'You have fitted in very well here, Alexandra,' she said.

'Thank you, Matron, I've enjoyed the work.'

'Even emptying the bed pans?' Matron smiled.

Lexie laughed. 'Not so much the bed pans.'

'What part do you find most satisfying?' Matron cocked her head and asked with genuine interest.

Lexie knew there were plenty of answers that would be appropriate but she said the truth.

'I like being so busy and tired that I don't have time to think or stress about my fiancé overseas and I hope that the more I support the sick and injured, the more chance there is that James will be equally as cared for by some nurse on the other side of the world.'

Matron nodded. 'I understand. I guess to some degree that answers my next question—why you have requested an overseas posting. You know VADs are not usually posted overseas, that's not to say there are not some VADs serving in European posts and on hospital ships. It will subject you to more danger than you face here.' She stopped for effect. 'You may see things that you are not yet able to handle. Have you given this some serious thought?'

'Yes, Matron, I've thought about it a great deal.'

'Do you speak any languages other than English?'

'Not capably, Matron. Just very basic French and Italian as taught by my tutors ...' Lexie stopped talking realising she was creating a picture of herself as privileged. 'I pick up languages very quickly.'

'Can I ask if your fiancé is your only motivation to be posted, Alexandra? You know the chances of running into him are slim?'

'Yes, of course, Matron, I realise I may never see him. But I want to do more and being near the front ...'

Matron cut her off. 'I know you are running to someone, but are you running away from something, Alexandra?'

Lexie's mouth dropped open. She stiffened, debating what to say. Matron waited, not saying a word.

Lexie sighed. 'Yes, both, Matron, running to and running away.'

To Lexie's surprise Matron laughed.

'Well, I always appreciate honesty. It is your business of course and I think you are level-headed enough to have thought about the consequences. I will talk to Katherine as well but I assume her motives are driven by a desire to go with you. Would that be correct?'

'To some degree, yes. But Kitty, that is Katherine, is loving her nursing training, Matron. She has a real aptitude for it and she wants to take it further. She is applying so we can go together, but I think it is what she wants as well.'

Matron nodded. 'I suspect you are right. I am going to approve your transfer.'

Lexie's face lit up. 'Thank you, Matron.'

'But I can't guarantee when a posting will come through ... it may be two weeks or two months and I can't guarantee where you will go. I assume you know that? You might end up in Algeria, Naples or Singapore.'

'Yes thank you, Matron, I am happy to go to any location as required.'

'Be careful, Alexandra and remember, you can always come back.'

Lexie stood up. 'I will remember that, Matron, thank you, thank you very much.'

Lexie pulled the office door closed behind her and walked back down the hallway. She grinned with delight.

I'm on my way! On my way to you, James, and I have got myself out of an engagement for good.

Father, you can't force me to marry Anson when I am not in the country now, can you?

She laughed with relief.

*****

Samuel Taylor patted his coat pocket; the envelope was still there. His blood pressure rose every time he thought of his daughter's insolence; the humiliation that a promise given by both families two decades ago could be destroyed because he could not control his daughter.

And to blatantly send Anson Howell home empty-handed. She will marry that boy and she will do as she is told. He almost hissed the words as anger fuelled him to walk faster. He stopped outside the War Office in Whitehall.

Samuel Taylor checked again that he had the envelope and then entered the cream, ornate building. Stopping at the front desk, Samuel Taylor advised the young man at the counter that he had an appointment with Henry Hanks. He was directed to the second floor and escorted by another young officer to Hank's office. Declining an offer of tea and a seat, he paced, stopping at the window to look out over the city. It looked battered and lacklustre.

Taylor turned as he heard the door open behind him.

'It's been a long time.' A trim soldier resplendent in a perfectly pressed uniform extended his hand.

'Henry, you're looking well.' Samuel Taylor greeted him. 'The short back and sides becomes you.'

Taylor saw Hanks glance at his own reflection in the window and run a hand over his perfectly groomed hair, flashing an expensive watch and gold jewellery. Hanks was always a ladies' man and Taylor knew how to bend him to his will.

'And you're looking well too, Sam. Please, sit.'

They sat opposite each other on brown, dimpled leather chairs.

'I hear business is tough?' Hanks asked.

'The war has been good for some and not so good for others.' Samuel Taylor shrugged. 'It depends on what you manufacture. Speaking of which, did you hear that Howell and I are tendering for a couple of the manufacturing contracts.'

'I did. Ambitious.'

'Do you think so?' Taylor asked, surprised.

Hanks shrugged. 'Probably not, knowing you two. Frank Theroux has a good stranglehold in that area though and a sound reputation for fair price and reliability ... he's your main rival I imagine. So, is that why you are here? Sorry don't mean to cut straight to business but you know how it is ...'

'I certainly do.' Taylor leant forward in his chair. 'Henry, this contract means a lot to Howell and me, more than you know. In fact, we need this contract to consolidate our families.' Taylor cleared his throat, he wasn't one for begging. 'Many of the traditional industries, that is, some of our investments, aren't doing as well since the war as you just alluded to ...'

'I understand ... but I'm not even on the committee or ...'

'I know,' Taylor cut him off. 'That's not what I want from

you. As you said, we have really only one major competitor, the current incumbent.'

'Theroux.'

'Yes,' Taylor acknowledged.

'I thought you and Theroux moved in the same circles. Why wouldn't you approach him about partnering?'

'Firstly, I barely know the man and I have a business partner of course, Edward Howell. Second, why would Theroux consider partnering when he is doing it successfully now?'

Hanks nodded. 'Yes, fair call.'

Samuel Taylor continued. 'You know Frank Theroux's son, James, is stationed somewhere in France at the moment.'

'No, I didn't know. I heard Frank's wife died a few years ago.'

'Yes. Anyway, what we need is … we need Frank to lose interest in this contract.' Taylor rose and walked towards the window.

'I'm not following you, Sam,' Hanks said running his hands down over the sharp pleat on his trousers.

'I want a telegram delivered to Frank,' Samuel Taylor announced. He turned, rocking on his heels, his hands firmly planted in the pockets of his pants. He waited for Hanks' reaction.

'What sort of telegram?'

Samuel Taylor did not speak.

Hanks laughed, then stopped. 'You're serious?' He rose and moved behind his chair.

Taylor continued. 'I want a telegram sent to him saying that his son was killed in action … you can retract it a week later, after the contract closing date and say it was a mistake, he was presumed dead but has been found alive. It's just temporarily putting him out of action.'

Hanks' face was stony. 'I'm not sure I am hearing this right. You want me to tell a man who has already lost his wife, that now his only son has been killed in action and put him through a week of agony, so that you can win a contract? And then, after ruining his life, send him another telegram a week later apologising and saying look what we found—your son and he's alive.' Hanks' voice continued to rise finishing in a yell.

Taylor leaned against the window frame, crossed his arms and nodded. 'Precisely.'

'You're out of your mind and you are a heartless bastard. Christ, Sam, what the hell is wrong with you? It's not just money … you're playing with someone's life here.'

Taylor moved quickly to the desk and slammed his hand down. 'Just money? This is my family's future and Howell's too for that matter. This is the difference between keeping homes that have been in our families for centuries, of preserving some heritage for our own children, against losing everything …'

Hanks cut him off. 'You have gone way too far, Sam. I won't do it. I would never do that. Now get out of here before I mention to the committee the stunt that you tried to pull.'

Taylor walked to the opposite side of the desk and standing next to Hanks, he pulled an envelope out of his pocket.

Hanks gave a mirthless chuckle. 'Don't think you can buy me. I don't need money.'

'Oh, I'm not offering you money, I'm offering you your head on a silver platter.' Taylor dropped the envelope on the desk.

Hanks stared at him, then slowly reached for the brown envelope and slit it open. Inside he found two photographs. They were grainy but there was no doubt as to the identity of the subject in each of them. Hanks swore under his breath, as he stared from photo to photo.

Taylor smiled. 'So how is your lovely wife? I'm guessing she doesn't know about this. If I release these, you can kiss your career and your marriage goodbye, Henry. It's a bad time to be looking for work but you could always volunteer for active service.' Taylor walked back to the window. 'I hear they need men with experience in France. You've got the haircut for it,' he smirked.

Hanks put the photographs back into the envelope and put the envelope in his pocket.

'I've got copies of those, naturally,' Samuel Taylor said. He moved to the door. 'I need the telegram to go out the last week of September, that's next Monday, a week before the contract bid ends. That should do it.'

'You'll pay for this,' Hank muttered.

Samuel Taylor stopped, his hand on the door knob. He shrugged. 'It's war.'

Chapter 16

'Christ almighty,' Sandy swore. 'We're never going to get out at this rate. Pull over, Scribbler.' In front of them, the road was completely blocked for as far as they could see with a parade of displaced people, abandoned vehicles and cattle wandering aimlessly with no sense of urgency.

James pulled the lorry over to the side of the crowded road. The second platoon vehicle pulled up behind him and the men got out.

'We're not going to make the coast until this time next year at this rate,' Sandy advised them. 'Leave the vehicles and start walking.' Sandy looked around. 'We're going to need to go overland. If we stay behind this crowd we're stuffed. Grab whatever you can carry, including some water, and move out.'

'But we don't know where the Germans are, Corporal. What if they are over that hill?' the same inquisitive soldier asked again.

Sandy frowned at him. 'Son, what's your name?'

'Private Chamberlain, Sir.'

'Chamberlain, what did you do before you joined the Army?' Sandy asked.

'I was studying physics, Corporal.'

'Figures. Here's the equation—A-we need to get to the beach quickly or we'll miss the evacuation. B-if we continue in the vehicles or walking with this crowd, we'll never make it in time. If evacuation equals 'C', what should we do?'

The young man frowned.

'Go overland, Corporal.'

Sandy thumped him on the back. 'Well done lad, we'll make a soldier of you yet.'

Two soldiers on motorbikes began to weave their way up the side of the road, throwing dust over the walking crowds and carts.

Sandy flagged them down. Reluctantly they stopped, noting a superior officer was ordering them to pull over.

'Got room for two passengers?' Sandy asked before issuing an order regardless.

The soldiers nodded.

'Two of you get on,' Sandy ordered 'and when you get to the beach, tell them to wait, more are coming.'

Sandy pushed the young scientist, Chamberlain, onto one bike while muttering 'thank God', under his breath and the second seat was taken in a flash.

'Lucky bastards.' Misty watched them go.

'The rest of you get your gear and let's go,' Sandy yelled.

The men scurried to grab whatever they could and follow Sandy across the field.

*****

They had been walking for about five hours when Sandy signalled behind him to the remaining half-a-dozen men. They ducked

120

down low behind the grassy embankment. Up ahead on a small rise was a timber hut with an enemy half-track troop carrier out the front. A number of German soldiers could be seen sitting on the front steps. James was pleased to stop, even if it was only for a moment; the hours of walking across the country had tired all the men.

'If we're not walking, we're waiting,' James grumbled, rubbing his sore calves.

'You're soft, Scribbler.' Misty ribbed him in a hushed voice.

'You'd know, baker boy,' James fired back with a grin.

"Shh, how many?' Sandy asked Shorty.

'Four, that I can see.' Shorty lowered his binoculars. 'We can go left and leave them to their own devices but the odds of them not seeing us are pretty remote—they're on the high ground—or we could take them on. If we come up on them from behind and position ourselves on their flanks, they'll have no idea of our numbers.'

Sandy rubbed his brow thinking. 'I don't want to take them out, and I don't want any bloody prisoners. Besides we don't know how many, if any, are inside or if they're expecting reinforcements.' Sandy looked at the road running past the house.

'If we don't take them out, then we're going to be watching our back for the next day until we get to the beach,' Shorty said.

'I could eat them?' Ham suggested flippantly. 'I'm starved.'

Sandy shook his head. 'You're a big help, Ham. I'll bear that in mind. Now shut up. Christ, I'm on the road with the Marx Brothers! Swap places,' he ordered Shorty, nudging in front of him.

Sandy surveyed the scene. The hut appeared to be a run-down farmhouse. Parts of the roof were missing and the fence had been destroyed.

'That place would do nicely for the night if those bloody Germans weren't camped outside,' Sandy muttered looking through the binoculars at the four enemy soldiers sitting, smoking on the steps.

'Okay,' Sandy turned to his men. 'We're going to have to deal with them. Shorty, take the Stooges and head to the back. Misty, Scribbler and I will approach from the front. We'll set off a decoy blast and see if any more run out. If it's just the four, we'll pick them off. If a horde of them run out of the house, Shorty, then you will set off a second decoy blast from behind to confuse them, then come around, head north as fast as you can, and we'll regroup. Don't do anything until I set off the first decoy. Got it?'

'Got it,' they agreed.

'Let's go.' Sandy led the way. Shorty peeled off through the trees towards the back of the property with the four young Stooges following like ducklings.

James strained to move low and fast; his legs had fallen asleep and the cold had set in, stiffening them.

Sandy stopped about 200 yards short of the house, a tree canopy providing cover with just enough clearing for a good view. Suddenly, Sandy froze.

'Do you hear that?' he asked.

'There's a bloody motorbike coming.' Misty strained to see further down the road. 'It's coming from behind us!'

'Well there goes that plan; it'll be more of them.' Sandy swore under his breath. 'Scribbler, round up Shorty, tell him to abandon the plan and catch us up. Don't get seen for God's sake; we're going to have to watch our backs from now on. Let's get out of here.'

'Done.' James glanced around and running low, headed back

across the meadow, camouflaged by trees. He felt Sandy's eyes on his back before he heard them heading deeper into the cover of the trees.

✷✷✷✷✷

By now the rider was approaching faster but Shorty still couldn't see or hear him. He was waiting for the decoy signal from Sandy.

'You reckon everything's okay, Shorty?' one of the Stooges asked.

'Does seem to be taking a while.' Shorty strained to catch a glimpse of Sandy and his team near the house.

Then he heard the approaching motorbike. 'Uh Oh.'

Shorty raised his binoculars to his eyes and looked down the road. Emerging on the road between the trees was a German dispatch rider, a machine gunner in the sidecar.

'Christ,' he whispered.

'Shorty!'

Shorty jumped.

'Scribbler, you idiot, you scared the living daylights out of me,' Shorty cursed.

'Good thing, I wasn't the enemy.' James thumped him on the back as he squatted down beside him. 'The plan's abandoned. C'mon, we're out of here, got to catch the boys up in the woods.'

'Yeah, thought as much.' Shorty passed over the binoculars while he put his pack on. He signalled to the ducklings to fall in behind him. James lifted the binoculars to his eyes and followed the noise of the motorbike. He focussed on the rider and let out a low whistle.

'Bloody great timing. Imagine if that had come ten minutes after we'd opened fire.'

'You said it,' Shorty agreed.

123

The rider was in full sight now; turning down the road where they were concealed. He stopped in front of the shack and the man in the sidecar jumped out. The four German soldiers rose and saluted. Three more came out of the house.

Shorty and James exchanged looks.

Shorty gave out a low whistle. 'We would have been up against it. Wait until they go in and then we'll move,' Shorty whispered.

James nodded his agreement.

The soldiers moved into the house, one loitering for a while, to put out his cigarette before following the others in.

'Let's go.' Shorty was up, James indicated for the other privates to fall in next and he brought up the rear, struggling to keep up with Shorty's six-foot-four stride. They weaved through the trees away from the house. James could see the mist from his own breath, his body yet to warm up again. He was hungry, cold and tired but pleased to be moving. Shorty and the lads were getting away from him and he panted to keep up. The light was fading.

Just got to get back with the others and far enough out of here to be able to rest, he coached himself, pushing ahead.

He heard a sound; a crack from a gun and that was the last thought James had before hitting the dirt, unconscious.

Chapter 17

Frank Theroux heard the knock at his front door for the second time before he remembered he would have to answer it; he had given the staff the weekend off. There was so little to do around Autumn Manor these days with only himself in residence and if Mrs. Atkinson left a casserole, he was perfectly capable, he told her, of heating up his own dinner for a couple of nights.

Mrs. Atkinson took the opportunity to call on her sister who had not been well and whose son had recently been called up. She was uncomfortable leaving Frank Theroux but he bustled her out of the house along with the gardener, telling them not to return until next week. The younger staff too was given time off and happily made their own plans for the weekend.

He heard the knock again, this time louder.

'Coming,' Frank Theroux called. He didn't receive many visitors other than a few church folk. He had enjoyed Lexie's visits, but now she was away and he had to content himself with her letters, his work and worrying about James day-in, day-out. He walked down the hallway. Through the glass door panels he could see his visitor was a male, slim and in some sort of uniform. He stopped; a bolt of pain in his chest made him reach out and lean on the timber wall of the hallway.

Frank Theroux steadied himself, drew a deep breath and moved the remaining six paces to the front door. He reached for the handle, somehow knowing his life would change in a few moments and he opened the door.

There in front of him stood a telegraph boy. The young man turned to face him and removed his hat. He would not have been 18 years of age. His bicycle leant against the terrace post.

'Mr. Frank Theroux?' he asked.

Frank nodded.

'Sir, the Land Ministry regrets to announce that your son, Private James Theroux, has been killed in action. Letter to follow.' He stumbled with the words and handed Frank a slip of paper with the exact wording he had just said aloud.

Frank nodded again.

The young man swallowed. 'I'm sor … ry, sorry, sir.'

'Of course.' Frank nodded. 'Thank you.'

'Can I do anything, to help, sir?'

'No, thank you.' Frank stepped back and slowly closed the door. He walked into the front room where the sun was streaming through the large windows and stood there, alone.

*****

'Over here.' Sandy waved to Shorty as he came through the undergrowth.

Shorty groaned with relief. 'We've been walking for an hour, I never thought we'd catch you.' Shorty dropped down beside Sandy and Ham.

'Yeah, we're like the wind,' Ham agreed.

Shorty gave him a wry look. The Stooges followed moments later, dropping their packs and squatting on the ground. Ham passed water supplies around.

'One, two, three, four … where's Scribbler?' Sandy frowned.

'Right behind me,' one of the Stooges answered.

Sandy could see the clearing for about 100 yards. 'How far exactly is right behind you?'

Shorty turned his six-foot-plus bulk and looked back in the direction he had just come. He swore an oath under his breath.

Sandy sighed. 'We'll give him five minutes and then we'll have to go back for him.'

'Bloody Scribbler! I lost him, I'll go back for him. You two go on,' Shorty said.

'We'll all go back for him,' Ham agreed with Sandy.

'Better still Shorty, you lead Ham and me back along your trail. The rest of you stay and recover. Misty, you're in charge,' Sandy ordered. 'Don't move unless you are under fire. I don't want to have to look for you lot when we get back.'

*****

James struggled to sit up. His mind racing. *Sniper shot, was it a sniper shot? Did they see me? Where's Shorty? Am I going to be a prisoner? Do they take prisoners or shoot to kill? Lexie; I promised her I would come home.* He struggled to his knees, staying low behind a hedgerow.

The shack was a fair distance away now and down the valley. Still, he could see the silhouette of the man from the sidecar scanning the hillside with his binoculars. Resting against the man's leg was his rifle.

Could he have seen me and had a lucky shot? James waited. *No one was dispatched or was running after him. Maybe he thought it was a deer or something,* James hoped.

He saw another person appear next to the German. He

couldn't see their features only their outlines. They weren't racing into action to find him. The German with the binoculars picked up his gun and went back inside, the other soldier following.

James hung his head, relief sweeping through him. He didn't realise until then that he had stopped breathing and he drew a long breath to make up for it. Despite the cold, the sweat was running down his face. *Okay, got to move. Getting dark.* James tried to rise but couldn't get up from his knees. A wave of hot and cold flushed over him. *This is not good.* He waited a few moments then forced himself to a squat position, steadied himself and inched himself to his feet. When everything had stopped spinning, he began to follow in Shorty's footsteps.

*****

Shorty stopped and looked around. Ham almost ran into the back of him.

'I came this way. No hang on, it was this way.'

Sandy rolled his eyes.

'Definitely this way,' Shorty assured him.

'Let's go,' Ham urged. 'It's getting dark and Shorty will be impossible to follow in the dark. If it was you, Sandy, we'd be right. You'd be like a beacon with your white skin.'

'And you'd be like a fire beacon with that bloody red hair,' Sandy retorted.

'Yeah, sorry, should have been me that got lost, oh but that's right, I'm a bloody good soldier.'

'How did I know he was going to go and do his own thing?' Shorty jumped into the discussion.

'He's a writer for chrissake. He's probably been inspired by a tree and has stopped to write a verse. Couldn't you look behind you at least once?' Ham suggested.

'Writer, reporter, whatever, that's no excuse. I'm a mechanic but you don't see me racing down to have a look at the engine in the German lorry do ya? He can't be that far back,' Shorty assured him.

Sandy rolled his eyes again. 'My father told me to become an officer, but no, I wanted to get down and dirty, be with the real soldiers.'

'Well you got your wish.' Ham thumped him on the back. 'C'mon you would have been bored as an officer. All that sitting around planning manoeuvres … dull, dull, dull.'

*****

The three soldiers had been walking for about fifteen minutes when they heard a noise.

'Drop,' Sandy ordered. The three squatted behind cover. 'Listen.'

The noise sounded like an animal or something stumbling through the bushes.

Ham raised his rifle to his shoulder. Shorty followed suit.

'Don't fire unless I give you the signal,' Sandy whispered.

They waited. The rustling noise came closer. Sandy strained in the fading light to identify the shape coming towards them. It was low, swaying.

'It's him,' Sandy hissed. 'Wait.' He grabbed Ham's arm as he began to leap up. 'Let's just make sure he's alone and it's not a trap.' He signalled for Shorty to go around behind James. Shorty silently moved out.

James was in full view now, but they waited.

Shorty signalled the all-clear from behind, and they rose from the hedge and grabbed him.

James reeled back in fright.

'It's us, relax, you're okay,' Shorty assured him.

'Deer,' James mumbled.

'Hello dear, to you too,' Ham answered.

'No. He probably thought I was a deer or … random shot …' James slurred his words.

'You're shot?' Shorty panicked. He winched the pack from James' back, saw the pool of blood on his shirt and pushed him to the ground.

Ham scurried for the first aid kit as Sandy lifted James' shirt.

'Scribbler, you're the luckiest pen-pusher alive.' Sandy sighed with relief. 'It's just a graze. Enough to make you giddy and take a bit of blood, but you're still a pretty boy. Your kit took the brunt, especially your mess tin.'

'We need to let Mr. and Mrs. Kit know.' Ham nodded sadly.

James chuckled and then winced. 'Sorry gents.'

'Yeah you should be. We're late for dinner.' Ham continued. 'Having said that … you do look a bit like a deer.'

Sandy shook his head. 'C'mon, let's get a swab on this and get moving. You'll live Scribbler. We've got about three days of walking ahead of us to get to the beach at this rate so you haven't got time to loll around recovering. Sorry, mate.'

*****

It was Father Ranken who discovered Frank Theroux's body.

Frank wasn't in church that morning and Father Ranken was concerned. It wasn't like Frank to miss mass. It wasn't that he was a religious man, but he attended to honour a promise to his wife. It was her attempt to keep him on a straight path to heaven. Father Ranken knew Frank's routine; he always went to work on the Sabbath, but he at least attended mass on the way to work. Today, he was absent.

Father Ranken waved the last of his parishioners off and, gathering his hat, walked the several miles to Autumn Manor. He normally was a guest at Mrs. Huntingdale's for Sunday lunch, but he had to give his apologies today to check up on Frank. She had other guests and he wouldn't be missed. He was pleased to have a change and a long walk.

Father Ranken reached the front door of Autumn Manor. No one was in sight.

Odd, he thought.

He knocked and waited; there was no answer. He looked around and found that the place was deserted. He called out but his voice reverberated around the empty property.

Father Ranken took a few steps to peer through the window of the front room. He saw the silhouette first; a man hanging from the large central ceiling beam.

'Frank!' Father Ranken gave a strangled cry and stumbled backwards, falling to the ground.

*****

'How are you holdin' up, Scribbler?' Shorty looked behind him to check James was still there.

'Fine, just fine,' James panted, sweat running down his face while the cold air chilled his body.

They had been walking for three hours; the moon provided enough light to see by and the trees provided enough of a canopy for protection. They could hear the occasional sound of firing in the far distance and when high enough, the odd light flickered in the sky from afar.

'You reckon we're on the right track?' Misty asked, 'seems like we're all alone out here.'

Sandy frowned. 'What do I look like? A dud with a map? Of course we're on the right bloody track. It's just that we've been off line for almost a week and the others have been moving at the same time.'

Misty stumbled, grabbed a branch and steadied himself. 'Sleep walking,' he muttered.

'We'll stop for the night as soon as we find some good cover,' Sandy promised. 'Just keep heading north and keep your eyes out for anywhere we can rest up.'

Chapter 18

Carrie ran up the front driveway of her family home, her pace restricted by the skirt of her suit and the dress heels on her leather shoes. She breathed in short, sharp gasps. She called for her mother, as she ran through the house.

'Good heavens, what is it?' Moira Taylor appeared from the porch with a watering can in her hands. 'I'm here.'

Carrie bent over, gasping for air. 'It's James and Mr. Theroux.'

Moira looked behind Carrie and out to the front entrance.

'They're not here, Mother!'

'Of course not,' Moira realised. 'James is at war and his father …'

'They're dead,' Carrie burst out and began to cry.

'What?' Moira stepped back. She placed the watering can down on a table and raced to Carrie, clutching her by the shoulders.

'What are you saying?' She shook her.

Carrie pulled free and fell back onto the railings. 'It's true. I was just in town with Emma and Father Ranken passed us. He was so distracted he barely noticed us and I called to him. He was really distressed and he said that Mr. Theroux had passed away and then we walked with him because he wouldn't stay to talk. He said he had to notify next of kin or find next of kin, but there's none, because James is dead too!' Carrie wailed in pain, loud sobbing cries.

Moira shook her head and guided Carrie to a seat. She sat down next to her daughter.

'Carrie, stop. Stop, please. You're not making sense. How do you know James is dead?'

'Father Ranken found a telegram saying that James was killed in action. He found it on the counter. The kitchen counter at the Theroux house.'

Moira gasped. 'And Frank? Mr. Theroux?'

'He hanged himself. After he got it. That's why he wasn't in church.'

Moira Taylor covered her face. Carrie reached for her and the two women held each other.

'I have to go to Lexie,' Moira said. 'But I must speak with Father Ranken first to understand what happened. Where's Mrs. Atkinson and the staff?'

'I don't know. Neither does Father Ranken.'

Moira pulled a handkerchief from her sleeve and wiped her face. 'I'll leave now, to see Father Ranken. Then tomorrow, I'll go to London.'

'I'll come with you,' Carrie said. 'Let me.'

Moira nodded. She rose and left the room to fetch a coat.

Carrie turned and looked out across the lawn. 'My poor James. I loved you, James. Oh Lexie …'

*****

James shivered; he desperately needed a break. He could no longer feel his legs, they were functioning automatically, had been for miles. The area where he was hit felt like it was on fire;

burning and constantly itchy. He stopped and leaned against a tree, sliding down its trunk to the ground. He winced, extending his legs a little.

'You'll feel worse for stopping,' Ham called to him.

'Just five minutes, just till Misty catches up.'

Shorty and Ham stopped near James and squatted, waiting for Misty and Sandy who were bringing up the rear.

James closed his eyes and inhaled: despite the rancid smell of men who had not washed for days, he could smell the crispness of the earth and the woods. The smell reminded him of Autumn Manor—racing down the front steps into the garden, across the grounds and down to the stables.

*****

James drifted into a shallow sleep, thinking about his favourite horse, Azure. He hurried to get dressed; he was going to ride to meet Lexie at the stonehouse. He applied a little cologne, attempted to brush his dark hair into place before it fell forward and ran a hand down his face; smooth enough. He couldn't sleep last night for thinking about her; her eyes, the way she held his gaze just long enough to express so much, her beautiful dark hair and her manner—so graceful, so smart and that smile. James felt a dull ache from the separation; her threatened arranged marriage always hanging over his head.

He straightened his jacket and left the bedroom, closing the door behind him. Avoiding the main staircase in case his father found a job for him, he went down the servants' stairs and out through the servants' entrance. The brightness of the day hit him; the blue sky, the green of the hills, the gardens before him and the brace of cold air. He stepped up his pace towards the stables.

135

The stable hand had Azure saddled and ready. James ran his hand down her mane and whispered in her ear before mounting and urging her into a trot. She seemed to understand and lent herself to the task with equal enthusiasm.

The stonehouse was a generous name for nothing more than a pile of old brick stones at the top of the hill. Once a functioning cottage for the groundsman, it had taken its share of beatings from storms that passed through the hills and valleys and over the past fifty years had become a rubble. James comfortably rode up the hill and turned full circle. She was coming: her dark hair loose and flowing, her face radiant from the cold air.

James dismounted and waited for her. He reached for the reins from her horse. Lexie slid off the saddle into his arms. He kissed her lips and groaned.

'I've missed you. You have no idea how much I missed you.'

Lexie placed her hands on his face. Her eyes were moist. 'Oh James, I couldn't sleep for waiting to be here this morning.'

'It's cold,' he shivered. 'Are you cold?'

'No,' she answered.

'But I'm so cold,' he shuddered. He woke with a start, seeing his legs extended in front of him and his army-issue boots where moments ago he was seeing Lexie's face. He closed his eyes again and felt dizzy.

He heard a voice.

'The sun's coming up, we've got to get moving.' It was Sandy speaking.

Did we sleep? James looked around. *Did I sleep here on the ground?* James felt Sandy beside him taking his arm and helping him up.

'Got to keep walking, Scribbler, you'll freeze to that tree if you stay there any longer,' Sandy was saying.

James nodded, disorientated.

Sandy frowned at him. 'C'mon we've got to keep moving. You all right?'

James looked around. He shivered. People were trudging past him; men, women, children.

Who are they? When did we get back on the main road? Have I lost an hour, a day?

'What's up?' Misty stopped near them.

'Scribbler,' Sandy said. 'Do you know where you are?' He continued to address James.

James could hear the voice but his mind and body were focused on walking.

'He needs to get that wound seen to and probably needs some blood too,' he heard the voice speaking again.

Misty grabbed James by the arm and slung it over his shoulder, supporting James' weight.

'C'mon, Scribbler, we'll stop soon.'

James automatically put one foot in front of the other.

'That's the way,' Misty said.

'Bugger, where's Shorty now?' he heard the voice say.

'He's ahead,' Misty nodded. Sandy scanned the crowds and saw him. He wasn't that hard to miss with one kid on his shoulder and another on his back.

'Oh, right, I didn't see him pass me.' Sandy spoke again to James. 'Hang in there, Scribbler, we're going to stop soon. It's just not safe right now.'

'I'm okay.' James removed his arm from Misty's shoulder, stumbled and straightened himself. He continued to focus straight ahead, walking like a drunken man. His eyes bored into the back of an old man dressed in a full suit and felt hat, holding the hand of a young boy no more than ten years of age.

It was hard to see who was leading whom. The old man limped slightly. James matched his step, keeping the same trudging pace, focusing on that and that only, while around him, military vehicles and horses passed by carting people and possessions and covering them in dust. Dozens of soldiers in various forms of attire and bandaging, struggled on by foot, some on crutches, or supported on the shoulders of other soldiers.

James wanted it over. At the end of this is Lexie. He increased his pace. At the end of this is Lexie.

'Whoa, Scribbler,' Misty called, 'pace yourself'.

'He's lost it.' Sandy shook his head, transferring his rifle to his other shoulder. 'I need to get him onto one of the passing lorries.'

James kept going. He visualised the stonehouse just around the next corner. If he kept walking, if he could get away from everyone, the stonehouse would be around the next turn and she would be there.

No one else would be there, because they don't know about it, just Lexie—waiting for me, got to get there, she's waiting for me.

*****

Lexie washed her hands. She still had an hour left of her shift but she had received a message to come to the nurses' administration area immediately.

What now? she thought. *Maybe our posting has come through,* she brightened at the thought, happy to be removed from her shift to get that news.

She dried her hands and quickly walked up the hallway. As she swung open the doors, she stopped in her tracks.

There waiting for her were her mother and sister. Lexie could tell from their faces what had happened. No words were necessary.

She couldn't remember walking towards her mother, or taking her arm and stumbling towards the entrance, out through the large front doors of St Bartholomew's. She remembered reaching for Carrie, with her ghost-white face and allowing them to take her home.

*****

James kept his focus straight ahead. Over the next rise would be the stonehouse and Lexie waiting for him. He didn't hear Sandy; he couldn't hear any of the noise around him—the sounds of humanity; people wailing, marching, distant bombing, tanks thundering past.

'Scribbler, I've got you a ride.' Sandy ran up past his men to stop James. 'Whoa, Scribbler, stop.'

Sandy grabbed his arm and James spun around. His eyes were blank. He stared without recognition.

'Scribbler, you need to see a medic. I've got a ride for you.' Sandy steered him to the side of the road. James pulled away. He stumbled back into the stream of people and picked up pace. He was over twenty yards in front before Sandy realised he had broken away again.

Shorty caught up. 'What? Doesn't he want the lift?'

Ham fell behind. 'Kids today, they're so ungrateful.'

Sandy shook his head and started to walk. 'He's off in la-la land. Got no idea where he is or who I am.'

'Shouldn't we do something about that?' Shorty continued.

Sandy shrugged. 'Sure. What do you suggest? No, let him walk. He's still standing. When he gets there, wherever he thinks he's going and collapses, we'll treat him then. He's got enough left in him to keep going for a while yet.'

*****

139

"So good of you boys to join us.' The Platoon Sergeant looked Sandy and his motley soldiers up and down. 'You're bloody lucky we're still here and trying to get a lift out or you'd be on your own.'

'Yes, Sergeant.' Sandy said. 'We've been walking for …'

'Yes that's evident,' the Sergeant cut him off. 'Got any rations left?'

'No, Sergeant.'

The Platoon Sergeant nodded towards a makeshift tent. 'There might be something over there. Get a feed and some sleep. We'll wake you if we can get transportation.'

He saw the Platoon Sergeant do a quick head count before turning his eyes back to the sea.

'Yes Sergeant,' Sandy snapped. He turned to his men and indicated for them to make for the tent. 'Can you walk another thirty feet to the food?' he asked.

'We'll crawl there if we have to,' Ham said. 'C'mon boys,' he said to the Stooges who looked beaten. The older men looked even worse. They stumbled along; a handful of straggler soldiers moved out of their way.

James was more interested in sleeping than eating, but tagged along. He accepted several cans of food handed to him and followed the others out of the tent. He fell onto the sand to eat. Misty leant over, opened a can for James, put a fork in it and thrust it into his hand.

'Eat, Scribbler,' Misty said.

They ate in silence.

'Going to finish that can, Scribbler?' Shorty watched him.

'Can't,' James answered.

'Good.' Shorty stuck his fork into James' can and removed a sausage, swallowing it in two bites. 'And that Spam?'

'Is that what it is?' Ham looked at his own can.

'Let him eat,' Sandy ordered. 'Eat Scribbler, that's an order.'

'Need to sleep.' James swallowed.

'Finish that can, then you can sleep,' Sandy said.

James nodded. He forced another morsel into his mouth, chewing mechanically. After a few more bites, Sandy rolled his eyes, removed the can and gave it to Shorty.

When they finished, they headed to a communal area and grabbing a blanket each, bunked down.

James shivered. He felt the other members of his squad piling in around him. He was asleep within minutes. Too exhausted to think, to feel, even to miss Lexie.

✶✶✶✶✶

'But we don't really know for sure.' Lexie dried her face. She shivered and accepted the wrap her mother passed her.

'Darling, there's witnesses who report these things.' Moira took her daughter's hand as they sat on the bench in the grounds of the family home. Carrie sat on the grass in front of Lexie.

'Not every lad who died in the Great War was ever found or their body brought home,' Moria said. 'It will be the same in this war. Mr. Theroux received a telegram.'

'But we haven't got his identity discs or his body, so he might be alive. It might be wrong … it could be, couldn't it?'

'It could be,' Moira conceded.

'What did the telegram say?' Lexie persisted.

'We haven't seen it,' Carrie told her. 'Father Ranken found it on the kitchen bench at Autumn Manor. Father Ranken said the telegram stated that James was killed … killed in action,' she choked on the words.

Lexie put her hand on Carrie's shoulder.

'Poor Frank,' Moira whispered.

'It's the best thing,' Carrie said.

'Carrie! Taking your own life is a sin,' her mother reminded her. 'You can't think that it was the best option.'

'He lost his wife and then his son,' Carrie said. 'What a miserable existence it would have been for him. He had already lost so much weight since Mrs. Theroux died, it would have only been a matter of time.'

'He had friends and he had a new family.' Moira looked at Lexie.

'If Lexie, Father and I died, would you want to live on with just your friends?' Carrie put the question to her mother.

'I would have to. It is not for me to take the life that God has given me at a time of my choosing. That is the call of our Maker.' She crossed herself.

Carrie rolled her eyes. 'I'm just saying I understand why he did it.'

'Me too,' Lexie agreed. 'It was too much for him to bear. I'm not sure how to bear it either. Please, don't be offended, but I need some time just to sit here alone. I'll be okay, really.'

'Of course.' Moira said. 'Come Carrie, we have chores to run.'

'But remember, we are nearby whenever you need us,' Carrie rose, assuring her sister.

'Thank you.' Lexie nodded.

She watched them walk through the garden and back to the house. A flash caught her eye; she saw her father standing in the window frame of his study watching her. Lexie turned away and buried her face in her hands; she rocked back and forth with grief. She didn't see her father's hand make its way to his heart, she didn't see that maybe he did have a heart after all.

*****

Samuel Taylor sighed. There were always casualties in war, he told himself and Lexie was one of those casualties. But he hated to see her so pained. He tried to turn away but was absorbed by her grief.

For a week it had continued. He thought she would be over it by now. He hadn't counted on the intensity of her loss. Samuel Taylor had loved like that once before, a long time ago now. Lily. He couldn't say the name without some emotion, even two decades later. She was perfect and they had promised themselves to each other. Samuel was to propose on her return from a trip to the East with her father. But Lily never returned. On her way back to him on the ship, she had died of typhoid fever. Four weeks she fought it, her father had said. A skeleton in the end when Lily's spirit finally slipped away leaving her body racked and destroyed.

She had promised to return to him, it was only six months and she would write constantly. But he never saw her or touched her again. Never had the chance to kiss or hold her. All his plans and dreams were gone from the day she boarded that ship.

I'm sorry, Lexie, my dear, he thought. Now he needed Anson to step up and wed her while she was needy and vulnerable, and before James is found to be alive. Samuel cleared his throat and moved away from the window, returning his focus to the business at hand—the contracts he had now won.

Chapter 19

James felt better. He had slept soundly, his skin had stopped burning and he was even hungry. Beside him, Shorty groaned, again.

'Shut up,' the men of the squad said in unison.

'It's all right for you lot,' Shorty answered. 'You don't know how hard it is trying to sleep in cramped conditions for hours when you are a six-foot-four.'

'Cry me a river.' Misty shook his head. 'Would you rather be warm or comfortable?'

'Both! It's hard enough beating the women off when you're tall and handsome, but at this rate, I'll never walk again.' Shorty continued to moan.

'You're an idiot, Shorty.' James started to laugh and it caught on. Soon, they were all laughing uncontrollably.

Sandy appeared and dropped down beside them. The men sat up, Shorty untwisting his legs from his makeshift bed.

'What's got into you lot?' he asked, reaching into his pocket for a cigarette and offering them around.

'You laugh or you cry,' Misty offered.

'Do you think there will be any French beauties on the beach today?' Ham asked leaning towards Sandy for a light. He took a puff and exhaled. 'You know, nice girls who like red heads?'

'Are there girls who like red heads anywhere?' Misty ribbed him.

'There'll be ugly Germans on the beach if we don't get out of here soon,' Sandy reminded his men.

'Well that's ruined my vision of sunbathing French beauties.' Ham jumped to his feet. 'Best get it over with then. Someone's got to arrive soon and give us a lift home, or maybe we should start swimming across the Channel.'

'Ham's right. Best to stay vigilant, let's go,' Sandy ordered, 'we've got to get on something floating—a boat, raft, anything and get out of here, otherwise forget the swimming, we'll be walking again back to the south.'

The threat of walking galvanised the men into action; they began to look for movement along the horizon.

*****

June 3, 1940

My darling James

I have had an awful, awful time. I'm in so much pain and I don't know what to do. Several days ago Mother and Carrie arrived to tell me that your father received a telegram advising you were killed in action. I have come home with them for a little while, but I need to get back to work, to be busy. But still somehow, my love, I don't believe it; I can't believe it. I still feel you here. I just don't get a sense that you are not with me anymore and until I get more information, some kind of confirmation like your I.D. discs or I speak with an eyewitness, I will go on dreaming of our future plans and writing to you.

Yesterday I went to the War Office and they couldn't find your name on the latest list of missing or killed in action. You weren't there. I asked them where this telegram was issued from and then I went there. They had a record of its delivery but couldn't remember where the order came from and you weren't on the list of names they had received. I don't know what this means, but it is enough for me to have hope. Mother is frustrated with me but Father Ranken said all hope is good.

The War Office suggested I try the Royal Engineers Records Office in Brighton. I took the day off and went there, unsure if they would help me or if the public even had access. But I was lucky. I stopped outside the building to check the address and a lovely girl who was going up the steps at the time helped me. I suspect she would have been in trouble for doing so. Her name was Margy and she works in the post room. Margy said part of her role and that of other girls with her, was to trace and forward mail to soldiers who moved to other units. But most importantly my love, was that she said they worked from Part 2 Orders. I don't know what these orders are or what they look like, but she said they hold the records of all serving soldiers and their various postings.

She had a box and in it were cards, each of which represented a soldier. It listed his name, rank, serial number and where he was. Then it was filed alphabetically. Every unit and every company had their own box and when I told her yours, she found your card. The part that gave me hope was that the Part 2 Orders did not list you. You were not listed as missing in action, killed in action or missing presumed dead. That means you are alive! She couldn't help me any further because the room was filled with sacks of mail from Dunkirk and Margy said they had their work cut out for them. She hustled me out, but I had enough information to keep me happy.

James my love, I know you will be worried now about your father and how he took the news. I don't know if you have been told, I'm sorry, I have terrible news to relate. Your father was distraught and at the thought of a life without you and your mother; he has taken his own life. I am sorry to have to tell you by letter, but I don't know how else to let you know. I assume you will get a telegram or your commanding officer will tell you soon enough if he hasn't already, but I felt it was my duty to say something.

Where are you? Please spare me the pain that I know you are now going through with the loss of your father. I am suffering the same worrying about you and need desperately to know you are alive. I am sick with distress, but I will be taking that overseas posting soon and I will find you myself if I have to. I will ask every soldier I meet, do they know you? Have they seen you? I will show them your photo and I will cling to hope.

Darling, the funeral for your father is tomorrow and I will be there, along with all his friends and staff. Father Ranken is officiating. He found your father hanged with the war office notice of your death nearby. He checked in on your father because he was not at mass on Sunday. I know the telegram is an error, but it has exacted a terrible price, a life. I will be there on your behalf tomorrow and I will ask Father Ranken to write to you, even if he doesn't believe you are alive, for my sake at least, in the hope that it will be of some consolation to you.

Please, please, I beg you, make contact with me somehow.

Yours forever,
Lexie x x x

*****

James looked around. He estimated nearly fifty soldiers were left behind, waiting to be evacuated. Everyone was doing their best to stay hidden in the daylight which was no mean feat. To his right, James could see Sandy was staying close to the Platoon Sergeant, determined to get his own men aboard anything seaworthy. Behind him, James turned to see other members of his squad ordered to work on the restoration of one of the partially destroyed ferries in the hope of getting it going again. He was left sitting in the shell of a boat hull on the beach, filing a first-hand account about the evacuation for the paper.

He titled the article *Waiting for a rescue vessel*, knowing that the sub-editor would most likely change that anyway. He saw Sandy walking towards him.

'Corporal.' James began to rise.

'Stay put.' Sandy waved him back down.

'What happens if we can't get transport?' James asked.

'Is this you or the story asking?' Sandy pushed his helmet back off his forehead.

'Will the answer vary?' James asked.

Sandy nodded. 'We're stuffed without transport and we're going to have to set off on foot again if nothing comes soon. The Germans are everywhere and … well, you know the rest. For the purposes of your article, we know that the British Government is doing everything in its power to rescue soldiers remaining at Dunkirk … even those like us who were unlucky enough to arrive after the main evacuation.'

James smiled. 'Well, we're in good company.' He nodded toward the Platoon Sergeant.

'Yeah, but his orders were to be the last off. He's coming with us. Anyone else that arrives after us is on their own.' Sandy shook his head.

'When did the last lot go?' James asked.

'About ten days ago according to the Platoon Sergeant. There's not much food left, so if we don't get something in a day or so, we've got to start walking.'

'Christ, ten days … maybe that's it, maybe no one else is coming,' James thought out loud.

'No, there have been a few ships, even destroyers, in that time but they've all been sunk or had to turn back,' Sandy frowned.

'Great,' James sighed.

'We've got a couple of amateur radio hams amongst us; they've been sending Morse Code, so maybe …'

Sandy and James heard a cry. Looking up into the bright sunlight, they saw a number of men running to the shore. Sandy jumped up.

'It's an MTB! Thank God.' He pulled James to his feet.

'A what?'

'A motor torpedo boat. Get to the beach front now,' Sandy barked as he raced up the beach to alert his remaining men. He could see the lads were already on their way toward him. They had seen it themselves. Misty tripped in the loose sand, rolled and leapt up running without missing a beat. He grabbed Ham's arm as he streaked past him.

'Come on, last one on board is a rotten egg.' He whooped with joy.

James froze and looked skyward. Overhead, he heard plane engines approaching fast, German bombers. He heard the Platoon Sergeant yell out orders to drop and he fell flat on the sand. Turning, he saw that everyone had done the same. James saw some of the other soldiers grab their rifles, for what good it would do to shoot at the bombers. The rifles were choked with sand and only the odd one succeeded in firing.

The noise of gunfire and exploding bombs terrified him as he lay with his arms covering his head, buried half in sand. He could hear Ham's fast breathing beside him. After a few minutes it was silent. James raised his head and saw half a dozen men rising off the sand or coming out of the bushes around the edge of the beach.

The MTB had disappeared from sight. When the skies were finally clear and it was safe, the Platoon Sergeant called the survivors together. James could feel the disappointment coming off the men in waves. Several soldiers dropped to their knees and others walked in circles, their hands on their heads in despair.

'Our rescue boat will be back to try and get us off,' the Platoon Sergeant assured the group. 'It's big enough to take those of us left. In the meantime, we have work to do.' He indicated the dead soldiers lying on the sand in the aftermath of the German air attack.

*****

June 6, 1940

My dearest James

Still no word from you. Where are you my love? I lie awake at night refusing to believe you are gone but the doubts are overtaking me. We have heard that everyone has long since been evacuated from Dunkirk and returned to England. Some have been shifted out again. Did you get home? Have you been shipped out again already? Are you still in France? I will keep writing, believing you are alive until I can no longer feel you or I get proof to the contrary. If you can, please send me a sign even if you only have time to write one line saying that you are okay, I will treasure it and expect no more. If you are imprisoned somewhere, please try and send word with someone. If you have left this earth my darling, please come to me in a dream; send me some sort of sign, please.

How I miss you ... how I love you. I know your last letter by heart now. I picture you sitting there writing to me, looking scruffy and thin and perfect in my eyes. I have one of your first letters with the names of some of the men in your squad. I am currently writing to the families of Sandy, Ham, Shorty and Misty to see if they know where you are or if they have heard from their own loved ones.

I am back at work now and I have been to the War Office once every week since that dreadful telegram, but they don't have you on any list. You are still alive then in my mind and I won't give up that hope. I just don't know how your name originally came to be on that list and from where it came. Neither do they. Even though I have had no word from you, I expect I'll get a bundle of letters all at once, given my address may change while the mail is in transit. How exciting that will be; enough for me to read and absorb for hours on end! What I wouldn't give to see you.

I have to get to my shift now but know that every minute of every day I ache for you. I see you in every soldier that comes in and hope and pray that you are safe and well. I am yours and please, please, my love, be careful for me. In the early hours of the morning as I lie in bed, I am tempted to give in to the possibility that you are no longer on this earth. I try to accept it, I try to think about a future without you, but I can't. Where are you? Be alive, please. Where is your body? Where is your heart?

Lexie x x

'Look at that.' Shorty sighed with contentment. 'What a beautiful sight, hey Scribbler?' he nudged James.

'You said it,' James agreed, taking in the cliffs which appeared almost white. He closed his eyes and raised his face to the warmth of the sun.

'God it's good just to sleep again.' Misty stretched out on the deck of the rescue boat. 'Wonder what happens to us now.'

'You could use a shower,' Ham suggested, wrinkling his nose.

Misty shook his head. 'Good thing you smell so good.'

Sandy came up beside the men. He had an air of always being prepared no matter what time of the day or night it was.

'Corporal,' James greeted him, while Misty offered a nod.

'Lads, we're arriving in Dover around seven this morning. There'll be trains waiting for us.'

'Going where?' Misty sat upright.

'Don't know yet,' Sandy shrugged. 'Guess we'll find out soon enough.'

'Reckon there'll be any ladies with a cup of tea and a slice at the train station?' Ham asked with renewed enthusiasm.

Shorty brightened. 'Every chance. Didn't your girl do that for a while, Scribbler?'

James opened his eyes. 'She did. But she's working at a hospital now. I hear the tea and slice ladies are more mother types than girlfriend types.'

Ham shrugged, 'I'm not fussy.'

Misty shook his head at Ham for the second time.

They heard the boat engines begin to slow down as they made their way closer to shore. The men rose.

'Home,' Shorty smiled.

'Doesn't it feel great?' Sandy agreed.

'It'll feel better when I put my feet on dry land … English soil,' James said looking longingly at the shoreline.

'Soon enough, my lad.' Shorty thumped him on the back, 'soon enough.'

*****

'This is bloody terrific.' Charles Robson, Editor of The Daily Mail smirked at the copy in front of him. He paced the floor of his assigned office at the country newspaper's premises which he deigned to visit occasionally to check on operations.

'See, Theroux was a good choice to send.' Robson justified his decision, a decision that had niggled at him since receiving the thirty pieces of silver from Frank Theroux. Robson turned to the Weekend Editor, John Gibson. 'Don't change a word, run it as it is.'

He read an extract aloud. 'The craft, an MTB (motor torpedo boat) came cruising along the coastline; its crew looking for stray units like ours. Risking their own lives to pick up their fellow countrymen, these brave seamen were attacked by German bombers before we could get on board.

'The waiting soldiers on shore grabbed their rifles, some

choked with sand, and tried to bring down the fast-moving targets in the sky. We watched with despairing hearts as the MTB pulled away from shore and left us stranded. At least they weren't hit. The same could not be said of those of us on the beach. The German aircraft bombed and machine gunned us, leaving only a handful of us alive.

'The surviving men, including yours truly, waited undercover near the shoreline for their return. Finally, we could hear the approaching sound of the MTB. I have never been happier to hear any sound in my life.

'We waited, trying to be patient and praying to God, ironically the same God the Germans pray to, to let us get aboard safely and return home to our beloved Mother Country.

'Fortunately, the beach was flat and given the design of the MTB, it could get close to the shore. Numbering off and with as much stealth as possible, we removed our heavy coats, leaving them on the beach and made our way to the waterline.

'We were almost up to our necks in water as we waded in and tried to pull ourselves on board. Our two leaders—Corporal Shaun *Sandy* Gibson and the Platoon Sergeant William Southey were the last to board, ensuring all of their men were safe.

'Thanks to the blessed work of the MTB's crew, we headed safely away from Dunkirk beach towards our home shores, praying for any other poor stragglers who may arrive in the days to come and find themselves left behind.'

Charles Robson grinned. 'It would bring a tear to the eye.'

'That it would,' Gibson agreed. 'Do you want to remove the part about the German God?'

'No, run it word-for-word!'

Gibson nodded.

'Bloody good choice,' Robson said again, seeking Gibson's endorsement.

Gibson cleared his throat. 'By the way, have you heard about Frank Theroux?'

'Heard what? Did he keep his contract after all? That would be justice for Theroux given Howell's ruthless pursuit of it.' Robson reached into the top drawer of his desk for a cigar.

'No,' John Gibson said. 'He got a telegram.'

Robson stopped and looked up. 'A telegram?'

'Yes, but apparently it was a mistake,' Gibson told him. 'The War Office sent a telegram saying James was killed in action. But now we've found James Theroux very much alive.' He tapped on the filed article.

Robson exhaled. He looked out of the window, running his hand over his chin. 'Poor bugger,' he muttered. 'I hope you're running a story on that—a father's grief put right, the joy on finding his son alive after the agony, etc.'

'Frank Theroux is dead. He hanged himself after getting the telegram,' Gibson announced. 'Nothing to live for, I guess.' Gibson grabbed James' article and left Robson's office, closing the door as he left.

Charles Robson dropped into his chair.

*****

June 5, 1940

Dearest Lexie

I haven't heard from you in such a long time … I imagine your letters are looking for me. At last I can write to you and let you know that I am safe. In fact, I am heading back to England as we speak. I may be able to deliver this letter in person. Imagine if I walked into the hospital one day! I'm not sure I could let you go.

For the last few weeks, seems like years, we have been trying to get out of Dunkirk; walking, destroying machinery, hiding from the Germans. I wonder if I'll ever sleep again without the sound of artillery in my ears.

The last letter I got from you was when you were doing your training in the hospital and getting your first taste of the wards and long hours. I know you would have written many times since then, so eventually I expect to get this enormous pack of letters that will be like reading a book. I can't wait. When you were talking about your cooking I nearly ate the page. We have been so hungry. On the road, walking endlessly every day, we had virtually nothing to eat. Ham found an Oxo cube and thought it was Christmas. What a ham he is … you should have seen the performance he put on unwrapping it. Then he boiled it in a pan. That in itself was an ordeal as all of our matches were soggy from wading through creeks. But we eventually got a fire lit thanks to Misty persevering with his magnifying glass, some dried paper and twigs. Ham boiled this one pathetic Oxo cube, beef-flavoured incidentally, and Ham poured the 'soup' into our tin mugs. We all drank this weak mixture like it was the best thing in the world. It was fun though and good for our morale. Since we got rescued however, we have had tea and a corned beef sandwich. I never thought anything could taste so good as that sandwich did.

Lexie, I am proud of you and admire what you are doing. It sounds like you are working around the clock, but I worry about the gruesome sights you will see and wonder if you will be able to forget them after the war is over and move on. I hoped you would stay at home, maybe keep volunteering at the canteen and not subject yourself to some of the awful things we are capable of doing. Just last week we stumbled on a pile of corpses. I won't go into detail; suffice to say that I couldn't tear my eyes away. There is something fascinating and macabre that makes you want to look; maybe it's the relief that but for the grace of God I wasn't on that pile. But the stench was overwhelming. It is still in my nostrils. We covered them as best we could, mainly for the sake of their families, the victims are past caring now. Lex, please go home. Please go home to your mum, visit my dad, pour tea at the canteen.

Speaking of my father, I haven't received anything from him for a while now. Perhaps his letters will arrive with yours. Is he okay? Did he get the contract renewed or have your father and Howell secured it?

Anyway, must go for now my love. Will write again soon but know that I am on my way home to you, even if it is only for a brief period. My best to Carrie, Kitty and your mother, my respects to your father, and all my love to you.

Yours, James xxx

*****

Lexie grabbed the newspaper greedily. She gasped, covering her mouth with her hand and then she laughed.

Lexie leapt up and ran from the canteen, down the hall to find her best friend. She saw patients raising their heads curiously as she ran past wards. She knew the Matron would haul her over the coals if she was caught running in the hospital hallways. Lexie didn't care.

She put her head into one ward but there was no sign of Kitty.

'What's up?' Emma, one of her nursing friends asked.

'Have you seen Kitty?' Lexie said breathlessly.

'Smoko.' Emma tipped her head towards the outside door.

'Thanks.' Lexie ran out through the side door to the hospital garden and saw Kitty sitting on a bench, her feet up on the fountain.

'Kitty!' she screamed.

'What?' Kitty jumped up.

'He's alive.' Lexie pulled her back onto the seat. 'He's alive,' she said the words slowly. 'My James.'

Kitty inhaled sharply. 'How do you know?'

Lexie thrust the newspaper at her and watched as Kitty's eyes scanned the pages.

'He filed a story on the boat after evacuation from Dunkirk … it's dated after the telegram! It's his story, filed in his name. It means he's on his way home.'

Kitty grabbed Lexie and held her in a tight embrace. 'Thank God,' she whispered. 'Thank God.'

Lexie cried with relief, offering snatches of thanks in prayer.

They sat holding each other for a while, enjoying the good news, until finally Kitty pulled away.

'C'mon,' she nudged Lexie, 'your boy is fine, but there's plenty inside who need us.'

Gratefully, Lexie jumped up and went back to work.

Chapter 21

James trudged off the vessel, following the other bedraggled men of his platoon. His body was stiff and every step took some effort. *Ham was right,* he thought. *We are a motley lot.* Uniforms that were hardly recognisable, different levels of attire, unshaven and filthy. He walked down the gang plank and joined the other soldiers that merged with his own platoon as they were herded onto waiting trains.

'Home,' he whispered and smiled. He inhaled. Doesn't smell like home, but it is home nonetheless, he thought.

He pushed into a carriage, moved to the back and fell into a seat. Other soldiers followed until the carriage was full. Sitting next to a window, James put his forehead on the glass and watched the scenery as the train slowly began to pull away from the station, heading north-west through the English countryside. An hour later, he woke with a start. James looked around. Everyone seemed to be dazed; sitting in silent thought, exhausted and not used to not being on guard. *I must write about what this feels like for the paper,* he thought. *To sit and let your guard down for the first time in months.*

The train pulled into a station and the sight of the ladies in their uniforms handing out cups of tea and sandwiches, had an emotional effect on many of the soldiers. James scanned the ladies looking for Lexie's face. He knew she wouldn't be there, but he had to search, she was the only woman he longed to see and hold. Alighting from the train, he gratefully accepted a sandwich and a cup of tea from a woman who would have been about his mother's age. When she said 'welcome home my brave lad,' he almost burst into tears.

After an hour, the men re-boarded and the train continued its journey through the countryside.

'Still no idea where we're going?' Misty leaned forward in his chair to ask Sandy.

'I've been here the whole time you have,' Sandy answered. 'You think I've got some kind of telepathy?'

'Yes, Corporal, I do. You knew we'd be the best bunch to hang around with after all,' Misty added.

Sandy laughed and lit a cigarette. 'That just proves I've got no idea.'

After what seemed like hours and hours of rolling along, the train slowed down and Ham read the name on the station sign out loud as they passed.

'Porthcawl, any takers for Porthcawl?' he asked.

The train came to a stop and the men struggled to their feet. James stepped from the train and stretched. This time, they were shuffled along to waiting buses.

Enough, James thought. *Just let me lie down somewhere that doesn't move for a few hours at least.*

'It's a hat trick,' Shorty said. 'Boat, train and bus. Any chance of a plane tonight?'

'God I hope not,' Misty added. 'I need to move a bit. Can't sit for too much longer.'

'Not much longer to go lads,' the bus driver said overhearing their conversation. 'We're no more than ten minutes from your last stop today.'

'Bless you young man,' Ham said to the driver as he passed him on the way up the bus steps.

The elderly driver chuckled and shook his head.

James dropped into a seat next to Ham and waited as the last of the men relieved themselves, smoked or stretched and then boarded the buses. Within five minutes they were off again and were pleased to find the driver was right, the bus pulled up on the outskirts of Porthcawl near an old warehouse. James entered the building, gratefully took the offered bowl of soup and a blanket, found a corner and soon fell sound asleep.

*****

James woke early the next morning and pushed himself up on his elbows. Hundreds of men were still asleep all around him. Others were seated on windowsills in the sun or smoking on the front steps of the warehouse. He had a plan. If they were to be given a few days to themselves, he had plenty of time to get himself to London, to St Bartholomew's hospital to surprise Lexie.

James found Sandy attempting to shave using the reflection of the window and a donated razor.

'Sleep?' Sandy asked.

'Better than I have for ages,' James answered.

'Me too. Good not to be rocking.'

'I want to go to London, Sandy, to see my fiancée. What's the story here?' James shuffled his feet, desperate for the right answer.

Sandy turned to look at him. 'You've got a seventy-two-hour leave pass. Effective now. That do you?'

James grinned. 'You bet. Thanks Sandy.'

'You might want to clean up first,' Sandy said, but turned to find James was already out of earshot.

*****

James hit the shower, put up with the cold water and donned a clean shirt that all the men had been given on arrival. He dusted off his uniform and put it back on, flattened his hair and pronounced his appearance hopeless.

He couldn't believe the generosity shown to him once he got on the move. Food was pressed into his hand at the station, he rode the train free of charge and was patted on the back and complimented the whole journey. All he could think of was Lexie. He was on his way to Lexie. It was nearly two hundred miles by train to London, but that was nothing after the journey he had just endured.

James sat in his compartment and began to worry.

What if she's not there? What if she has a day off and no one knows where to find her? What if she's met a doctor?

James didn't get much time to dwell on this; everyone in the carriage wanted to talk with him and the other soldiers on board. He was happy for the distraction as the Welsh landscape passed by his window en route to London, otherwise every minute would have seemed like an hour.

*****

He arrived mid-afternoon. Passing through the hospital's grand gates, he nodded to the statue of King Henry VIII. Soldiers were everywhere, so he was hardly noticeable; visiting, sitting in the sun recovering, hobbling on crutches or being wheeled in chairs by nurses.

James' heart was beating so fast in his chest that he was sure he looked as though he should be admitted.

Was I this nervous going into battle? He felt flushed and anxious as he searched for Lexie's face everywhere, expecting to see her at any moment.

Deep breaths, he told himself.

So much had happened since he had stood in the grounds of his garden, wearing his suit and offering Lexie champagne, his hand and his kingdom. He chuckled at the memory, which helped him relax. *Madness,* he sighed, looking around as he walked to the administration desk.

A mature lady peered over her glasses at him. Her name badge read Mrs. Wilson.

'Can I help you?' she smiled.

'Yes, please, Mrs. Wilson. I'm looking for Lexie, uh, Nurse Alexandra Taylor please?'

'Is she expecting you?' she asked looking at the day's roster.

'Definitely not,' he answered.

Mrs. Wilson looked up and smiled. 'Welcome home young man.'

'Thank you, it is good to be back.'

'Well, you are going to make one young lady very happy.' Mrs. Wilson looked around. 'I'm sure Matron won't mind on this occasion if we don't page Nurse Taylor. Perhaps you would like to surprise her?'

James nodded, holding back his emotions. 'Yes, thank you. I've dreamt of it.'

She nodded and looked at the list again. 'You will find Alexandra in the main wing, on level two, my dear. Take the stairs to your right. Now don't give any of our patients a heart attack with your reunion!' she warned.

James laughed. 'I promise I'll do my best to be restrained. Thank you.'

She nodded.

As he turned back before climbing the stairs, James saw she was still looking at him and smiling. He gave her a wave and vanished up the staircase, two at a time. On the second level, he looked around. Three nurses were in the hallway but none of them was Lexie. He glanced through the door of the first ward. Soldiers were playing cards, or lay bandaged and strung up. He gave a nod to a few of the men and continued down the hallway, straightening his jacket and hair one more time.

I should have got flowers or stockings or something, he realised. *Never mind, she'll have to make do with just me.*

He felt so close now that it increased his anxiety. He saw two nurses in the next ward but not Lexie. One asked which patient he was looking for and he replied it was a nurse. He said her name but the nurse didn't recognise it. James tried the name 'Lexie' and the nurse's face lit up. She clapped her hands together.

'You must be James.'

James smiled, delighted that Lexie spoke of him. 'She's mentioned me?'

'Non-stop.' The young nurse rolled her eyes. 'Two doors from the end on the right.'

'Thank you.' He ducked out of the room and increased his pace. *Two doors from the end on the right.*

James stopped. He could hear her. She was laughing at something another nurse was saying. Then he saw her; Lexie was applying a dressing to a soldier's arm. James couldn't move; he stood still watching her. The angle of her chin, her dark hair tied up to reveal the milky white skin of her neck. She laughed again, this time at something the soldier said and then, for just a moment, she blinked rapidly, as though holding back tears and returned her concentration to finishing the bandage.

James heard her say, 'there, you're done!' as she rose and brushed down the skirt of her uniform. She turned towards the door and saw him.

James smiled, his eyes locked on hers. Lexie gasped and stepped back, bumping into a steel cabinet. Neither of them moved. He had been thinking for months about what he would do at this moment and all he could do was stare at her, as though the scene wasn't real.

'Lexie,' he said her name and immediately she ran towards him. At last; his arms were around her, feeling her pressing against him. He kissed her lips and held her tightly, never wanting to let go in case it was a dream and he should wake up. Behind them, the room burst into applause and Lexie pulled away, tears streaming down her face, flushed with embarrassment. She turned to her nursing friend and the patients.

'Ladies, gentlemen,' she said, 'this is my fiancé, Private James Theroux.'

It was James' turn to go red. He bowed slightly, reached for her hand and said, 'you must excuse us,' as he pulled her out into the hallway.

Lexie took the lead. Not stopping, she led him out of the hospital wards, down the stairs and into the garden. She led him around the side to a private area and pulled him down onto a seat beside her.

Lexie put her hands on his face and their eyes remained

locked for a long time before she spoke. 'I knew you were alive, I could feel you in the world.'

James kissed her slowly. He stopped to hold her again and inhaled her scent.

'You are the most beautiful sight I have ever seen.' He gazed lovingly at her.

'And you are my dream come true, but messy,' she teased him.

'Stopping to get cleaned up properly would have delayed me another half-an-hour.'

'You look perfect.' She held him again. 'Can we just stay like this? Cancel the war?' she asked.

James chuckled. 'Leave it with me, I'll organise it.'

Lexie pulled away. 'How long do we have?'

'I got a seventy-two-hour pass this morning.'

'And then?'

'I don't know, but for seventy-two hours you're mine,' he said.

Chapter 22

Getting time off was no problem for Lexie. Everyone understood the need to grab those few precious moments together and Lexie would have left nursing rather than miss spending the time with him. Even her fellow nurse roommates looked after her; moving to other quarters and leaving Lexie to have their small and crowded room for herself and James.

Lexie wanted to make love but James had protested. Lexie was more pragmatic.

'I want to give myself to you,' she assured him. 'It's a different world now from our champagne days. We'll never have that again and I want us to feel love, make love and share this now.'

James agreed, 'War makes you want to grab every precious moment. But we'll have plenty of time, the rest of our lives, to make love. I want to get married now … today!'

'Today!' Lexie exclaimed.

'Yes. I want you to be my wife when I leave. We can still have the big celebration when the war is over. Marry me now, Lex?'

Lexie gasped. 'Yes, of course,' she said excitedly, 'it's the best idea I've heard since you proposed!'

James grabbed her and spun her around. She pummelled his shoulders until he put her down.

Lexie continued. 'But we haven't got our banns ... if we visit the vicar now and he reads them out at mass tomorrow morning, we could get married in the afternoon.'

'Or we could get a special marriage licence ... I heard someone on board a ship did that because they didn't have time for banns.' James shrugged.

'Maybe, but let's try the vicar first—I'm sure he will do that for us—he has done quite a few ceremonies in the last few months. Then, my love, our last day-and-a-half together can be our unofficial honeymoon. I want us to squeeze everything we can in this little window of time so we have happy memories to hold us together ... to help replace some of the gruesome ...' she didn't need to say more. 'I want you to have all of me.'

'I want that more than you know,' James said.

Lexie began to plan. 'We won't have time to get Mother and Carrie here, and it is best that Father doesn't hear anyway, he might try and stop it.'

'I agree,' James said. 'Just ask Kitty if she will be one of our witnesses and maybe Esther or Fran ... Frances?' he stumbled recalling her friend's name.

'Franny.' Lexie nodded.

'As long as you and I are there,' he said.

'Yes.' Lexie embraced him. 'Perfect.'

*****

The next day, early in the afternoon in the hospital chapel, James and Lexie exchanged their vows in front of Father Albert Walker, Kitty and Franny to whom the matron gave one hour off. James wore his uniform, Lexie wore a pale pink dress that she borrowed from one of the nurses and the bridesmaids, Kitty and Franny, wore their best dresses. They signed the marriage certificate, witnessed by Kitty and Franny and dated it the 8th June, 1940.

The hospital kitchen had baked a miniature wedding cake for the occasion, using what little rations they had and all five guests shared in it at the end of the ceremony. Kitty threw her homemade confetti over the couple as they walked out of the chapel, promising Father Walker that she would clean it up later.

The rest of the day was theirs alone. Franny gave Lexie a silk negligee from her collection as a wedding gift—pale cream and impossible to get during war time!

For the first twenty-four hours they barely surfaced. Lexie bathed and cared for him, fed him what food she could get and they made love like they might never have the opportunity again. They walked and talked of all the things they had seen and felt. They spoke of his father's death; of her father and Howell Snr winning the contract with no competition; of Moira and Carrie working at the station canteen serving refreshments to the soldiers; of Misty, Ham, Sandy, Shorty and Gunna, and of Aunty Jo in Australia and Uncle Will still away at war. They spoke of Autumn Manor and filling it with children and calling their first son, Frank.

That first day was blissful and when night came neither could sleep. Time was going too fast and sleep meant losing hours and hours that they couldn't get back to share together.

Then, inevitably, it happened; the morning came when James had to catch the train back to Porthcawl.

*****

Lexie could barely touch James or look at him for fear of collapsing in tears. She vacillated between pain, tears and anger. They stood together on the platform of the train station, oblivious to the people milling around them.

'I want you to tell the matron you want to make up for the time you were given off. I want you to work every shift you can get for the next few weeks, so you drop into bed exhausted at the end of every day and fall immediately to sleep. Then,' James continued, 'I want you to wake up and get straight back to work again and soon, you will see, you'll feel better and stronger.'

'Is that what you did when you left me the first time? Tried not to think of me at all?' Lexie asked.

'Yes,' James answered truthfully.

Lexie pulled away but James pulled her closer.

'If I had thought about you, I would have been despondent, less attentive, and more vulnerable to the enemy, viruses, you name it. Instead I kept as busy as I could … digging trenches, doing spotter's duty, anything, everything. Because the moment I thought about you, I couldn't operate. I dreamt about you. I spent any downtime I had writing to you.'

'All I ask is that you stay safe.' Lexie buried her face in his shoulder. 'You know my love that I am here waiting for you.'

'And you will write as much as you can?' he asked.

'It is when I feel the closest to you,' she said. 'I suspect we are both going to get a huge bundle of letters after seeing the piles of mail at the Royal Exchange.'

'I hope so.' James sighed.

They both looked up with dread on hearing the train pull into the station, and they held each other until the last boarding call. James took Lexie's hand and walked to the carriage.

'Goodbye for now, Mrs. Theroux.'

She smiled with pleasure and then shook with sobs.

He stood on the step and gave her one last kiss. Neither spoke as the train pulled away and they watched each other until they were out of sight. Lexie turned around to leave and saw Kitty standing near the exit, waiting for her. She rushed to her best friend and into her embrace. Eventually, they linked arms and left the station to return to St Bartholomew's.

*****

'Hey, Scribbler's back, miss us?' Ham called, nudging Misty as he spoke.

'You have no idea, Ham,' James answered. 'I almost came back early, but I thought it might get me discharged on the grounds of insanity.'

Misty hooted with laughter as he thumped James on the back. 'Well we're the first back. I tell you, if the Corporal isn't back on time, he's going on report.'

'Boot shining and pressing our uniforms,' Ham agreed.

'And a sorry state yours is in too,' James noted.

'I didn't have it on much,' Ham winked. 'And you?'

'A gentleman doesn't kiss and tell.' James walked past him to see what food was in stock.

'Hmm, I'll take that as you did well. How is the lovely Miss Scribbler?'

James sighed. 'She was a sight to behold. And lads, it's official, she is now Mrs. Scribbler.'

'Well done.' Ham whooped and shook James' hand. Misty thumped him on the back again.

'Quick honeymoon,' Misty stated.

Ham shook his head. 'Stupid bloody war. Ah, here's the missing two.'

Shorty and Sandy had arrived.

'Lads.' Sandy nodded.

'Corporal,' they answered in unison.

'Get ready … tonight we ship off to Baghdad.'

*****

August 1, 1940

Dear Lexie,

I can't believe you got to see James and have nearly seventy-two hours with him. How wonderful to know he is alive and well. Although it would have been nice to see him here too even for just a few hours, instead of keeping him all for yourself.

Mother and I have been doing our canteen duty and really enjoying it. You are right though, it is a long day and we are both exhausted afterwards but it is so rewarding. I have been proposed to twenty-seven times and been asked out at least a hundred times. I'm going to a dance tonight to welcome some of our boys while they are on leave.

Anson has also been visiting me. I'm not sure whether he misses you, likes me or whether this is another one of Father's bright ideas, but he has been very sweet and good company. He even picked me up from my canteen shift one day last week and Mother and I were driven home in style. He's not that bad, in fact he's rather dashing and I am feeling quite spoilt.

Next week, in case you have forgotten, I turn eighteen and I too can enrol to study nursing if I want to. I'm not sure yet, but will think about it. I'm fairly busy as it is and I don't want to be too tired to go out with Emily at night to the dances. Anson said we have a duty to keep ourselves fresh and attractive to brighten the day for the men doing their duty during this grim war. Yes, I know what you will say to that, but is it so wrong to want to look nice and feel pretty?

Anyway, must be off now. Emily and I are trying to get enough good fabric to make some new dresses. There's so little available and we'll be wearing hessian sacks next if we can't find anything good. The curtains are looking promising, especially the ones in your bedroom! Take care Lex and write or visit soon.

With love
Carrie xx

*****

'Where exactly is Baghdad?' Shorty asked.

'Iraq,' James answered, 'it's the capital of Iraq.'

'Okay.' Shorty shrugged, no wiser. 'Will we like it there?'

'Maybe for a summer holiday,' James said. 'Gets warm there.'

'Good!' Misty exclaimed. 'I could use a little sunshine. How warm are we talking?'

James shrugged. 'September, let's see; just over 100 degrees.'

'Get out of here!' Ham sat up straight. 'I'll fry. Look at this red hair and pale skin. I have to preserve my natural assets. Sandy, can't you get me sent to Switzerland. I hear that cold climate preserves your looks?'

Sandy shook his head. 'I know where I'd like to send you! See that platoon that's shipping out now?'

'Very funny,' Ham smirked. 'You'd soon miss me.'

They continued to watch one of the platoons loading bags onto a lorry in the yard.

Sandy put his hands behind his head and leaned back. 'Rather be going on our cruise in the sun than overland any day.'

'I'd be a little more enthusiastic about it if there were no Germans at sea,' Shorty added.

'Yeah,' Sandy agreed. 'Nothing's perfect.'

James thought of Lexie and smiled.

Chapter 23

Lexie stopped and looked around. She realised it was the first time she had stopped for hours. The wards were overflowing with casualties; the theatres had worked non-stop since around five p.m. when the first of the German bombers dropped their bombs on the East End and central London.

Lexie stared in disbelief; this was London—London at war, it couldn't be happening. None of it felt real; it was like walking through a movie set. The windows were covered with sticking paper in criss-cross patterns to prevent splintering. In some wards there was no glass left in the windows and she could see through one of them that it was now dark outside. What had happened to the day?

Lexie licked her lips and tasted dust and dirt. Behind her the doors of the hospital swung open again and an elderly lady with blood running down her face, stumbled towards Lexie. Disorientated and having used the last of her energy forcing the door open, she began to sway. Lexie ran to her and reached her just in time.

'You're safe now, I have you,' Lexie assured her, lowering the elderly lady into a chair between an old man, sleeping, and a mother with a child in her lap.

'I'm sorry dear. Sorry to be a nuisance.'

'No, no,' Lexie shushed her. 'You're not a nuisance at all.'

'I wasn't fast enough to get out of the way,' she continued.

'Many weren't fast enough, don't you worry about that,' Lexie assured her, observing the blood pouring down the elderly lady's leg and the large blood stain on her blouse near the shoulder.

'I'll just find somewhere private, so we can remove your blouse and assess your injuries. Just a minute, I'll come straight back for you,' Lexie promised. 'Will you wait here?'

The elderly lady nodded and closed her eyes.

Lexie looked around. Half a dozen nurses were ministering to patients right there in the entrance hall. She raced into the nearest room, which already had more beds than it could sustain, and found a number of women being treated behind a makeshift curtain.

'Can I bring an elderly lady in, Sister? She has a chest wound and I need to remove her blouse to see the extent of the injury,' Lexie asked the sister in charge.

The sister looked around. 'We'll make room for her somewhere, bring her in.'

'Thank you.' Lexie returned and knelt down beside the old lady. She touched her to wake her.

'I've found a room, not far,' Lexie said before realising with shock that the elderly lady was dead.

A sob caught in Lexie's throat and she swallowed hard.

Stay in control, she coached herself.

The poor old dear, how far did she walk alone and in pain to get here?

This horrible, pointless war.

Lexie blinked away her tears, wiping her face with the back of her hand. She rose and let the sister know what had happened.

The sister nodded and briefly touched Lexie's arm before returning to her work.

Lexie moved to the exit; she had to get out, if only for a few moments. She passed more casualties coming in, her eyes glazed, not hearing their requests and questions.

Outside in the cold air, she moved into the shadows at the side of the hospital building and bent over, inhaling deeply. She allowed herself to cry a little, then wiped her face, straightened her uniform and breathed deeply again.

'Getting to you?' a voice asked from the dark.

Lexie jumped.

'Sorry, I didn't mean to startle you.'

'Doctor!' Lexie looked surprised. 'I thought I was alone … I'm sorry. A dear old lady just passed away before we could help her. But you would see that sort of thing all the time.' Lexie felt foolish.

'Doesn't make it any easier,' he stubbed out his cigarette. 'You're a VAD aren't you?'

'Yes. I've been here about six months, I should be used to this by now,' Lexie said. She noticed his face was lined and wearied.

'Sometimes it still surprises us. I'm really only twenty, look how it has aged me!'

Lexie laughed.

'Thanks,' he declared. 'Is it that obvious that I'm older?'

Lexie studied him. He was handsome in a conservative way; tall and wiry, short dark hair flecked with a bit of grey that did prematurely age him and wearing thin-rimmed glasses. She put him at about thirty years of age.

'No, but I know you couldn't have qualified as a doctor by the age of twenty.'

'Well said.' He smiled at her. 'What's your name?'

'Lexie, Lexie Taylor … um Theroux.'

'What sort of name is that?' he asked.

'Alexandra Theroux,' Lexie tried again, 'I was just married.'

'Ah, well congratulations. So, you go by the name Lexie? I can see why. The emergency could be over by the time we got your full name out.'

Lexie laughed again.

'I'm Adam Gardam.'

'Adam,' Lexie repeated, 'or Doctor Gardam in front of Matron.'

'Yes indeed, we wouldn't want to risk the wrath of Matron. He opened his cigarette case and offered one to Lexie. She declined.

Adam lit up. 'So you're doing general wards?'

'Yes, what few are left since the last bombing.'

'Hmm.' He studied her. 'What did you do before the war?'

Lexie blushed. 'I drank champagne and practised being charming.'

This time Adam was the one to laugh. 'I suspect you were good at it. Strange isn't it, how everything changes? Bet you never thought you would be doing this?'

Lexie shook her head. 'Never in my wildest dreams. You know, I can't remember what time I started my shift today … I feel I have always been here. I've done everything from bed pans to deceased reports.'

'I know exactly what you mean.' He exhaled smoke into the cold air. 'I've been looking at blood and wounds all day. I don't think any of the bodies I've touched had a face or was a real person; just one after the other, after the other. Still, at least we have some supplies here. Try doing what we do on the battlefield and making do with a swab and a needle and thread.'

They stood in silence for a few moments.

'Are you from London?' Adam asked.

'No, Gerrards Cross. Not far from here. But in some strange way, I'm glad I'm here. I would rather be here than waiting at home feeling useless.'

'So, this lucky husband of yours … where is he?'

'He's in … actually I don't know where he is now. He came back from Dunkirk, we had seventy-two glorious hours together and then he was shipped out again. I don't know to where yet,' Lexie said.

'I'm sorry.' Adam removed his glasses and began to clean them. 'What did he do before all this? Besides pour your champagne and win you over.' He winked at her, pushing his glasses back on.

Lexie smiled. 'He was a journalist before the war, and was to be sent to Europe as a war correspondent for his paper. But he enlisted instead and has been fighting ever since.'

'Very admirable,' Adam said. 'I've thought about going over myself.'

'But you're just as needed here.'

'So they say.' He stubbed out his cigarette.

'And you? Do you have someone waiting for you or here with you?' Lexie felt bold asking but had Kitty in mind.

'No. Unbelievable isn't it? A good catch like me,' he joked again.

Lexie wondered how much pain he masked with humour. They heard the whistle that heralded another explosion and Lexie saw Adam flinch.

Maybe that's why he's here, she thought. *Maybe he's been there and back already.* But she didn't have a chance to ask.

'Ready to go back in?' he asked.

'I am. Thank you, Adam,' Lexie smiled. "I feel better for the break and company."

'You're welcome. I make it a habit to leap out scaring nurses in the dark; seems to do them the world of good.'

Lexie laughed again. He bowed to let her pass first and she entered the ward again to find it looking just a little brighter.

*****

September 16, 1940

Dearest James

I can still feel your embrace and your touch. Weren't we lucky to have those few moments in time? I go over them in my head again and again like playing a reel of film. Mother and Carrie are so relieved to hear you are alive. You have given hope to us all, especially me.

As for my news, I am working long hours and you are right, it is a great remedy for heartache. We seem to be constantly awake and working, but I'm sure you know that feeling.

All of us and the hospital itself have been through an enormous ordeal; the Germans have started bombing the city and it is relentless. It started last week and they are calling it the blitz. Kitty and I have been on the night shift for the last few weeks (and some day shifts too actually) and it's getting to be a common thing to eat our breakfast in the evening, with the unwelcome drone of German aircraft flying over.

I lost a dear old lady on my shift tonight; she died within minutes of me leaving her the poor old soul. She was hit by shrapnel and had walked miles to get to the hospital, not realising how bad her injuries really were. Almost as soon as she sat down and I went to find a bed for her, she passed away. I guess there's some comfort in knowing she died in a safe environment with people around her. I wonder where her family are now. Perhaps they are dead too, or panicking in their search for her.

I've saved my big news for last. The Matron has agreed to Kitty's and my transfers. We will be posted overseas. I can't wait and I'm hoping and praying we will be sent to where you are … I know it's a bit naive to think that the odds of us seeing each other are better if I'm over there rather than here in London, but I'm holding onto that thought. Then I will be there to look after you if needed. Kitty has agreed to come with me and she's quite keen for the adventure. She has never been outside of England before, and I think she hopes to end up near her brothers. I'm not sure if she will still want to come though if she falls in love with Adam before we leave—that's Dr Gardam. I met him tonight and plan to matchmake them! They will be perfect for each other.

We don't know when we are going, but the Matron said it could be as soon as next week. We are on constant standby. I hope it is sooner rather than later. I have your photo and I will ask every person I meet if they know you or have seen you. You thought the Germans were tough to evade!

My love, the busier I am the better I feel. My thoughts are with you always, and I am overwhelmed with fear for your safety and my longing for you.

September 18:

Darling, I'm sorry I haven't got this letter in the mail to you yet but I was called away in the middle of writing it and only now can return to finish it, two days later!

But I have great news so it was worth the wait—we have a date for our posting. We are going late this week, in two days' time to be exact, but we still don't know where. Some of the nurses said that this has happened really quickly and we are lucky; I suspect Matron made it happen. She has a soft spot for Kitty and no one else would have got away with that tomboy haircut that Kitty got on Matron's watch. Matron is not sure how long we will stay in any one location, but that's fine, at least we may be in the same part of the world. I will feel closer to you then.

Mother is worried of course, Father can't look at me for wanting to kill me and Carrie is genuinely concerned. I was surprised that she reacted that way. We have never really been close, maybe she is growing up and thinking less about herself. Perhaps working at the canteen has helped. You know, I think you might be safe from Carrie—I think she has now set her sights somewhere else—Anson! Yes seriously, he is courting her. It is hard to be her age and have a crush on someone a million miles away I'm sure. Lucky for you I am more mature and much more capable of sustaining love from a long distance. How I miss teasing you and hearing your laugh.

Now I know what you will say about my posting, but trust me, I know it will be difficult and challenging working more in the thick of it, but it already has been challenging and I have survived. We work around the clock here and I have seen some awful things. Last week, I had to assist the senior nurses in surgery, we are just so stretched. I didn't think I would be able to stay in the room but I did. That poor soldier—we didn't have the drugs to help relieve all his pain—it was unbearable.

Add to that, last week, a bomb went right through the middle of our nursing quarters—it literally blew the windows out. Fortunately we were all at work in the wards so no one was injured but what a mess. Kitty, Esther and I lost nearly everything. Franny's bed and cupboard survived, so we are all wearing very nice underwear at the moment courtesy of her still-unknown-to-us benefactor! Several of the other rooms were completely destroyed, so we now have another three nurses in our room sleeping on mattresses on the floor. Luckily we all do different shifts and are so tired that we probably would have slept through the explosion even had we been in the room. Kitty has started wearing her tin helmet around permanently. It has caused much humour and cheered up a few people. Matron scolded her at first but then decided there was probably some merit in it (see, Kitty is one of her favourites, I would never have got away with that).

I am so excited that I may soon be closer to you, somewhere, somehow.

I love you.
Your Lexie x x x x

Chapter 24

'He is gorgeous.' Kitty dropped onto her bed and began to rub her sore feet after a twelve-hour shift in the wards.

'Who?' Lexie rolled over on her bed and studied Kitty.

'That doctor with the glasses, the one who stopped and talked with you when he was doing the rounds today.'

'Adam, Dr Gardam?' Lexie asked.

'Yes! How do you know his first name?'

'Because I have him earmarked for you!'

'What?' Kitty brightened.

'I retreated for a break and a cry the other day …'

'Oh I'm sorry, love.' Kitty stopped and looked at Lexie.

'No, it's okay. It was the day that elderly lady died in the chair … the sweet old dear. Anyway, I was outside gathering myself and I didn't realise he was standing about ten feet from me having a cigarette. There I am snivelling away like a drama queen. It was most embarrassing but he was charming.'

'Gee, and you didn't smell someone smoking ten feet away from you. You were distressed.'

'It was the day of the dock bombing. The air was full of dust and smoke. The cigarette could have been smouldering right next to me and it would have blended in. Anyway, he's nice, really nice, Kit.' Lexie said, with excitement in her voice.

'Is he married?' Kitty asked, moisturising her hands and gazing at her wedding ring finger.

'I made a point of asking, just for you,' Lexie teased her. 'Well actually, he asked me first if I was writing to someone and I told him about James, but he said he was free as a bird.'

'Really? Can't have that. A doctor, of all things … he must need someone to comfort him after those long shifts in surgery.'

'I've been looking for an opportunity to introduce you,' Lexie assured her. 'I just haven't had the luck to find you both in the same place at the same time.'

'I'll work at making it happen,' Kitty assured her. 'Kitty Gardam, Mrs. Adam Gardam. Mm, that sounds good. Would you be my bridesmaid?'

Lexie laughed. 'Sure, what colour would you like me to wear?'

'Let's see,' Kitty studied her, 'with that dark hair, I'm thinking something gold maybe or cream. Have you and James spoken about having a wedding party after the war since you didn't get one? Sort of reaffirming your vows in front of everyone?'

'Not exactly, but we've spoken about life after—the white picket fence, the whole thing,' Lexie sighed.

'Lucky you.'

Lexie reached for her hairbrush. Kitty moved behind her and took the hairbrush from her. She began to brush through Lexie's long dark hair.

'What I wouldn't give for a glass of champagne right now,' Lexie sighed. 'If you fall in love with Adam and he sweeps you off your feet, you don't have to come overseas with me.'

'I don't think that I'm going to be in love before we move out on Friday. It is Wednesday after all. But if I get an introduction, we could write! I have to be honest, even though I would love to be in love, I'm kind of happy not to have anyone to worry about. I already have my brothers fighting, I don't really want to be pining for someone else. Besides, this is the first time in my life that I've had any real freedom,' Kitty said.

'I know. Just last year we were both being groomed for marriage.'

'Now,' Kitty continued, 'we're needed. We're useful and we will be travelling abroad with our work. It might be the only chance I get to have a real adventure, even if it is in the middle of a war. Can you believe that by next week, we will be on our way overseas?'

'In the middle of a war.' Lexie repeated, biting her lower lip.

*****

September 21, 1940

Hello my beautiful wife,

I hope this finds you well and in good spirits. I hit an awful low after leaving you but I would not have traded a minute of our time together despite the fresh pain of separation.

We sailed away from England and the further we got from the shore, the more my heart ached for you. I can't say much, of course, but it's probably okay to say that we started the journey on a ship called the SS Atlantic. She used to be a luxury liner. So bizarre to be sleeping on the floor, surrounded by hundreds of men and looking up at a huge chandelier! Ham insists on dancing with the nurses onboard in the ballroom despite it being set up as a temporary hospital. He is truly a ham, but they love him.

Misty, who, you may remember is a baker, can't stay out of the ship's galley. It's not like there's flour, yeast or butter on board, but the cooks seem happy to have the volunteer help and he seems happy to be back to his true calling.

Shorty, all six foot four of him, has investigated the entire workings of the ship. He is a mechanic after all, and they let him down to check out the engines and all that stuff (you can tell I'm hopeless when it comes to anything mechanical).

I spend my whole time writing or listening to the Stooges talking up their adventures; they look older, more confident now. Meanwhile, Sandy just rolls his eyes and wonders how he got lumped with the lot of us. We'll gain a few new lads when we land and Sandy's in meetings every second minute getting updates and working out plans. We still miss Gunna. Once, I forgot he was gone and looked for him. Enough about that.

I am so glad we got that time together and so happy you agreed to marry me then and there. It has given me enormous strength. I think about everything we are planning when we both come home and move into Autumn Manor. Since Father's passing, Mrs. Atkinson has decided to go to her sister's place somewhere in Yorkshire. Kenneth said he is happy to remain to maintain the house and gardens. Mrs. Atkinson blames herself for agreeing to take the weekend off. She says Father was insistent but that she should have stayed regardless. They are very upset, as you can imagine. I'm just glad that it was Father Ranken who found my father's body and not Mrs. Atkinson on her return to work on Monday.

You know I would still prefer that you stayed at the hospital in London rather than accept an overseas posting. I don't want to be the type who tells you what to do, and I know after witnessing how you handle your father, that you would ignore me anyway.

But it's hard enough being here, and knowing that you may be in a dangerous war zone somewhere just adds to my list of worries. Please reconsider … for me. I don't think it would take much to persuade Kitty to stay, just find her a date. Please think about it, Lexie. I know there's danger where you are, but not as much as being in the thick of it.

Will sign off now as I can see Ham coming towards me and that's bound to mean trouble. I will start my next volume soon.

I love you my wife, my life.
Yours,
James xxxx

*****

They were on their feet again, the start of another day in the hospital when Kitty began to laugh. Lexie looked across at her and smiled as they struggled to move a bed whose wheels were refusing to go in the right direction. This was the fifth patient to be moved to a safer area; into the wards where there were still windows, or light or the roof wasn't dripping. Moving patients around was getting trickier as so many of them were crammed together and very few rooms remained functional. Some were capable of walking, others had to be wheeled in their beds, along with all their attachments.

'What's so funny?' Lexie asked.

Kitty started laughing again. It became infectious; the patient in the bed grinned.

'It's just that we must look so ridiculous,' she looked around. Lexie chuckled and soon they were all laughing. 'If I were you David,' Kitty addressed the patient they were wheeling, I would ask to see drivers' licences!'

'I hear some patients are being moved to the cellar,' Lexie offered. 'Don't think there's a drop to drink down there though,' she smiled at the patient.

The two nurses steered the bed through the open doorway and into another room. 'Make way, mattress brigade coming,' Kitty called which started a fresh bout of laughing at the absurdity of it. Kitty continued to keep the situation light. 'You won't catch us Hitler,' she said, 'we're going to keep moving our beds and hiding underneath them!'

By this time, most of the ward was laughing, including those patients who had been relegated to chairs, unable to assist with the lifting.

'No, don't keep trying, we're too tricky for you,' Kitty continued to everyone's amusement.

Lexie shook her head laughing. 'You're a card, Kit.'

A loud bang made everybody in the ward cower and sober immediately. The building seemed to shake and the sound of breaking glass could be heard on a lower floor. The lights flickered back off and then back on.

Kitty filled the silence. 'See, John,' she said to a patient sitting with his leg suspended and covered in plaster. 'I told you this floor was safer. Stick with me.'

'You're a doll, Kitty, you really are.' He winked.

Lexie joined in sensing everyone's nervousness. 'Kitty's right though. It's the room service,' she added. 'Much better on this floor.'

'And the cooking,' Meg, one of the nurses contributed. 'That three-course meal last night—water, rissoles and a cup of tea—marvellous!'

They all laughed thinking about last night's canteen offering: rissoles that had more bread in them than meat.

'I think it's the staff,' one of the young and handsome patients said smiling at Kitty, 'the nursing girls are alright up here.'

Kitty blushed and began to make a vacant bed.

*****

September 28, 1940

Dear Lexie

Well, I did it, sorry … I am now wearing a beautiful dress made from the curtains in your bedroom. The burgundy looks quite nice and I don't think you can tell it was once curtains. There's more left if you would like a new dress but I suspect you just want to hang around in those dowdy nurse uniforms and look the part.

So how are you? Are you still working those terribly long hours? Have you heard from our James? I saw Mrs. Atkinson a few weeks ago. She was packing up to return to West Yorkshire. Her sister lives there somewhere. Kenneth is going to stay to look after the gardens but the house will remain vacant until James returns and the two of you move in together. I suspect you know all that anyway as Mrs. Atkinson was going to write to you if she hasn't already.

Mother and I are still working at the canteen three days a week. I really enjoy it and Emma is there now too.

Now Lex, I need to tell you something which you might find quite surprising. I think I have developed feelings for Anson. I'm sure that won't upset you since you didn't want him, but he is so very sweet and he really looks after me. I understand now what you meant when you told me that one had to have something to compare to when trying to work out one's true feelings. I have been asked out a number of times and I have had many dances with charming soldiers, but my thoughts keep returning to Anson. I can't sleep some nights and I've caught myself smiling and humming like some silly love sick debutante! I hate to say you are right, so I won't. But I understand now what you meant when you said that you were constantly thinking of James and there was no way you would be able to pretend to be content with anyone else.

So I'm glad you did what you did for love.

Lexie stopped reading and smiled.

Esther looked up from the bed opposite. 'What is it?' she asked.

'I think my little sister might be growing up and falling in love,' Lexie said.

'Happens to us all,' Esther smiled returning to her needlepoint work.

Lexie continued to read.

I've also decided not to do nursing but to stay here and continue my part-time work in the canteen. Mother and I thought we might drop up for a day visit at the end of the month. Can you get some time off on a Sunday to see us?

Anyway must run. Much love to you. Oh, and Father is well but we never, ever see him since he got the contract. Mother did get a letter from Aunty Jo and she too has volunteered. She is working in administration and enjoying her independence.

Write soon. I love you, Lex.

Carrie xxx

Ps-even if I do say so myself, I look particularly fetching in your curtains. Even Anson says so but he doesn't know where the material came from so don't tell him please.

Chapter 25

Lexie closed the car door, picked up her brown port and turned to Kitty.

'Ready?' she asked.

'More than ever,' Kitty answered with an enthusiastic grin.

Lexie reached for Kitty's hand and squeezed it, relieved her best friend was travelling with her. They turned and watched as the car drove away, leaving them in front of Millbank Military Hospital, reporting for embarkation.

'It's not too late you know,' Lexie said, 'to change your mind and not come with me. I'll understand.'

'The car's driving away,' Kitty said.

'I could run after it!'

'Are you kidding?' Kitty playfully hit Lexie on the arm. 'You couldn't keep me away. Onward and upward.' Kitty picked up her port and took off.

'Onward and upward.' Lexie followed, grabbing her own port.

The two women walked up the front steps of the austere hospital. Before they had even opened their mouths to greet the administration person, she pointed and said, 'through the doors on your left, take a seat and wait with the other ladies, someone will be with you shortly.'

They mumbled their thanks and pushed open two large timber-framed glass doors. Inside the room sat more than thirty ladies, all with ports and embarkation orders. Kitty pointed to a couple of seats and they made their way through the maze of legs and ports with smiles and nods. The air buzzed with excitement and pockets of conversations were going on around the room.

'Hello.' Lexie greeted a girl on her left as she sat down.

The girl shook Lexie's hand and introduced herself as Sally. Kitty leant forward and exchanged greetings.

'Do you have any idea where we might be going?' Lexie asked as she straightened her skirt and removed her hat.

'Some of us heard it was going to be India,' Sally replied.

'India!' Kitty exclaimed over the noise in the room. 'Good grief!'

'Well some of the girls have been issued with tropical kits,' Sally explained.

Lexie, her face reflecting panic, looked at Kitty for a reaction.

Kitty patted Lexie's knee nonchalantly. 'Maybe we are not all going to the same place,' Kitty suggested. 'We haven't been given any kits, have you?'

The girl shook her head. 'But the staff was here much earlier handing them out. They might come back with more.'

'How long have you been sitting here?' Lexie asked.

'About two hours,' she replied.

'Oh well, best make ourselves comfortable.' Kitty settled back in the seat and began to observe the women around her.

Lexie whispered to her. 'Kit, what if it is India?'

Kitty shrugged. 'So be it.'

'But ... you can change your mind you know ... you don't have to come with me, the matron would welcome you back with open arms.'

Kitty looped her arm through Lexie's. 'Listen Lex, I am already overseas in my mind. I don't care where I go. Our boys will be there and I'll be useful. I can't go back to the city hospital now; that would seem way too tame. Let's just see where fate takes us. It's an adventure.'

*****

London, December 2, 1940

My darling James,

I received a letter from you just before I left London, but it was dated before your father received the telegram. It was such a shock to get it, especially having seen you since.

The good news my love is that I am back at St Barts. Yes, I suspected that would make you happy. Mother would die if she could see how I spent last night huddled with the girls and queuing just to use the bathroom, before we were all sent home—supposedly there was a drama at sea and our designated ship got reassigned.

Kitty and I had a little panic attack when we first arrived at the embarkation hospital as some of the women declared they were being sent to India. They had tropical kits already dispensed to them. But as it turned out, it was a split group. Some left by train to go up to Glasgow and then by sea to Netley Military Hospital in India, the rest of us were sent to Gourock, also in Scotland, to wait for a ship that would take us to Palestine. Kitty, God bless her soul, was still enthusiastic and keen to accompany me, but I have to admit I was terrified at the thought of going there and even more worried about Kitty. Imagine if something happened to her because I dragged her there—how could I ever forgive myself?

Anyway, we were prepared to see it through come what may. I was once frightened to go to London and look at me now. After the night of 'camping' with the fifteen other ladies, we left London by train to Oxford and Kitty and I got to have a stop-over night at home with our families. Mother cried every five minutes and this was only exacerbated by Carrie being jealous of my so-called 'adventure' yet not wanting to do nursing herself. I did not see Father, he is back in London on business.

I also got to enjoy the sandwiches and tea from the canteen volunteers when we stopped there en route, and I caught up with all the latest gossip. They were surprised to see this group of girls get off amongst all the boys, but happily fed us anyway and spoilt Kitty and me rotten.

The next evening, Kitty and I were shuffled off to the train station again and we travelled overnight to Gourock. How beautiful Scotland is; the scenery was breathtaking. I hope it manages to stay that way despite this war. Kitty and I were given a bunk so we got some sleep; more than we ever got on our nursing shifts.

Then, you'll be pleased to know, we got sent back. Matron was delighted to see us and so were our old roommates. So tomorrow we are back to our normal shift. Maybe this is meant to be … I will discuss it more with Kitty and decide whether we reapply or stay where we are. When we arrived back at the hospital, we ran into Dr Gardam, Adam. In fact, he was outside having a smoke as we pulled up and he carried our cases in. I introduced him to Kitty and there was definitely a spark. Remember, you have to deliver on your promise and stay safe. I miss you.

Love and kisses and hugs,
Lexie Theroux xxx (how good does that sound?).
Ps – St. Paul's Cathedral was bombed. The roof and altar are

*****

'War, what war?' Misty asked as he lay on the upper deck of the
ship, gazing at the blue sky. Beside him, James lay smoking a
cigarette and Ham sat reading, covered from head-to-foot to
avoid sunburn.

James nodded to the ladder from the lower deck and they
watched as Shorty appeared mounting the steps two at a time.
He strode over, stepping over men on the way, and dropped
down beside them.

'Enjoy it while you can lads,' Shorty said, 'we'll be ashore in a
few days and back to reality.'

Misty looked over at James. 'Who's the party pooper?'

James laughed. They sat in comfortable silence, listening to
the sound of the water as the engines powered the ship through
the sea and the occasional cheer as someone won a hand of cards.

Ham lowered his book and looked to the sky.

'Hear that?' he asked.

The men stopped and strained to hear.

'Plane coming.' Shorty jumped to his feet.

'Plane,' he yelled alerting everyone. An ominous feeling of
tension ran across the deck. Friend or foe?

Men got to their feet and scanned the sky. Only the rumble of
the approaching aircraft could be heard.

'Going to the engine room,' Shorty announced and ran
towards the ladder.

'Christ, we should get below, there's three of them.' Ham
pointed.

A loud ripping sound could be heard and the ship lurched, knocking them off their feet.

'We've been hit.' James yelled the obvious. Smoke was pouring across the deck as men scrambled to get the lifeboats released. The noise became deafening: the sounds of panic and pain and bombing. The ship was lurching out of control and all around him men were grabbing whatever they could to steady themselves. James looked around seeing everything as though in slow motion but yet, everything was happening fast, too fast.

Another loud explosion and the sound of splintering. More smoke. Men were screaming. James heard calls for the medic. He turned as yet another explosion rocked the ship and he fell to the deck with the impact. He saw men on the bow falling into the ocean. Hoses, extinguishers, everything once tied down had been torn loose and was hurtling through the air or rolling overboard. Water poured across the deck with a ferocious roar.

James heard a cry for help. Through the noise and smoke, he saw Shorty extending his hand. He hadn't quite got to the ladder before the next bomb hit and was thrown back onto the deck. Steam was coming off his clothes and James could see red on his leg. Blood, skin and bone exposed.

Shorty lay gasping.

'Christ.' James crawled towards him and began to tear strips of fabric from Shorty's shredded shirt, desperately trying to stem the flow of blood.

'Medic,' Ham yelled, waving down a young medic already attending other soldiers.

'Get down you idiot,' Sandy hissed pulling Ham down. 'You'll be hit too, just what I bloody well need.'

The young medic scurried over, chased by more calls for help. He scanned Shorty and quickly raised his eyes to James.

He shook his head.

'What does that mean?' James demanded.

'Sorry.' The medic rose.

'No, wait.' James tried to grab his arm but he had already scuttled off to attend to another soldier. 'Sorry! What the hell does that mean?' James yelled after him.

'It means it's too late.' Shorty looked up at James, gurgling the words through blood and coughing.

'Bull, it's not too late,' James hissed, continuing to stem the flow of blood. 'Sandy …'

Sandy leant down beside James and Shorty. 'I'm not God, kid.' He pumped Shorty's arm.

'Scribbler, write for me.' Shorty's chest heaved and blood ran from his mouth.

'Write? Write, okay, to whom?' The ship trembled again and James fell backwards. He stumbled back to Shorty. He was choking now on the thick smoke.

'Get in the lifeboats,' he heard the command.

'Go!' Shorty told him.

'No, quick,' James had a stubby pencil and pad in his hand.

Shorty groaned in agony and gurgled the words, 'My girl. Tell her …' Shorty stumbled. 'Tell her …'

'What's her nickname?' James took charge.

'Dee Dee.' Shorty's breathing was becoming laboured.

'I'll tell Dee Dee that you love her.'

Shorty nodded. Tears rolled down his cheek, he winced in pain and began to gasp.

'And, marry, I want to …'

'And I'll tell her that you wanted to marry her and spoke about her all the time,' James whispered.

Shorty smiled.

'And that she was the love of your life.' James finished, oblivious to the whistle of falling bombs and the screaming all around him.

Shorty smiled. 'Thanks …' His eyes rolled back.

James closed his eyes and swallowed. Another explosion made him jump; he opened his eyes, took the identification discs from around Shorty's neck and placed Shorty's hands across his body.

He heard the order 'Move out,' and he turned to Sandy.

'Forget it Scribbler,' Sandy shouted above the noise, 'Shorty's six-foot-bloody-four. He's going down with the ship. Leave him or we'll be going down too, get out now!' Sandy turned back to Shorty and muttered an apology that he would never hear.

James rose and started towards the lifeboats.

Chapter 26

They were in a rescue boat on the choppiest sea James had ever experienced and the size of the ship did nothing to buffer the waves or to quell his sea sickness. He scrambled to the rail and heaved the contents of his stomach over the side, wiping his mouth across his sleeve.

'I told you to avoid the hors d'œuvre, didn't I?' Ham called from nearby.

James retched again.

Sandy grinned. 'Leave the poor bastard alone, Ham.'

'Christ, he's been throwing up for an hour. You can't have anything left in your stomach, Scribbler.' Ham shook his head.

James crawled back towards them. 'Just give me land or shoot me, either is fine.'

'Yeah, almost there,' Sandy assured him.

He slumped back next to Sandy, Ham and the three new assignees to Sandy's squad.

'Is that why you didn't join the navy?' Private Briton, one of the new squad members asked James.

'Navy? I was supposed to be the war correspondent for the Daily Mail but somehow I enlisted in the army instead,' James answered.

The five men looked at each other and burst out laughing.

'Yeah, I suppose it is funny.' James couldn't help but grin.

'Here comes the boss,' Sandy warned them, as a Lt. Colonel made his way around the groups bunched on the ship's deck.

'Corporal, ready?' the Lt. Colonel asked.

'Ready, sir,' Sandy saluted and the Lt. Colonel nodded and moved on. Turning back to his squad, Sandy muttered 'five minutes, lads. Now keep your heads down, don't be heroes and run like you've never run before.'

The next thing James knew, he was being pushed down the ramp and into the landing craft. Within moments, the smaller boat was speeding towards the shore. The men choked on the black clouds of diesel smoke and the smell of fuel. Between uncontrollable bouts of sickness, James covered his mouth and nose with his hands to hold back the retching and block the smell.

Sandy pushed James' head lower. 'Heave in the boat if you need to Scribbler. If you stick your head over the side, it'll be shot off.'

'Yeah we can't smell your vomit anyway,' Ham called to him, 'the fuel wins.'

James put his chest on his knees; the sound of missiles hitting the water seemed to surround him. He gripped his rifle gaining some security from feeling it in his hands.

'Landing, get ready,' Sandy yelled. 'Priority one, get to the beach and drop.'

James raised his head, waited for the signal, and in turn, jumped out of the landing craft, following the men in front of him. He hunched low and pushed through the shallows as fast as he could, his chest tight from fear and exertion. On reaching the beach, he ran as if pursued by the devil himself, diving for cover behind a sand dune. Once he had his bearings, he looked to the left and saw Ham was beside him and Sandy, while several others of the squad, were no more than twenty feet away huddled behind an upturned car body. James saw a large stone house on a nearby cliff and pockets of scrub along the dune edges. He turned to the right and gasped. Through the grey haze he could see bodies floating in the water, red with blood; hundreds of them, like flotsam. Behind the bodies were the burned-out carcasses of ships, beached and derelict, left stranded.

The Lt. Colonel dropped down near Sandy and gave instructions, then ran on, not even staying low. James watched in awe at his leadership as he ran from group to group as though he was untouchable.

Sandy passed the orders along; the aim was to take the immediate beach precinct and claim the stone house to set up a defensive position.

'Wait for the signal,' Sandy instructed his men. The signal came to move and they headed down the beach, around towards the back of the house, Sandy leading the assault, heading directly into enemy territory.

James felt Ham nudge him to move; he nodded but his mind was glazed with fear. He rose to follow the squad, keeping his rifle at the ready, his finger near the trigger.

They were moving fast along the edge of the water, their legs feeling like lead, the water thick and heavy with blood and bodies. Around them, bullets whistled and men dropped. James fell, dropping below the water surface, his head submerged. For a moment, it was silent; nothing but the echo of water. He pushed himself back up and felt Ham grabbing him by the shirt.

'I'm not hurt', he mumbled, 'not hurt, keep going, go, go, go!'

One of his new squad members fell in front of him as if in

slow motion; a bullet burst from the back of his head, splattering James with blood and brains. But James kept running, pulling his legs through the water, keeping Sandy in his sights.

James heard a huge explosion behind him and felt Ham pummel into him. They both fell into the water again. James found his footing on the shallow floor of the ocean and pushed himself up. He turned for Ham and grabbed his arm, pulling him up.

'I'm okay,' Ham spluttered and spat out a mouthful of salt water, 'just the concussion wave from that hit, that's all, I'm okay,' he said convincing himself.

James glanced back. 'Ship was blown up,' he said and returned his gaze forward. He was almost there now. Sandy had made it, two of his new squad had made it and he was almost there. As he got closer, Sandy yanked him in and then grabbed Ham. James stumbled to the sand.

He laughed; the hysterical laugh of one who had made it against all odds. For a few minutes they squatted, catching their breath.

'Let's go.' Sandy staggered up and went further into the trees. The squad followed. In front of them, another platoon was already in position; Sandy's squad provided reinforcements.

Squatting and with the stone house now only a few yards from them, they took aim. On the signal, two soldiers threw grenades through the broken windows. Within seconds of detonation, the noise and smoke filled the premises and a dozen or more Germans ran out of the stone house like ants from a burning ant hole. The squad picked them off, James shooting with the best of them.

And then there was silence. The gunfire continued on the far side of the beach, but all James could hear were his ears ringing.

The platoon leader signalled an imminent move forward and Sandy instructed his squad to wait.

Shortly, the all-clear was given and they rose. James looked down at himself and then looked at Ham.

Ham grinned. 'We made it again, Scribbler, and you're on land.' He thumped James on the back.

James smiled. 'Like I ever doubted it.'

Sandy exhaled. 'Welcome to Greece, boys.'

Further down on the beach, James turned to see the Lt. Colonel still issuing orders and standing as it was bullet proof, moving troops along as more landing craft came into shore. There was no sign of the Stooges.

*****

Anna Howell extended her glass towards her brother.

'I take it that means more champagne?' Anson asked.

'Yes please.' Anna kicked off her shoes and swung her legs over the side of the cane chair. 'We must be nearly out of Daddy's champagne stock, how dreary and speaking of dreary, I am so sick of this war, when will it be over?'

Anson shrugged, filling his sister's glass. 'Not for a while if Father has his wish. He's doing rather well out of it.'

'What about you?' Anna turned in her cane chair to look at her brother. She studied his face; he was looking tanned and healthy. His square jaw which gave him the classic profile much admired by women, and his dark eyes were family traits that she shared in smaller proportions.

'What about me?' Anson raised his glass to her and gulped a mouthful. 'Mm, good.'

'Aren't you tired of hearing "after the war, after the war?" Don't you want to move on with your life? You know, get Lexie back here from that tiresome nurse charade that she's putting on, get married, start a family, all that?'

Anson shrugged. 'I tried that. I went up to London to see her about a month ago.'

Anna sat up straighter and studied him. 'You never told me that.'

'How remiss of me,' he teased her.

'I would have come with you and had a look at how London was doing.'

'It's not pretty,' Anson said. 'You're better off here,' he nodded to the splendid rural view stretching beyond their manicured acres. 'It's something isn't it,' he spoke as if to himself. 'One day, I'll be managing it all.'

'One day,' Anna agreed. 'So what did Lexie say to you?'

Anson shrugged again. 'She doesn't want to marry me, she wants to concentrate on her nursing and she wants me to move on.'

'Well now that James Theroux is dead, maybe you should talk to her again,' Anna suggested.

'He's not dead.'

'What?' Anna's jaw dropped open.

'He's not dead. The telegram was an error. I saw Carrie just the other day and she said he was not only alive but Lexie has seen him.'

Anna shook her head. 'That's unbelievable. His father ... Frank ...'

'Yes,' Anson agreed, not needing to say more.

They sat in silence for a while.

Anna turned to Anson again. 'You don't seem too upset about Lexie's refusal. You've met someone else haven't you?' she prodded him.

Anson shook his head. 'You have a vivid imagination.' He ran his hand through his dark hair. It was unfashionably long by the standards of the day.

'You have too!' She sipped her champagne and wagged her finger at him. 'Tell me, who is it? Is it that Anderson girl?'

'Norah Anderson! No, never.'

Anna studied her brother. 'You may as well tell me, I'll wear you down until you do.'

'Yes, you will, won't you?' He swallowed the remaining champagne in one gulp. 'Carrie.'

'Carrie Taylor!' Anna almost screamed.

'Yes, what's wrong with that?'

'Lexie's sister?'

'Oh come on. Lexie won't care, she's never really been interested in me. We were about fourteen when we had a crush on each other. She's had her heart set on Theroux for a while now. '

'It was Carrie who liked James, not Lexie, that's how it started,' Anna declared.

'Since when?' Anson's voice betrayed a hint of defensiveness.

Anna shrugged. 'Doesn't matter now, does it? Let's face it, you're a great catch big brother. So, how long have you been seeing Carrie?'

'Not very long. The idea only came to me recently, knowing how our fathers wanted the two families to combine our business interests … and when I ran into her the other day, well, we've met a few times now actually. She's looking good, like a lady. I've driven her home from her shift at the canteen some afternoons.'

'But she's a bit flighty isn't she?' Anna frowned.

'She's quite charming really. Besides, she's settled down a lot in the last few months. I suspect working at the canteen with the older ladies has matured her.' Anson smiled. 'She's a fiery little thing, always having a go at me.' A smile traced his lips, 'and she's quite pretty. But she's not Lexie.'

Anna smiled. 'True.' She studied her brother's face.

'You love Lexie, don't you?' Anna asked. 'You really actually do love her and want to marry her.'

Anson scoffed and turned his face away.

'Does she know?' Anna asked. 'She may feel the same about you but think you just want the marriage for convenience. You have to tell her, Anson. It might change how she feels.'

'I told her,' he snapped. Anson relaxed. 'It's over with Lexie. Besides I haven't got time for romantic love. I can't be distracted. I think Carrie will be better for me than Lexie. She's got a bit more go in her.'

'She's younger.'

'Only two years for God's sake.'

'Really? She seems so much younger,' Anna mused.

Anson continued. 'When she comes of age, we'll marry.'

'Goodness, you're serious! Have you told Father yet, or her father?'

'No. There's no hurry is there?'

Anna watched him as he shrugged and returned his focus to the grounds.

With all the girls that want you … what is this fixation with the Taylor girls? She wondered as she sipped her champagne.

'Mm, I guess there's no hurry,' she eventually responded, 'except Carrie's surrounded by soldiers every day … if she's such a good catch, you might not want to wait around for too long.'

*****

December 16, 1940

My dearest Lexie,

I hope this reaches you. I have received three of your letters at once—I can't tell you how excited I was. I didn't speak with anyone for about two hours, just went off with your letters and read them over and over again.

We have had a horrendous few weeks. I realise now that war is not selective; I thought I was the weakest link in our squad but somehow I have managed to survive when first Gunna and now Shorty as well have both perished. It was not by any great skills of my own but rather good fortune shining on me and not my comrades. Our ship got bombed and sunk but we got picked up by a sister ship. We had a lot of casualties and we lost a lot of men too. I can't believe we lost Shorty. The bombing just seemed to come from nowhere; one minute the sky was clear, the next, we could hear the drone and then there was smoke and mayhem. I'm sure you have seen for yourself first-hand the results of these awful things.

After we landed, we spent weeks on the move and I think I walked the equivalent of the entire length of England. We finally caught up with another platoon and spent two days just eating and sleeping. Then we were shipped out again! I can never sleep on those bloody ships, I swear I'm over the rail being sick the whole way and boy do I cop it from the boys. If the sea is at all choppy, it's all over. So you can imagine I'm so happy to see land that I don't care if there's a thousand of the enemy waiting there with guns, just get me ashore.

Anyway, we finally got into the landing craft, I broke the speed record for getting off the ship according to Sandy but nothing improved. The Germans were waiting above the beach and shelling us. We were like sitting ducks! You couldn't see a thing for the smoke and the noise was deafening. So I went from being sea sick on the ship to being sea sick in the landing craft.

The water was shooting up all around us and everyone was expecting to be hit at any moment but unbelievably, we all made it ashore in one piece. We grouped and positioned ourselves to see the beach—what you could see of it, that is, amidst the smoke and sea spray. It is probably the equivalent of being in a hospital ward during an air raid; the lights flicking on and off, smoke, people screaming and you are trying to do your job, I imagine.

We were passing messages back along the line from some of the lads that had spread out and I didn't realise that at one point I had been passing a message on to a dead man. The poor bugger next to me just looked like he was ready to fire—he was still holding his weapon with his finger on the trigger.

There was so much junk on the beach it was unbelievable— complete wrecks of vehicles and ships and you name it. It was like a marine ghost town for want of a better explanation. Really quite weird. But the strangest thing of all was when I hit the sand as a round of explosions went off to my right, I felt something sharp under my chest. When I pulled it out, it was a toy car; some little boy must have left it behind on the beach during peace time, maybe even buried it on the beach and couldn't find it. It was just so surreal and it made me dreadfully homesick for the life we used to have—what simple times they were.

Do you think life will ever be the same, Lexie?

Do you think one day, our son will have a toy car and will play peacefully on a beach while we sit wrapped in each other's arms, the sun shining down on us? Doesn't that seem like an impossible dream?

I think the toughest job though is that of the medics. We've only come across one real battle, and too late at that, but the casualties were high. It really shook us all up. Lexie, I don't know how these medics do it, or the chaplains for that matter. The medics run around, I swear they've got little more than a bandaid between them and yet they patch us up and send us back. The chaplains— well our one chaplain—is only a young man, straight out of the seminary and he's held men's hands and comforted them as he watched them die. I wonder how he will ever return to a normal life. Maybe he won't.

Forgive me for being so morbid in this letter but it does help to be able to write about some things. I could never tell you everything we've experienced; I'm not sure I can fully understand how I have been capable of some of the things I have had to take part in, but I know that you see the end result of some of it as our brave lads come in for repair.

Anyway, I don't want you to worry. As you can see I am still in one piece and the day ended better than it started. Our mission was to move and move fast and that we did! We were supposed to all make a run for an old stone house and take possession of it by cleaning out the enemy within. I was so scared, yes your hero, that I ran the fastest race of my life. My heart was thumping so loud, it was competing by itself with the noise of the firing and shelling.

It took us a few hours but eventually we managed to gain control of the area and then we were able to set up base. We've been here now for a few days and will move out tomorrow. We don't know what happened to the four young lads from our platoon that we called the Stooges. It was every man for himself, so they may be with some other platoon, safe and sound, but that's just optimism at its best.

Do you realise it is coming up to our second Christmas apart? I love you my beautiful wife. To say I love you doesn't seem enough when you are the only thing that keeps me going day and night. Take care for me, wait for me, stay beside me in spirit.

Yours,
James xxxx

*****

'Enjoying your honeymoon?' Ham offered James a cigarette as they dropped down next to the rest of their squad.

James shook his head. 'I think you're supposed to have your wife on the trip to make it official.'

Misty positioned himself back onto his elbows beside them. 'Blimey, plain ungrateful if you ask me. We take you on a lovely stroll, hundreds of miles through the length of Greece, with superb beaches ...'

Ham broke in, 'plus the excitement of being shot at or bombed, never a dull moment, and that's all the thanks we get.'

James chuckled. 'You're right lads. Downright ungrateful of me. On behalf of my wife and myself, my sincere thanks.'

Ham nodded. 'It's our pleasure. Don't mention it. What do you think young Briton?' Ham turned to one of the new squad members, Daniel Briton, wet behind the ears and keen to impress.

'Best holiday I've ever had,' he snapped back.

'There you go, Scribbler, that's the attitude to have, why I have a good mind to send you home!' He shook his head.

Sandy's voice interrupted their dialogue.

'Okay men, over here.' Sandy waited until the men packed in around him. 'Word is that the Germans have captured part of the old town and the Mole.' Sandy looked down, hesitated and added, 'it's not looking good boys.'

You could hear a pin drop.

'Keep your bayonets handy, but the word is that we might have to surrender.'

Groans were heard all around.

Sandy raised his hand for silence. 'There's a lot of them, not many of us. If we get the order to surrender, we'll destroy our weapons and anything they can use against us, then it's every man for himself once we're taken … if we are taken prisoner.' He looked around.

'I don't like it any more than you do, but keep your heads down, stay sharp and don't try to be a hero unless you have a guaranteed win in front of you. Understand?'

'Yes Corporal,' the men snapped back.

'And men, trust no one,' Sandy added.

Chapter 27

Lexie turned away to gag so her soldier patient would not see her reaction. She wiped her sleeve over her face and turned back to face him. He groaned as she began to cut away the bandages that had stuck to his skin with dried blood. She gave the young soldier a sympathetic glance. The smell was overwhelming; a combination of gangrene and rotting flesh, the wound crawling with maggots which actually were helping, not hindering, the healing process.

Kitty made a face at her, as she started the same process on a soldier lying next to Lexie's patient.

'You are the most beautiful thing I have seen for a long time.' The soldier's eyes were now fixed on Lexie.

'I bet you say that to all the nurses,' Lexie teased him.

'No,' he answered sincerely. 'You're the first nurse I've seen since I left home.'

'Well that improves my chances, doesn't it? So where is home?' Lexie asked, keen to keep him talking and distracted while she cleaned his wound.

He couldn't be more than 18 years of age, she studied him, *still full of sincerity and honesty.*

'Chester. Do you know it Miss?' he broke into spasmodic

coughing. Lexie reached for his head and held him up until his chest settled.

'Of course, I know Chester. It's beautiful.' She smiled at him before returning her attention to the wound. 'I'm almost done now. So what did you do in Chester?'

'Nothing much according to my father,' he grinned.

Lexie laughed, brushing away the flies as she continued to clean the wound. She glanced up at him again. *His father wouldn't recognise him,* she thought, *pale, gaunt and now lame.* She realised he was watching her and she quickly returned her attention to his dressing.

'I'm not going to be able to walk again, am I?' he asked.

Lexie saw Kitty glance at her.

'I can't say,' Lexie said. 'I'm not a doctor so I don't know if you will be able to or not … I'm sorry.'

He nodded.

'I do know though,' she continued, 'that we have some of the best doctors in England here. You'll be in good hands.'

*****

The surrender was not as frightening as James expected it to be; it all happened so fast. One moment they were scurrying along trying to stay out of sight, the next, they were facing the guns of a German patrol.

Maybe, he thought, *I'm too tired and war-weary to feel anything anymore.* Then, feelings of hunger and exhaustion flared up again and he realised he was still alive on some level.

'The farmer,' Misty hissed, 'that bloody farmer.'

Sandy nodded. 'Gave us food to look like he was sympathetic then turned us in.'

They were marched in the sun for several miles, shuffling along, before coming across more Germans and some lorries. They were herded into the lorries, the Germans cramming in as many as would fit.

James could feel his breathing quicken; he counted more than sixty men in the cramped, hot confines. He willed himself to stay calm. After travelling for less than half an hour, the lorries stopped and they were herded out again and onto a beach.

James searched Sandy's face for any insights. Sandy shrugged.

An English-speaking German soldier issued an order for them to strip. They removed their uniforms and were pushed into line and marched past two Germans with large canisters on the ground between their feet. James breathed a sigh of relief; they were being sprayed not shot. Then his relief turned to anger—sprayed like flea-bitten dogs—his emotions were short-lived as the spray from the disinfectant-smelling chemical began to burn his skin and he ran towards the water following the soldiers in front of him doing the same. James emerged from the ocean, his skin red raw. They re-dressed and were forced back into the waiting lorries, uncertain, stinging and hungry.

The next time the lorry doors opened they were at a camp. James heard Ham give a low whistle. Inside the camp fences were thousands of men. Thousands of starving, wasted men. James followed his troop, staring at the men's faces. Some were diseased, suffering from dysentery or viruses. Many were so painfully thin, that James wondered how they managed to stay on their feet.

'Men, while we have the strength, we need to think about escape,' Sandy whispered. 'In a month's time, we'll look like these men and then we won't have the ability or the will to save ourselves.'

James felt tears welling in his eyes. *My God,* he thought, *this is what my life has become. I am going to die here and I'll never see Lexie again.* He hid his face from the men, regaining his composure.

At the far end of the camp, laughter was heard and the men turned to see what was amusing the German soldiers. They were throwing pieces of crust into the sea of starving men who fought for it like seagulls. The Germans were laughing. James felt the anger build in him. If only I could file this story.

Behind him, he heard another lorry arrive.

'Holy crap,' Misty hissed.

James turned expecting to see more men being unloaded and pushed into the camp. But it wasn't the same as the lorries that had brought them and no heads were visible through the gaps. The smell reached them first and James gagged. The doors were opened and on the floor of the truck, piled up, were dead men. The German guards walked away shaking their heads.

'They're going to burn them,' Ham said watching the soldiers play with lighters.

'Offer to bury them,' James spoke up, surprised he heard the suggestion come from his own mouth. He looked at Sandy. 'We're fit enough.'

Sandy nodded. 'Agreed.' He went to the fence and volunteered his men to remove the dead and bury them. The German soldier in charge laughed, translated and nodded. He pointed a rifle at Sandy and then the truck. Sandy turned and nodded to James, who grabbed ten of the men and gagging, they went to pull the dead from the truck.

James put his shoulders back and made a vow. *I will get out of this place alive.*

*****

Lexie entered the hospital canteen and made straight for the help-yourself tea making facilities. She turned to see Kitty waving at her; she was sitting with Dr Gardam, looking very pleased with herself, Lexie thought.

Lexie raised a cup but they both declined. She filled her own cup and joined them.

'Hard day at the office?' Adam asked, rising to pull out a chair for her.

'Thank you.' She sank down next to Kitty. 'No harder than you two I imagine. Did you see those men this morning? It was so very sad and horrifying. I couldn't look … and then I felt guilty for not looking.'

Adam nodded. 'They're going to be sent to a special hospital for facial re-construction.'

'Oh! Do we have specialty hospitals?' Kitty asked.

'We do.' Adam turned to Kitty. Lexie noticed he looked at her with affection. 'Mainly just for facial wounds though. It's a very precise thing and as you can imagine, life altering for the lads and their families.'

Lexie shuddered. 'This dreadful war.'

'Have you heard from your husband?' Adam asked.

'Yes, thank you for asking after him.' Lexie smiled. 'I just got a batch of his letters but they are so old, from months before I saw him. Nothing of late. I suspect wherever he was sailing to, he should be there by now.'

'Did I mention I was the bridesmaid at their wedding and I caught the bouquet?' Kitty teased.

'Ah, the next to get married then without a doubt, soon I imagine,' Adam said making Kitty blush. 'Well, I've got to get back to the grind. See you for dinner?' he turned to Kitty.

'Wouldn't miss it, unless a bomb drops on us,' she smiled.

Adam rolled his eyes. 'You've done it now.' He nodded at Lexie, rose and left. As soon as he was out of sight, Lexie grabbed Kitty's hand.

'Oh my God, he's asked you out. I knew it, I knew you would be perfect for each other. See it's meant to be … fate! We weren't meant to go away, we were meant to come back so you could be with Adam. Soon we'll both be married, I know it.'

Kitty laughed. 'Whoa, steady up. Thank you for introducing us. And yes, I want all that, but I've known him for a minute.'

'True and my pleasure.' Lexie beamed.

'And it's only dinner here, where else is there?'

Lexie shrugged. 'It doesn't matter. Any time you can spend together is all that matters, not the venue. Does he have his own room?'

'Lex!' Kitty exclaimed in mock horror. 'How would I know? But I'll find out.'

Lexie sat back and sighed. 'I'm pleased. You deserve some happiness and he is so lovely.' She watched as Kitty pushed the loose strands of her hair back under her cap.

'It does make work much more enjoyable,' she agreed preparing to go back on the floor.

*****

'Being hungry is so bloody distracting, all I can think about is food,' Misty moaned.

'Then think to yourself,' Sandy grumbled.

'That piece of bread tonight really filled the hole,' Ham said and despite themselves, the men began to laugh.

'You're killing me, Ham,' Sandy chuckled. 'Not quickly enough though.'

'We're out of here tomorrow,' Briton said.

They turned to look at the youngster. He looked away, self-consciously and made a show of doing up his boot laces.

Sandy frowned. 'How do you know that, Private?'

Young Briton cleared his throat, looked around and then lowering his voice, he leaned in close to the men. 'I heard the soldiers talking about it. They said that we'd be leaving Corinth at daybreak and that they expected to lose a lot of us on the way, or get rid of some, was what they actually said. They're going to shoot anyone who doesn't look strong enough to make it.'

'What? They can't,' the men began to protest.

'Shh, shh,' Sandy put a finger to his lips. 'Keep it down, that could start a panic. How do you know this Briton? Do you speak Kraut?'

'Yes Corporal, a little,' he shrugged.

'Christ, why didn't you say so earlier?' Sandy swore.

'It never came up, Corporal,' Briton answered.

Sandy shook his head. 'Okay Private, from now on, I want you to be the eyes and ears of this camp. Eavesdrop on every German conversation you can and report back. Is that understood?'

'Yes, Corporal.'

'Good,' Sandy exhaled. 'Anyone else speak Kraut, Greek, read Braille or do anything extraordinary that you should tell me about?'

The men shook their heads.

'I can recite poetry while drinking a glass of water,' Ham offered.

Sandy shook his head. 'Very useful. I'll come back to you,' he smirked at him. Turning to Briton he asked, 'Did you hear where we're heading?'

Briton shook his head. 'No, but they said it would take five or six days to get there.'

James' jaw dropped open. 'Is that by foot or truck?'

'They were saying both,' Briton continued.

The men sat in silence absorbing this information.

'Well boys, we are going to be a lot better off than some of these poor sods; they won't have the strength to go a mile. We need to watch each others' backs.'

James took in the men around him as far as the eye could see and wondered how many would be left at the end of the journey.

*****

Private Briton's words proved true; the next morning, the men were lined up like cattle and under the threat of being shot, herded into lorries. James flinched as a skeletal man, unable to lift his own weight into the truck, was shot and thrown aside. The men behind him continued to climb into the truck. Every now and then, a shot rang out as someone failed to pass the first survival test.

James neared the back of a truck and easily pulled himself in. Without the guards noticing, he had given a frail man before him a push in and now extended a hand behind him. Moving to the front of the truck, he looked longingly at the sky before the timber door was shut and the bolt slid across from the outside. This time it was worse. James counted heads to keep his sanity and reached nearly seventy men with standing room only. James could see the men in his squad—it was of some comfort—their familiar faces amongst the other men, holding the ration of bread they had been given and two cans; one with drinking water in it, the other for urinating.

Beside him, he heard panicked breathing and moved his head to see young Briton and his equally as young mate, Private Jack

Hosier. James realised he was the mature one now; he was the man that they could look up to instead of the kid with the pen.

'You all right there, Brit, Jack?' he asked the two boys.

'Yes, thank you,' Briton said with wide eyes. Jack nodded beside him.

'You lads will be fine, just stick with me. You're young and fit. Bet you've run tougher marathons than this getting away from the law?' James ribbed with an aim to distract them.

The boys smiled at each other. 'We might have once or twice.'

James grinned. 'No doubt. This'll be nothing for you two then. Chin up.'

'We'll be okay,' Briton nodded.

One of the men started to pray and everyone fell silent to hear his words.

'Lord in heaven, hear our prayers. Let the world find peace again … return us to our loved ones …'

'Forget it,' another soldier hissed. 'If there was a God do you think he would let this happen?'

The praying soldier continued in his hushed voice. 'Don't turn your back on mankind, dear Lord. There are men who are still humane, who want to raise their families true to your word, who long to till the soil and see growth, who vow to live their lives in your footsteps. Don't give up on us, Lord.'

A few men muttered the words 'Amen' and then the lorry engine started, filling their confined space with noise and fumes. The vehicle began to move jerkily out of the camp. The men had little room to fall forward or back, absorbing the movements through their legs and backs.

The chaplain began to lead them in the Lord's Prayer and many of the soldiers joined in. James silently prayed for their lives. Within two hours on the road, the first man had died. There was nothing to do but leave his body lying amongst them.

Chapter 28

The lorry stopped and the rattle of the bolt was followed by the door being flung open. The men staggered out, stumbling to the ground, their limbs not functioning after hours of immobility. The stronger helped the weaker to their feet.

'Know where we are?' James asked.

'No,' Sandy answered. 'I saw a signpost that read 'Marbug an der Dran' or something like that, which is German, but we haven't travelled far enough to reach Germany. I suppose we must be in Austria.'

The German guard yelled for them to walk.

'You have to be kidding,' Misty hissed. 'I can barely stand.'

A loud rifle shot made them all jump and one of the prisoners fell to the ground dead. The soldier again yelled for them to walk. Suddenly, the pace picked up and they all stumbled forward. The German soldiers patrolled the line, hitting stragglers with their rifle butts. A walking skeleton fell in front of James and he reached for him. A young German soldier instinctively grabbed the man's arm and helped him to his feet, then stepped back. James gave him a grateful nod and took over supporting the man. They walked on.

The spasmodic sound of rifle shots kept them walking. An

hour later, they arrived at the camp. James glanced around; it was no better or worse than the previous camp. As they walked through the gates, the men were divided into work details.

'Look sharp,' Sandy muttered, 'you don't want to be sent to death row.'

James did his best to look capable. His stomach groaned with hunger; one piece of bread a day was not enough—he felt hollow. He came to the entrance gate and was directed to the left.

*****

Kitty sneaked into the nurses' shared bedroom after midnight and slipped off her shoes and dress. She lowered herself into bed and turned to find Lexie, lying wide awake and looking at her.

'All good?' Lexie whispered.

'Oh, he's just dreamy,' Kitty gushed. 'He's the best thing that's happened to me for a long, long time. I'm so glad that ship didn't take us away. Sorry Lex, but I really am.'

'So am I,' she whispered. 'Goodnight, Kit. Sleep well, if you can!'

'Night, Lex.' Kitty smiled and closed her eyes.

*****

'Nice to get out and get some fresh air.' Ham inhaled, 'not to mention a little exercise.'

James chuckled as he followed in line, away from the camp, across the fields towards the road. 'I love how you see the bright side of everything, Ham. You're a living treasure.'

'Better than whining isn't it?' Ham cast a meaningful glance at Misty.

'Yeah, yeah,' Misty responded. 'Just because I can't be Joe Jolly because I'm bloody starving and I don't want to spend all day working on a road like a chain gang and sleeping on a timber bloody floor at night.'

'Spare a thought for some of those other men,' Sandy added. 'Cleaning duty. Would rather be here than there.'

'I reckon I could have slept standing last night, I was so wiped out,' James added.

The men heard the command to halt. They stopped, dropping their tools, and waited for instruction.

Sandy moved behind James to stand next to the younger men.

'Listen up,' he whispered to them. 'Pace yourself today okay? We're going to be out here all day, so don't go too hard.'

The younger men nodded.

'I heard the last group had to dig graves, Corporal, trenches, you know, to bury people in,' a lad spoke up.

'Son, by the looks of this road, we'll just be cleaning it up. Keep your head down and do what you're told. Follow my lead.'

'Yes, Corporal,' he nodded.

'Good lads.' Sandy smiled at them. 'We'll be alright. We need to keep our morale up, that's how we'll win. Besides, Briton overhead the guards saying the Red Cross wanted to inoculate us against typhus, so we're not forgotten.'

Ham shook his head and clucked his tongue.

'What?' James asked.

'Look at us. They've shaved our heads and there might be nurses coming. My hair was my best feature.' He ran his hand over his prickly scalp.

The younger men began to chuckle.

'Now, I'm just going to have to get by on my charm,' Ham sighed.

'More for me then,' Misty quipped.

James grinned at them both. He looked away, taking in the scenery. *This mountain road would have been quite scenic, before it was blasted into oblivion and we were brought in to open it up again,* he thought. He followed the lead of those around him, picking up the shovel and beginning to dig. He was starving, lacking the energy to do a full day's work, but they had been promised an extra ration at lunchtime. That was something to look forward to.

*****

Lexie heard the siren and the droning of the German bombers. She felt the tension rise in the ward. Injured soldiers flinched, some ducked under blankets as though that would provide some cover and the nurses waited for the impact. All day, Lexie had been flinching; she felt as if her shoulders were permanently hunched. Casualties had been pouring in; first a few, then more, then hundreds. The nurses moved in a blur, trying to determine the level of help needed and where to put patients. Every inch of floor space not needed for walking was taken by a seat or bed for a wounded soldier or civilian.

Some wailed in pain as they sat waiting, others rocked in silence. Lexie saw Kitty rush in and look for a patient. She found him and began to lead him away. Others called out to her and Kitty glanced at Lexie, who offered a supportive smile.

Lexie heard it again; more sirens, more droning and then, a different sound. An older man sitting on the floor bleeding from a head wound yelled out, 'bomb, everyone down.' Patients screamed as people ducked under furniture and covered their heads. Lexie looked around quickly. Before she could react, the hospital windows shattered. The noise was deafening and she felt her nurse's cap blow off. She fell to the floor. For a moment there was stillness and then she heard the moaning begin. She pushed herself up and looked for injuries on her own body. All clear. Glancing around, she saw Adam ever so briefly as he raced by, two nurses trailing behind him. The matron came in and ordered all the nurses to put their helmets on. Lexie would have to return to her room to get hers. Franny ran past.

'I'll get them, Lex,' she called. Lexie nodded. She turned to survey the damage. People were picking glass out of their skin and off their clothing. A woman screamed and called for help, frightened by the sights around her. Lexie moved to her side, took the woman's hand and pulled her close for just a moment, before releasing her to the care of a stranger.

Lexie could see through the window frames where the glass had been blown away. Outside the building had been levelled. The chapel where she had married James just six months ago was gone, razed to the ground. She heard her name called and turned to see Franny tossing the helmet her way. Lexie grabbed the helmet and called her thanks. She felt silly putting it on but did so anyway. She found her kit again and began to dress wounds as best she could, offering encouragement and support, freezing at the sound of the sirens, coughing on dust and hearing the imploring calls of the injured.

She saw a young woman about Carrie's age, lying near the window, staring at her. As Lexie got closer she noticed the woman was pinned by a large shard of metal. Lexie dropped down beside her.

'What's your name, sweetheart?' Lexie asked.

Blood gushed from the young woman's chest and Lexie knew there was no saving her.

'Ruby,' she whispered.

Lexie took her hand. 'I'm Lexie. You're doing fine, Ruby, just fine. I have a sister about your age. Her name's Carrie.'

Ruby smiled. 'I always wanted a sister. I have two brothers.' She coughed and winced with the pain of moving. 'One's dead.'

Lexie nodded.

'Will you tell my mother … I'm sorry,' Ruby said.

'Of course I will, I promise.' Lexie wondered what she had to be sorry about, maybe just being another child to cause her mother grief. Lexie reached over and closed Ruby's eyes. She was gone now. She choked on a sob, regained her composure and moved to the next person.

*****

Ten hours later, with glazed eyes, Lexie sat across from Kitty in what remained of the cafeteria. The windows were gone and shelves had been shaken from the wall. They could still make a cup of tea though.

'I have no idea what the date is, what day of the week it is and if the sun has gone up or down.' Lexie closed her eyes, her hands wrapped around a cup of tea and her legs stretched out underneath the table.

'I hear you.' Kitty leaned on one elbow. 'Was that a 24-hour shift? Did we go to bed last night?' Kitty turned to look out of the window. 'Oh, it's still light.'

Lexie began to laugh and Kitty joined in.

'Oh, Kit, do you ever wish I didn't get you into this?' Lexie asked.

'Are you kidding?' Kitty straightened up. 'I can go home anytime. I'm useful here … besides, I've met the love of my life.'

'True,' Lexie said, 'you're right, you owe me.'

Kitty hit Lexie's arm playfully. They sat in silence for a while.

'Poor Adam,' Kitty sighed.

'I know, I saw him for a few moments running back and forth,' Lexie said. 'This is as bad as I've seen it since last year, since September, you know when that little old lady died from the bombing. I still think of her, after all we've seen.'

Kitty nodded. 'I can't believe it's getting worse.'

'Matron said the docks and East End are in bad shape. They've estimated the dead at over seven hundred already,' Lexie lowered her voice.

'I reckon we've had close to a thousand through here today … last night … yesterday, you know what I mean.' Kitty sighed.

"I wonder if it will ever end,' Lexie said. 'What will it take to end it?'

*****

They had been shovelling for what seemed like all day, but James knew from the position of the sun that it had only been three or four hours. A lorry pulled up and they were given a lunch break.

'What are you going to have, Scribbler?' Ham asked.

Sandy chuckled.

Ham continued. 'I'm watching my weight, so I was thinking of just having a piece of mouldy dry bread and some dried fish if they have any.'

James couldn't help laughing. 'That sounds good, I'll have the same.'

They walked towards the lorry and were given a serving of dried fish and a mug of broth. They ate hungrily.

'What was in that?' Sandy asked draining his tin mug.

'Bit late to ask now isn't it?' Misty suggested.

'He wants the recipe,' Ham said. 'Chef's special.'

A German shouted an order for them to return to work and with a groan the men pulled themselves up off the ground. James turned to see one of the men behind him was still sitting. He extended his hand to help him up, but the man began to cry.

'Hurry, take my hand,' James hissed. The guard walked toward them. In a split second he was behind the man and delivered a blow to the back of the man's head with his rifle butt, splitting it open, in front of James' eyes.

'Work,' the German yelled and James hurriedly stepped back into line.

Chapter 29

The train carrying Lexie pulled into the familiar station she knew so well—home. The platforms were crowded: soldiers everywhere, their families seeing them off and on, paper sellers, canteen ladies serving tea and sandwiches and the ever-present station conductor in command with his whistle. Smoke from the train mixed with the soldiers puffing away on their cigarettes and the air had an edge of excitement about it. Lexie saw Carrie waving before the train had even stopped. She was still in her volunteer canteen uniform and beside her, wearing the same attire, was their mother. Lexie smiled. *How far we've all come from the princesses we were only a few years ago!* She waited until the door was thrown open and stepped down from the train with her small bag in tow; Lexie ran towards them.

'We've missed you.' Carrie wrapped her arms around Lexie. 'You missed my birthday!'

Lexie laughed. 'I know … the blitz … I wanted to get away but …' she couldn't finish her sentence before her mother hustled Carrie aside and stepped in to embrace Lexie.

'You look well, my dear, tired, but well,' Moira Taylor said.

'I am. It's good to be home though, even if it is just for a few days. I've missed you both.'

'Come and say a quick hello to the canteen ladies, while we hang up our aprons—don't worry, you won't be put to work—and then we'll head home,' Moira said.

'Home,' Lexie smiled.

'Yes,' Carrie said, 'you can do nothing for a few days except sleep and catch up on all our news. Anson's coming to drive us home.'

Lexie laughed. 'Oh good,' she exchanged looks with her mother as she followed them into the canteen.

*****

Anson Howell was different, Lexie observed. Still strikingly handsome, especially in that dark three-piece suit, but somehow more contained, less arrogant. *Maybe we've all grown up*, she thought. Lexie noted he was charming to her and very attentive to Carrie who teased him and he seemed to love it. Anson opened the door of his stylish Austin Saloon and Lexie and Moira slipped into the back seat. He closed the door and raced around to open the front passenger door for Carrie, before making his way to the driver's side.

'Goodness, I haven't travelled in anything except a train for the longest time. What a luxury.' Lexie sank back into the plush leather seat and breathed in the cleanliness of the interior.

'Perks of helping the war effort.' Anson smiled as he started the car.

Hmm, Lexie thought, unable to equate his absence from fighting due to business with her own man who was putting his life at risk.

'I imagine you must be very busy, now that you've won that big contract that once belonged …'

231

Anson cut her off. 'Yes, it has required quite a lot of restructuring and we have tight deadlines to produce and deliver goods that the war office needs, as you can imagine. But still,' Anson continued, 'I try to get away from the office for a short time every afternoon to pick the ladies up if I can. Can't have them walking home after being on their feet all day.'

Lexie watched as Carrie patted his hand and gave him a grateful smile. She turned her face to gaze out of the window, overwhelmed with missing James. *Where are you, my love?* She watched the streets go by and as they passed the turn off to James' house, Autumn Manor, Lexie stretched to look up the lane. All she could see was a line of trees. *Our home,* she thought, *that's my real home now.*

Several miles further on, Anson turned the car off the road and they pulled up outside the Taylor family home.

'I'm afraid I can't stay, but I'll catch you before you leave, Lexie,' he said taking her bag and carrying it to the front door.

'Yes, thank you for the lift and for looking after Carrie and Mother.' Lexie smiled at him.

'The pleasure is all mine,' he said straightening his tie. He nodded to Moira and gave Carrie a wink before jumping back into the car and heading off down the driveway. They watched him drive away.

Carrie sighed. 'He's really quite lovely isn't it?' she said.

Moira Taylor smiled. 'I believe he is, dear, quite a gentleman.'

'He's changed.' Lexie picked up her bag and followed her mother inside. 'He seems more … settled, content, something. You might be just what he needs, Carrie.' Lexie smiled at her sister.

'Perhaps we are good for each other,' Carrie agreed following Lexie up the stairs to the bedrooms.

Lexie opened her bedroom door and stepped back.

'Good grief,' she said looking at the palatial room. Her hair brushes were laid out on the duchess, the pristine white bedspread and plush pillows looked so inviting and sunlight streamed in through the bay window where the curtains once hung. 'I had forgotten how big it is. I've been sleeping in a room half this size with four other girls.'

'You'll sleep well tonight then.' Moira turned away. 'I'll go down and get the kitchen to make some tea.'

Lexie turned to Carrie and pulled her into the room. She hugged her.

'What's that for?' Carrie smiled and pulled away.

Lexie dropped onto the bed. 'A few weeks ago, this beautiful young woman, Ruby was her name, died in front of me. She reminded me of you. I told her about you.'

'It's scary isn't it?' Carrie said. She walked to the window. 'I know you don't approve, but I'm glad Anson is here. I'm glad I don't have to go to the station and see him off like the other girls do. I'm glad I don't have to worry every minute of the day whether or not he's okay.' She turned to Lexie, 'I know that's selfish but why wish pain on yourself?'

Lexie nodded. 'I understand, I really do. I don't know where James is. I haven't received a letter from him or any word since he sailed, months and months ago. I know, well, that is, I choose to believe he's fine and I'll get all these letters at once, but the waiting and the imagining when you see the injured soldiers that come into the hospital ....' Lexie rose and went to the duchess. She ran a brush through her hair. 'I'm glad to be a VAD, so exhausted every day and night that I don't have time to think about it around the clock. I feel a bit lost here.' Lexie looked around, 'I need to go back as soon as I can … in a couple of days, I need to be back.'

Carrie moved to her side and took her arm. 'Then I will make sure that when you are not sleeping, you are always totally distracted and busy. We'll go and see Jonathan at your new home, Autumn Manor. He'll be happy for the company.'

Lexie's eyes lit up and she clapped her hands together. 'That would be lovely!'

Carrie continued. 'We'll help the ladies at the canteen, you will sleep, we'll visit Kitty's parents and Father Ranken, he always asks after you, and we'll stay out of Father's way. But now, we'd better get downstairs or the tea will be cold.'

Lexie laughed. 'Will we fit all that in?' She headed to the door.

'You bet. You wanted to stay busy, consider it done.'

Lexie gave Carrie a grateful smile and linked arms.

'Oh and we should try and shop for my wedding dress.'

Lexie stopped on the spot. 'What?"

Carrie raised her hand to show off an extremely large sparkling diamond.

'Oh Carrie, that's wonderful! Goodness me, my little sister is engaged to be married.' She hugged Carrie and then pushed her away to look at the ring once more. 'No wonder Anson picks you up every day. Can't have any of those soldiers making eyes at you.'

Carrie laughed. 'He is a little possessive.'

Lexie looked at Carrie's face. 'I'm happy he makes you happy, I really am.'

'Really?' Carrie asked.

'Very, very happy. We must drop in on Anson too so I can congratulate him for winning over my beautiful sister. Father must be delighted.'

Carrie shrugged. 'I guess so. He has all his ducks in a row as the saying goes … the contract, Anson for a son-in-law and another daughter who married well …'

'Yes, hopefully that will cheer him up a bit. Is Mother happy?' Lexie asked.

They heard Moira's voice calling up the stairs.

'Let's go.' Carrie led the way, 'and yes, she's happy for me, for us! I think volunteering at the canteen was a great idea of yours. It's given her new friends and something to do. I think Mother is really happy; content for the first time in a long time, maybe ever. It's funny how all our lives have changed.'

Lexie agreed. 'The war has brought some good along with the bad.'

*****

They were sound asleep when the doors to the hut burst open and the Germans rushed in. Dazed, the men woke to find rifles pointed at them.

'Up, up,' the order came.

James and the men around him stumbled to their feet. They were herded into the parade ground, under-dressed and shivering from the cold. The yard was already full of men from other huts; hundreds of them stumbling, shivering, trying to understand what was happening.

James fell into line beside Sandy. He looked up at the moon. It can't have been much past midnight. It seemed odd to him to see the moon and stars out, ever the same. He calculated they had been at the camp now for over three months. They had been replaced on work detail by more able men. Now they shuffled around the camp of a day time trying to fill the time and not think of their hunger. James could count his ribs. Sandy looked the worst; his face so gaunt he was hardly recognisable. Misty was holding it together but James was worried most about Ham—he had a cough that racked his body.

They stood in lines, in silence, while German soldiers walked along the lines, looking closely at each man. A senior officer marched onto the grounds and stood at the front of the group. James could no longer feel his feet. To his left he saw a man shivering violently until a German soldier threatened him and he froze, trying to keep his bony frame still.

A translator stood next to the senior officer and began to speak.

'Tonight, there has been an attempted escape.'

Several men groaned, knowing what was to come.

Sandy and James exchanged looks. They had been studying the camp, studying how they could get the men out.

James heard a noise from behind and looked around to see three men being dragged to the front of the camp by German soldiers. Their legs dragged behind them. The Germans stood them against the fence. The men kept their heads bowed. James did not know them. Beside him, Ham tried to disguise a hacking cough. It wasn't wise to draw attention to yourself.

The translator continued. 'Any person attempting to escape will not only himself be shot, but will condemn ten other men to death.' The senior officer nodded and guards ran into the mass of soldiers, picking soldiers at random and dragging them to the front. Men yelled in fear. One of the three escapees begged for mercy for the men and the German soldiers laughed, allowing him to wail.

Terror gripped James.

'Don't look up,' Sandy whispered. 'Don't make eye contact.' James passed it along to the younger men near to him.

James heard someone nearby cry out and he cast a glance to see young Jack Hosier being dragged to the front. He looked at

James, at Sandy, at Ham and Misty—his face contorted with fear. Sandy lowered his eyes.

'Christ.' James panicked.

'Scribbler, look down, be quiet,' Sandy hissed, 'that's an order. You can't save him.'

James dropped his eyes. He heard Briton sobbing beside him. Then it began, each shot, slow and deliberate. James felt each one—the reverberation through his own body.

When there was silence, James looked up. Jack lay dead on top of another body. He was only eighteen years old.

The Germans ordered the prisoners back to the huts. Some soldiers stepped forward to collect the bodies but they were turned back. James led Briton away; Jack would have to lie there until morning.

Chapter 30

James shuffled over to Sandy, Misty, Ham and young Briton, all sitting smoking in the sun; barely recognisable. He dropped down beside them and winced from the impact of his bones on the dirt.

'What's up, Scribbler?' Misty asked.

Ham coughed, wheezed and looked up at him. 'You look like the cat that got the cream.'

'Did you have to say cream?' Misty groaned.

James looked around. 'I've got two potatoes.'

'Well no need to boast,' Ham added. 'I've got two bunions and a sore back.'

Misty began to chuckle.

'No seriously.' James looked around and seeing no one near, pulled them out of his shirt pocket. 'A kid just handed them to me through the fence. Just like that.'

The men looked at the potatoes. They were starving.

'But it could be dangerous eating them,' James added. 'I read somewhere in my other life that starving people have to take fluids, like soup, before they can eat solids again.'

Sandy looked around. 'We're managing bread. Besides we'll starve to death if we don't eat. Anyone not want to risk it?'

They all shook their heads. James gave the potatoes to Sandy, who with a quick glance around, pulled a strip of metal from his shoe and cut the raw, dirty potatoes as best he could. He handed out the pieces and they immediately slipped them into their mouths.

'Nothing's tasted this good for ages.' Misty sighed. 'Even raw and dirty.'

James thought about the potato. *Don't go there,* he restrained himself as visions of Mrs. Atkinson's baked potatoes made his mouth water.

'Good of you, Scribbler, to share,' Sandy nodded at him chewing the hard lump in his mouth. He held up one remaining small quarter and offered it back to James.

James nodded to Ham.

'Couldn't fit it in, honestly.' Ham patted his bony stomach frame.

Misty shook his head and Sandy turned and gave it to Briton. He shoved it into his mouth before anyone could protest and then burst into tears.

James patted him on the back. 'It's okay kid, next one you have might be cooked by your mum, hey?'

Briton nodded. 'I've got news too.'

James studied the young man; he had aged a hundred years since Jack was shot. His face was lined and gaunt, his eyes dull.

'What news?' Sandy turned to face him.

'I heard the guards say a Red Cross load had arrived.' He looked down at his boots. 'I didn't know whether to mention it or not because they were going to go through it first and take out food and any stuff worth having.'

Misty groaned. 'Typical.'

'We might get letters though,' James brightened.

*****

London, 11 March 1941

Hello James, my love,

I finally got your letter, the one from the ship. Thank God you were picked up after the bombing. We hear so many stories of drowning and even soldiers taken by sharks because there's no rescue boat. For the rest of my life, I will pray for blessings for the captain of the ship that picked you up. I wonder where you are now?

I took a few days off and visited home. It wasn't the best time to be away and Matron said to me that hospitals were not here for my convenience but she gave me a wink so I took that as approval to go! Kitty also got time off to go home for a few days at the end of this month and Adam is going with her. I suspect she wants him to meet her parents and he may want to ask Mr. Mills a certain question. How exciting it would be to have some happy news.

It was great to see Mother and Carrie and the big news is that Carrie and Anson are engaged! I think they are both very happy and well suited. He is different with her; he lets Carrie boss him around and laughs and enjoys it, but he also watches over her and protects her and she seems to need or want that from him. Maybe she is more afraid of all that is happening around her than she cares to admit. They haven't set a date yet but I suspect that won't be until later, when we are all home again and can celebrate in style. Sometimes I wonder if this ghastly war will ever end.

We had an awful bombing of the city just recently. We counted nearly seven hundred injured people through the hospital doors over the course of a single day. Can you imagine? I think it was meant to be that we didn't get our overseas posting. Kitty and Adam are together and given the amount of drama here, I'm just as useful no doubt on England's shores as overseas.

We have been moving the beds around like crazy, as different wings of the hospital are bombed or become useable again. There are no porters of course, the young men are all off at war, but there are some older gentlemen who help out and between us, we are getting very good at it. I have also spent a lot of time under the beds in the last few weeks with the nurses and patients. The bombs drop unexpectedly and we don't always get a warning. The children poured in after the last round of bombing and we put mattresses on the floor for them underneath the hospital beds. Some are injured, others are with injured mothers or grandparents and have nowhere else to go.

Kitty and I calculated that we did thirty-six hours straight, or we think we did. It's hard to tell because night rolls into day and sometimes the sirens just seem to go on continuously. We have become quite immune to them. Kitty and I look like the living dead after our shifts ... good thing you aren't here to see me. Franny still looks beautiful though, even after a two-day continuous shift; she's amazing that girl. It's quite funny because you find doctors and nurses sleeping in the most peculiar places—in the canteen, over desks, even on a patient's bed in one case ... it was a civilian patient. One of the nurses, Iris, fell asleep on a sandbag. The matron was not happy but it was quite funny really and her nickname is now Sandy.

The mortuary also took a hit from a bomb. Isn't that awful? I know it is good in the sense that the patients are already dead, but quite disrespectful really. One of the doctors actually fell into a crater in the hospital caused by a bomb. Luckily it wasn't deep and he could be pulled out but odd to say the least.

Darling all my news is just more of what you are living I'm sure. On a cheerier note, I visited Jonathan at Autumn Manor. He had a tear in his eye when talking about you and your father. The house and gardens are in perfect shape as you would expect but I think he is lonely. He's living in the groundsman's cottage by himself and with the 'family' he once had around him now gone, it seems such a vast, empty space. What a shame Mrs. Atkinson couldn't have asked her sister to come and stay with her at Autumn Manor, rather than leaving to go to her.

I also caught up with Anna Howell. I'm not sure she knows there is a war on—she looked wonderful and so well groomed. By contrast, I need a haircut and I had no nails to speak of to highlight my engagement and wedding rings. Kitty and I dropped in on Father Ranken too. He was pleased to hear that you and I got married, but surprised. He still thought I was to marry Anson. He sends you his blessings for a safe return.

It is getting warmer now and I think of us sitting in our garden in the spring. What a wonderful picture. I send my love, hugs and kisses to you, my husband. I'm sorry I don't have socks knitted or biscuits baked to send you. I'm a rather hopeless, untraditional wife aren't I? But I care for all the soldiers as I would hope some nurse may care for you if ever there was occasion. I annoy the Red Cross regularly trying to find out where you might be. After receiving your letter I did find out that your ship had landed in Greece. That was the last I heard. You are in my thoughts and prayers non-stop my love.

Lexie xxx

✻✻✻✻✻

'I'm worried about Ham,' James whispered to Sandy as they huddled in the bunks trying to get comfortable enough to sleep. 'He won't complain, but he's got dysentery bad, although he tries to hide the stomach cramps and that cough's not getting any better. He needs drugs.'

Sandy nodded. 'I know, but there's not much we can get our hands-on. Young Briton said he could get hold of some when he was doing the cleaning shift. I don't know though … he's not the savviest kid on the block and if he's caught, it's death by firing squad—and probably not only for him. I don't want to risk that.'

'I'll talk to him. See if there's any way I can get them.'

Sandy lifted his head to look at James. 'Scribbler, what then? After Ham's had the drugs, how do you stop him and all of us from starving to death? We're going to get everything going around—we've got no immunity. This is the worst possible situation,' he lowered his head. 'All I can do is try and stay alive to lead you men, but lead you where? Instead, I get to see you all die one by one,' he swallowed.

'God, Sandy, none of this is your fault,' James patted Sandy's shoulder before dropping his arm in exhaustion. 'And you do keep us alive. I would have tried to save Jack and we would all have been shot. But … but it's Ham….'

Sandy tucked his knees tighter to his chest. 'No,' he eventually said, 'you can't risk getting the drugs. It's a short-term fix at best and Briton's too green to pull it off.'

'Right,' James sighed. 'I'm not sure I can …' he stopped and swallowed.

'What?' Sandy pushed him.

'Ham keeps me going, keeps us going. All I do is think about bloody food all day and when I'm not thinking about food, it's because I'm so exhausted from a simple act like walking to take a piss that I can't think at all. Ham, you know, he's one of us originals …'

Sandy nodded. 'Okay, I get it. Have a chat with Briton and see what we can do, but I'm doing it. If Briton can get me in, I'll get them, not you two.'

'Done.' James stumbled to his feet and shuffled away, lowering himself next to young Briton who was rocking back and forth in the corner of the hut looking at the sky.

*****

'Christ, Scribbler.' Ham's eyes were huge. 'You scared me, I thought it was the grim reaper.'

James grinned. 'A good looking grim reaper?'

'No a bloody skinny one with a big stick.' Ham put his head down again. James noted the effort to lift it seemed to drain him.

James sat down on the floor near Ham's bunk. 'We're going to try and get something to help with the … the cough and pain. How are you feeling?'

Ham turned on his side. James could see the frame of his skeleton. 'I've felt better to be honest, Scribbler.'

James smiled. 'Yeah, you've looked better.'

'Promise me something,' Ham started.

'Sure what?'

'Don't do anything stupid to get me a remedy, okay? Seriously, Scribbler, it's not worth it. I'll be fine. I'm just conserving energy really.' He launched into a racking cough. Blood appeared on his hand; self-consciously, he wiped it on the blanket.

'No, don't worry,' James assured him. 'Sandy and I are going to help young Briton with some cleaning tomorrow. He's seen some sulphur drugs lying around.' James lowered his voice and looked around. 'Might help … worth a try anyway.'

Ham nodded once. 'Hey, wouldn't be the first time I've swallowed something unknown.'

James put his hand on Ham's shoulder. 'Can I write anything for you?'

'No, but thanks. Maybe later I'll feel like whipping up a novel about a good looking young man who goes on holiday to Greece and ends up in Austria.' Ham sighed and smiled at James. 'I'm ready to go home, Scribbler.'

'Me too, Ham, me too. Sleep.' James pushed himself up off the floor.

*****

Sandy woke up first, he didn't sleep much, just turned from one position to the next, trying not to think of the sorry state of his squad, food, and ways to get comfortable. He glanced over at his remaining men—at Ham. Private Harry Haines, studying to be a lawyer … and a comedian. He was gone. Sandy could tell by his colour.

He wanted to yell. He wanted to run out into the courtyard and shoot every German he could find, bayonet them, feel his hands tighten around their necks until they fell to the ground. But instead, he pushed himself up into a sitting position and cried; guttural crying that shook his body.

Behind him, James stirred. He winced, jarring himself as he hurriedly sat upright on hearing Sandy's anguish. 'What is it? Are you all right?'

Sandy straightened and wiped his face on his sleeve. 'It's Ham.'

James raised himself out of bed, falling over. He crawled to Ham's side.

'Ham.' He shook him. 'Wake up, wake up, Ham.'

Men woke around them. Misty shuffled over.

'Oh Christ,' he swore looking down at the pale corpse in front of him.

'Ham!' James said again. 'We're going to get something today, something that might help …'

'He's gone, Scribbler.' Misty sniffed behind him.

James lowered his head onto Ham's chest and wept, unashamed.

Sandy came up behind him and put his hand on James' shoulder before shuffling back to his bunk. Eventually, James removed Ham's identity discs. He struggled to his feet, his face a mask of anger and handed them to Sandy.

Sandy pocketed the discs then grabbed James pulling him down to the bunk. James tried to fight him off but was too weak.

'Scribbler, listen to me.'

'Get off me,' James hissed, tears rolling down his face.

'Listen to me,' Sandy shook him. 'You won't say a word about this. Your anger will only lead to trouble and could be dangerous for all of us. That's an order, Private, do you hear me?'

James nodded. The life ebbed from him.

'You've got a wife waiting for you. Don't put her through the pain of losing you. Do you hear me, Private?' Sandy asked again.

James sniffed and pulled himself together. 'Yes, Corporal.'

Sandy nodded. Behind them, Briton pulled the sheet over Ham's face. His boots had already been taken.

*****

April 1941

Dear Lexie

I love you. I can't write much, I am very tired. I am a prisoner in a camp with thousands of men—maybe not so many now, we've been burying up to ten men a day for the last few months. The work and the hunger gets them. Then there's the illnesses ... blood poisoning, diphtheria, dysentery ... plenty to choose from. Imagine if it was winter, that would wipe half of us out. I don't know when you might get this letter ... there's only been one Red Cross drop since we've been here.

I cling to you, Lexie, to get me through.

Ham died. I struggle without him. He was our rock. He died before our eyes and we couldn't do a thing about it. His spirit to the end was so uplifting. Some days, I don't know how to carry on, so I thank God for you and I try and think of home but I can't imagine it anymore. I was put on burial duty about a month ago. I don't dig but I fill. So far from our world all of this, isn't it? I threw dirt on Ham's body like he was a stranger, covering him until I could no longer see him.

Sandy is bad too. He's a walking skeleton. He's always thirsty but water goes right through him. Misty is doing the best of us all. He got some kitchen duties and I think he's been able to sneak a bite every now and then. No one would begrudge him that. Maybe Gunna and Shorty got the best deal, getting out early and fast. Some of the young lads are just haunted. Briton rocks all day. His best mate since they were young lads, Jack, was shot randomly in retaliation for an attempted escape he had nothing to do with.

I wrote to Shorty's girl giving her his last message. She wrote back thanking me. I got her letter the same day I got your last one which was about the ship not sailing and you being sent back to London. That made me very, very happy, my love, thank you.

I am sorry that I can't be more upbeat and I probably shouldn't tell you all these things but know I am trying hard to survive for you, for us. Lexie, if anything should happen to me, to separate us, I want you to be happy my love. I want you to find love again and I want you to move on with your life.

I love you my wife. James xx

Chapter 31

Dr Adam Gardam pulled a daisy from behind his back and presented it to Kitty.

'It reminded me of you,' he said, 'sunny and happy.'

She clapped her hands with delight and accepted the flower.

'Thank you, there is something wonderfully fresh about a daisy, isn't there?' Kitty cut the stem and slipped it behind her ear. She was wearing her best frock, one of the few dresses that she had at the hospital. Adam told her he wanted to speak with her privately, so they linked arms and walked away together. She was hoping he was going to propose having met her parents, but only Lexie knew her dreams and she didn't let herself get carried away in case he just wanted to talk about the weather.

'You look beautiful.' Adam leaned in and kissed her. He looked around. 'Isn't it good to get away from the hospital, even just for an afternoon?'

'I know. It seems to take every minute of our lives,' Kitty agreed.

They strolled in silence, enjoying the warm spring weather. They came to a small park and sat on a bench, Adam gallantly wiping it clean before Kitty sat. They watched the ducks landing on the lake.

'Imagine being a duck, carefree and so oblivious to all of this,' Adam said.

'They are probably a little less well-fed I'd say since the start of the war,' Kitty suggested.

Adam chuckled. 'Aren't we all? I'm surprised they're not on someone's dinner table.' Adam cleared his throat. 'Kitty, I wanted to talk with you about two things …'

Kitty turned, putting her elbow on the back of the bench and facing him.

'I have a couple of ideas and I wanted to hear what you thought of them,' he started. 'But, it's important that I say up front—not to bribe you or soften you up, mind you—that, you are the most wonderful thing that ever happened to me.' He took her hand and kissed it.

Kitty touched his face and waited until he looked up. She regarded his warm and weary eyes, his hair greying just slightly at the temples and the kindness in his face.

'That's how I feel too,' she said. 'I love my work but you have brought more joy to it, to me. I feel alive.'

Kitty noticed Adam breathed a sigh of relief. He turned to face her.

'I know we haven't known each other that long, maybe eight months or so, but I've learnt how short life can be and I've learnt that if you have something that is wonderful, then you should grab it,' he said sincerely. 'Miss Katherine Mills, would you do me the honour of agreeing to be my wife?'

Kitty's smile lit her face. 'It would be my honour,' she answered immediately, 'yes, I will!'

Adam threw his head back and cheered. 'Thank goodness. I thought you might say no.'

'Why?' she asked surprised.

'C'mon, I've seen all the looks you get around the hospital. I know you must get asked out a hundred times a day … I can't believe you ever looked my way.'

Kitty studied him. 'Adam Gardam, you are the most sincere, down to earth and modest man I have ever met, not to mention handsome and a man of good taste!'

He rolled his eyes at her.

Kitty continued. 'Believe me when I say, no one comes close to you. No one. And I can't wait to be Mrs. Gardam.'

Adam held her face between his hands and kissed her. He stopped only to pull her closer and hold her in an embrace.

'I can't wait to tell Lexie,' she said. 'But what was the other question. You had two questions didn't you?'

'Ah yes. The other is for your consideration and please take your time, I don't need an answer straight away, in fact it won't happen for a matter of months, I have to serve some time at the hospital …'

'What is it?' Kitty prodded him.

'Yes, I'm getting there … but I want you to know I won't force you and I won't go without you but …I've been asked if I would consider serving aboard a hospital ship.'

'Hospital ship …' Kitty repeated.

'Yes. There is a danger of being bombed at sea, more danger than being bombed in London. But they sail to pick up injured soldiers, treat them on board and bring them home. We might sail as far as Egypt or Greece or even Singapore.'

'On the ship the whole time?' Kitty asked.

'Pretty much. But we'll go ashore occasionally when it's safe. Not much different to our work now … we don't go ashore much.'

She laughed. 'You're right. This is the first sunlight I've seen for a while.'

'Just think about it. Don't think about marrying me,' he added quickly, 'I'm taking that as a yes, but think about the hospital ship. I've had time to so I'm clearer of mind. Perhaps Lexie might come too?'

Kitty brightened. 'She did want to go abroad. Do they take VADs on the hospital ships?'

'They do indeed, especially when the VADs come with a doctor,' he said.

'Ah, yes, I imagine that helps,' Kitty smiled.

Adam stood. 'C'mon let's go for a drink to celebrate being engaged, I can introduce you as my fiancée.'

Kitty stood. 'We could do some window shopping for rings too if there's any windows left intact.'

'You mean you want a ring?' Adam asked.

Kitty gave him a wry look.

He smiled at her. 'I have one already picked out, but of course you get the final say. Come on, let's go and I'll show it to you.'

*****

Sandy heard James call out. He was too weak to go to his aid.

Everyone expects me to be able to save them, he thought. *I can't save my own men. I'm losing them all. Got to do something. Save my men ....* He turned. He heard James call out again but someone answered him this time and Sandy drifted back into delirium.

He felt someone shaking him awake.

'What is it? What?' he opened his eyes and focussed on Briton. 'Young Briton, are you still here?' Sandy asked.

'Uh, yes Corporal,' he answered, confused.

Sandy continued. 'I can't save you lad, it's every man for himself.'

'It's James, Corporal, uh, Scribbler … he's lost it I think. He's calling for someone called Lexie and he told me to get his father.'

Sandy groaned and struggled up to a sitting position.

'You're a good lad, Briton,' he shooed him away and looked across at James.

James was on his side, staring straight back at Sandy, his mouth open slightly. A pen and a scrap of paper lay beside him.

'I'm sorry, Scribbler. I'm sorry I can't save you all … it's every man …' he let the sentence fade away. Scribbler had not blinked. Sandy was staring into dead eyes.

*****

It was the Red Cross that broke the news of James Theroux's death, officially recorded on April 30, 1941. After failing to locate a living relative, they found the name and address of his new wife, and arrived to break the sad news to her in person. Samuel Taylor was home, working in his office and he answered the door. He nodded solemnly, accepting the formal notice and advised he would break the news to his daughter, it was his duty after all he told them. He thanked the two Red Cross officers and closed the door.

Returning to his study, he picked up the phone and requested a number, waiting to be connected. His solicitor came on the line. Samuel Taylor advised him that his daughter was now the legal owner of the property called, Autumn Manor, at 1 Arcadia Lane and that she had requested the property be added to the family's property trust. He agreed to provide the appropriate signed paperwork in due course.

Next, he rang a local agent and advised them that the property was to be leased out. The new tenants could choose to keep the housekeeper and gardener, or let them go as they saw fit. He hung up the phone, lifted his jacket and hat off the rack and headed to Autumn Manor to break the news to the groundsman. *Least he could do,* he thought.

Then, he continued to plan; he would drop into the station canteen to inform Carrie and Moira. Moira could tell their daughter. He wouldn't mention the property just yet. *Leave that for another time. They could talk about it after the war.*

He smiled, 'now I completely own you, Theroux. Worked out better than I could have hoped.' A vision of Lexie wiped the smile from his face and for just a moment, his thoughts of Lily surfaced again.

Chapter 32

'Hospital ship?' Lexie repeated Carrie's words. 'Why, I've never thought about it … well thought about staying on the ship permanently that is.'

'Neither had I,' Kitty said, continuing to flash the large engagement ring on her finger. 'My fiancé suggested it.'

Lexie grinned. 'You're impossible. How do you feel about it?'

'A bit nervous. I don't know if I would find it too much, being on board all the time. I guess it is worth a try and we could always get off, that is if you agreed. I'd want you to come; it has to be the three of us.'

'You were prepared to drop everything for me, Kit, so I owe you at least the same.'

'This is a bit different though,' Kitty said. 'We could be bombed at sea or torpedoed.'

'Aren't they supposed to be immune from attack?'

'Yes, and so are hospitals,' Kitty pointed out.

'Hmm, good point.' Lexie looked at the missing windows around them in the hospital canteen.

'We will be surrounded by injured men, day in and day out.'

'Compared to now, where we only see them a few moments a day?' Lexie joked.

Kitty sighed. 'True. But I'm just making sure you are aware of the reality of it. We might drown if we're bombed.'

Lexie shuddered, 'that I don't want to think about.'

They sat in silence for a while.

Lexie shrugged. 'I think we should definitely consider it. When will Adam know?'

'He's got a few months here to do yet, maybe in four months or so,' Kitty said. 'Shall I say we're open to the idea?' she asked. 'We can decide finally when the pressure is on.'

Lexie offered her hand and they shook. 'Ay, ay, Captain,' Lexie said, 'Let's consider sailing.'

*****

Lexie made her way down the long hall leading to Matron's office. This time, she was worried—she had been summoned. *What now?* She ran over the last few days in her head, wondering if she had done anything wrong. Outside Matron's office, she straightened her cap and dress, inhaled and walked in.

The moment she saw her mother and Carrie sitting opposite Matron, Lexie knew what had happened. She began to back out of the door and her mother rose, following her. In her hand, she held the fibre identity discs belonging to James; there was no mistake this time. Lexie sank to the floor.

*****

The remaining month of spring and then summer passed in a blur. Lexie felt no consolation in the words and prayers offered and felt no incentive to go on. She could no longer feel James in the world. People tiptoed around her and she performed her duties in a robotic fashion, refusing to go home where she would have all day to dwell on having no future with James. At night she lay awake, wondering about his last days and why she couldn't feel him leave the world. How many more letters would arrive from him, giving her hope when she knew this time, there was none? She also knew Carrie and Kitty tried to hide their happiness from her, but she didn't want that. She wanted them to feel what she had felt with James and she told them so.

And then one night, she dreamt of him. As vividly as though he was standing there beside her, touching her, kissing her hand. He was as she had last seen him. In her dream, James touched her face and when Lexie awoke, she remembered he had spoken one word to her and one word only; live.

That morning, it was a light work day at the hospital. Lexie sought Kitty out and tapped her watch suggesting morning tea. Kitty nodded. They made their way to the canteen.

'You look different this morning.' Kitty studied Lexie's face. 'Calmer. What's happened?'

'I feel calmer. I dreamt of James. He came to me,' she told Kitty about her dream. 'And now, I know exactly what I want to do.'

'Well, okay then. What?' Kitty asked.

'The posting, it's soon isn't it? She didn't wait for an answer, 'I want you and Adam to stop stalling because of me and let's sail.'

Kitty grinned from ear to ear. 'You'll come with us? Yes!' she whooped out loud. 'I'll let him know.' She kissed Lexie on the cheek and raced away, leaving her half-filled cup.

Franny came in and watched Kitty running out. She turned to Lexie. 'Something you said?'

Lexie laughed. 'Yes, but all good.'

'Can you stay five minutes more and have a cup of tea with me?' Franny asked.

'I've got all day.' Lexie smiled feeling a little better, a little lighter, even if only for a little while.

Chapter 33

Lexie stopped suddenly and Kitty ran into the back of her. Lexie mumbled an apology as she stood gaping at the large white ship in front of her.

'It's truly impressive,' Lexie said, 'it looks too big to be able to stay afloat on the water.'

The hospital ship was painted bright white with a large red cross on either side. There was an air of excitement buzzing around the vessel as the crew and medical staff boarded and their families and friends prepared to wave them off.

'A floating life saver,' Adam agreed, coming up behind them both and carrying their three ports. 'Are you worried?' He searched Lexie's face.

'Oh no, quite the opposite,' she turned to smile at him. 'I'm just admiring our new home.'

Kitty shivered. 'It's chilly, let's go on board and get this next part of life's journey started.'

Adam laughed. 'I feel like I should break some champagne against the hull or something.'

'Oh my God, if you got your hands on champagne, the last thing we would do is break it against this ungrateful boat,' Kitty exclaimed.

'Ship,' he corrected her. 'All aboard then?'

'You two go ahead, I'll be right behind.' Lexie waved them off.

'Lex … we don't have to …' Kitty began.

'No, believe me, I want to. I just need some time to absorb it all.'

'Righty-o then.' Adam nudged Kitty up the gangway before him.

Lexie turned back and waved again to Franny and Esther, who stood behind a wire fence barrier. Franny blew her a kiss and crossed her fingers for luck. Lexie smiled and returned her gaze to the ship.

She took a deep breath of the cool morning air and took her first step onto the gangway.

Kitty's right, this is the start of a new journey. That first step had been easy and she continued until she was aboard and then turned back to look at how far she had come.

'I'm leaving so much pain here,' she said in a whisper. 'I might collect it when I return, but for now, I'm leaving it behind me.' She breathed deeply again, expelling the memories from her body. 'From now on, I'm new,' Lexie continued. 'New in this role, new in this world, until I work out what to do … without …' she stopped herself as Kitty appeared at her side. They waved to the girls again and then Kitty took her arm and led her into the depths of the ship.

*****

October 12, 1941

Dear Carrie

We are sailing at last. It all seemed to happen so quickly. After you left, we bade Matron and the girls' goodbye and caught the train to Liverpool. Our ship was there waiting, it had docked several days earlier to drop off a number of injured lads and stock up on provisions before it could set sail again with us on board. Franny and Esther surprised us and came to see us off. The matron gave them a few days' leave and even though unnecessary travel is discouraged, none of the soldiers on the train seemed to mind the presence of two young ladies. It was very sad saying goodbye to them after all we have shared, but I am happy to be starting something new. Our first port of call is Freetown in West Africa. Can you believe it? I didn't even know where it was, I had to look it up. Adam suggested we don't get too excited though as he heard it is very hot there and quite dirty. Isn't everywhere dirty at the moment? It should take us about two weeks to get there.

The ship is amazing and of course they were delighted to have Adam on board, I think Kitty and I are just a bonus. It is really like a hospital only on water—there are 504 beds, 78 medical staff and 110 crew members.

Luckily, I've made a few friends already. The pharmacist is a charming gentleman by the name of Gerald Hughes—no, don't get any ideas, I'm not ready for that yet—but we do enjoy a chat over a cup of tea. He's about thirty years old and tall and thin. He is losing his hair which makes him look older. The nurses I've spent some time with are a good lot, especially Liz—a brazen American with wild red hair and loud features—she's a bit like a younger version of our great aunt Pippy … all woman! She's one of my cabin mates. She is so irreverent; I blush all the time around her because she is so direct. Liz is always teasing Gerald and he blushes as badly as I do, but he tries to give back as good as he gets; they may be a perfect match yet.

We've also got some nurses on board that we are dropping off at ports of call along the way, but Liz says she is on board for the long *haul. It is wonderful to have two funny and bright people like Kitty and Liz around me. They must think I'm an awful drag, but I try not to be, in company at least.*

Gerald told me that they have had over four hundred patients on board on a past occasion. It will take me weeks to meet everyone but the nurses I have met were very welcoming and they seem keen to have new people on board, especially if you can play cards. I have been told that our ship is relatively small, especially compared to some of the troop ships that carry thousands.

The ship is entirely painted in white except for large red crosses on all visible surfaces. All of our ship's lights are left on at night so that the enemy can tell it is a non-combat ship; Kitty jokes that the large red crosses are just target marks. We are lucky to have a convoy of ships of all sizes around us and I feel safer in their company. It's quite a sight to behold, like having a royal escort. It is very odd though being in these ships that weren't built for war. Ours must have been a wonderful luxury liner in its time. A lot of the fine trimmings have been removed but you can't escape the gilt and marble. The ballroom has become an operating theatre. Equipment is scarce but Adam says that we'll get by. A couple of times in the past the crew has had to give blood; luckily there's a good mix of blood types on board. I am B-negative but as yet, I haven't been asked to donate.

I heard that last trip there were quite a few deaths on board, some soldiers with terrible burns. Several of the boys were buried at sea. I thought the deceased would be stored, but not so. The corpses were covered and slid off a beam into the ocean, with anyone who could attend paying their respects. I guess we just don't have the room to be a floating mortuary as well, although I've heard from Gerald that some ships do have mortuaries on them.

Kitty still really loves the work despite the sea sickness, but I think that once she is married, after the war she will happily just be Mrs. Adam Gardam. I on the other hand am not ambitious to be anything more than a VAD. As part of my role, I have to ensure the patients who can exercise and who should be exercising do so. So I will be spending many an afternoon walking around the ship, arm in arm with an injured soldier and sharing our stories. It is very sobering and I feel honoured to be able to play a role in their recovery.

Sorry, I am all over the place in this letter. Anyway, once we left the safety of the shore, the weather deteriorated and the conditions became dreadful. The ship rolled and pitched from side to side. We were all green but by the next day it settled down a bit and I felt fine. Kitty, as I mentioned, is still terribly sea sick, it hasn't settled for her. We may even have to give up the idea of working on a hospital ship and go ashore if she does not develop her sea legs soon. She has been sick since day one with no improvement in sight. Adam wants to get married on board and Kitty is all for it—then they can share a cabin of course. I share with a number of girls including Kitty and Liz.

Anyway, enough about my nautical adventures. Carrie, thank you again for coming to the hospital to see me off and thank you especially for making the trip to see me all those weekends after James' death. I must have been such morose company, but still you came and sat with me, held my hand and distracted me with talk of all things. I'm so very grateful. Could I ask you to keep any letters from James that may still arrive? I want to have them all. It really was a great comfort to me to have you nearby and I won't ever forget it. Please tell the ladies at the canteen that I am doing fine.

Now, in your next letter, I want to hear all your happy stories and your plans for your marriage. I want to know when, where, what you will wear, what colour the flowers will be, who is best man, who are your bridesmaids, what will Mother wear, will we have to cut up more curtains and more!

Give my love to Mother and Father and a hug for Anson. Write soon if you can. It is lovely to get a dose of news from home. I love you.

Lexie xx

*****

Despite the threat of enemy fire, enemy submarines, torpedoes and the constant reminder of danger with the presence of the supporting convoy, it was a beautiful day on the ocean. Kitty straightened up and inhaled the salt air. She was thinner, her eyes ringed by dark circles made more apparent by her pale face. The ship was rarely steady, and she gripped the railings, her knuckles white, her feet apart and balanced. She turned from the waist to talk to Lexie sitting behind her on a bench, reading.

'Lexie, you know how you owe me a favour?'

'Do I?' Lexie frowned.

'I'm sure you do,' Kitty continued.

Lexie chuckled. 'Yes, my love, what can I do for you?' Lexie put a bookmark between her pages and rose to stand beside Kitty. She held onto the rail as the ship lurched forward.

'Push me overboard now,' Kitty ordered.

Lexie laughed. 'Oh Kitty, you poor thing, I'm sorry you are so sick. I wish I could share your load, then you would at least only be half as sick.' She rubbed Kitty's back as Kitty turned and leaned over the rail, her chest retching again.

'Think how wonderfully thin you will be on your wedding day … not that you weren't thin before,' Lexie added. She looked along the ship's deck at a scattering of other white-faced medical personnel.

Kitty groaned and wiped her face with her handkerchief. 'I was fine yesterday, it's only when it gets rough … the motion … I thought the bigger the ship, the less rocking.'

'Supposedly. I can't believe I feel fine, so far,' Lexie said. "Kit, you know, if the illness keeps up, you may have to consider not working on the ship … you might have to talk Adam into working in a hospital somewhere that we dock. I'm sure any hospital would be grateful to have you two.'

'Three,' Kitty corrected her. 'I've been thinking about that too, what I would do if I couldn't cope, but it's only been a short while. I'm sure I'll be fine.' Kitty tried to convince herself. 'If not, I won't be able to come home after the war unless you send a big liner to pick me up,' Kitty continued, 'the biggest ship you can find that doesn't move at all in the water except to go forward.'

'Mm, consider it done. I guess playing a game wouldn't help?' Lexie asked.

Kitty retched again. 'I need to lie down.'

'Of course.' Lexie looped her arm through Kitty's and helped her along the deck and down the narrow ladder to their cabin below.

'Can you wake me when the sea calms down?' Kitty asked, lowering herself onto the bunk.

'No. I'm going to let you sleep for as long as you can. Who knows, the war might be over when you wake,' Lexie said.

*****

The next ten days passed in much the same fashion—sunny skies, Kitty leaning over the edge of the ship being ill and everyone else enjoying social nights of games and dancing while they still could be had. No one had ever been happier to see land than

Kitty as Freetown came into sight. She didn't care if it was dirty or old or hot, it was land. Her spirits were not even dampened by Adam breaking the news that they would only be staying for the length of one day to load supplies, water fresh fruit and fuel. She didn't care; she had dreamt of spending the day on solid ground and intended to make the most of every second until it was time to board and sail.

That evening, the ship was abuzz; the word was that they were heading to Alexandria to pick up some soldiers and nurses and take them to Tobruk, along with some supplies. There they would evacuate the wounded, hundreds of them.

This is it, Lexie thought, *the first time Kitty and I will be put into action.* She finished helping make up the beds and, straightening up with a groan, she headed to the upper deck. She found Adam and Kitty sitting, smoking. Liz was playing cards with Gerald at a nearby table.

'Have you finished those beds yet, Lex?' Liz yelled out in her loud accent followed by a laugh.

'Yes, and thanks for your help,' Lexie teased her.

'Lexie.' Kitty waved her over and patted the seat beside her.

Lexie dropped down beside them. 'Is it true? We're sailing into action and have wounded to pick up?' she asked.

Adam nodded, exhaling smoke. 'Up to five hundred wounded, I've heard.'

'Full house,' Kitty added.

'I just hope we'll have enough antibiotics,' Adam added.

James was never far from Lexie's thoughts and it saddened her to know there was no point searching for him amongst the faces of soldiers she would encounter.

Chapter 34

The port of Alexandria came into sight; Lexie strained to see it through the morning mist. It looked peaceful from afar; no tourists of course, and no soldiers in sight, just the shadow of buildings starting to appear and a small flotilla scattered around the harbour.

Lexie looked around; everyone able to was standing on the deck, watching the entry. Kitty came up beside her, more excited than most to see land.

'I can smell land.' Kitty inhaled and smiled.

Lexie did the same. 'I can smell … something … like a spicy smell.'

As the ship pulled closer to the port, the water changed from dark blue to an inviting green and a warm breeze carried the smell of spices and salt water in the air. As the mist lifted, the buildings took on an industrial appearance, they looked sunburnt and brown.

'Alexandria,' Lexie rolled the word around in her mouth. She turned to Kitty. 'Liz said they had a few days here last time and it's a beautiful old city.' They watched the shore coming closer.

'I don't care if it was built yesterday,' Kitty groaned, 'I just want to feel the earth beneath my feet and no rocking. I want to be the first to get off and the last to get back on board … not a second too soon back on the ocean!'

Lexie grinned. 'Okay, so you're saying you've had enough of the sea life?'

Kitty rolled her eyes. 'I hate the constant movement. Do you like it? Because if you do, I'll survive it for you and Adam,' Kitty continued as they watched the crew undertaking the ship's docking procedures.

'I like any change at the moment, on land or at sea. What does Adam think?'

Kitty shrugged. 'He's been so busy, to be honest, I don't think he's noticed.'

*****

Shore time in Alexandria was never going to be long enough for Kitty's liking. In just a matter of hours they would be leaving and sailing closer to the action, sailing into the war. Liz told the girls that she had found out from Gerald, who had found out from one of the doctors, that Tobruk was under siege and the only way in now was by sea.

'The plan,' she whispered to them, full of news and self-importance, 'is to leave Alexandria tonight in darkness, sail in convoy during the day and arrive in Tobruk in darkness. We're going to drop our supplies, pick up survivors and get out fast!'

And Liz's information proved to be true. As soon as the sun had set, the hospital ship pulled out of Alexandria's port with its additional cargo and passengers and began the journey through the night and day, surrounded by its small convoy.

The next night they sailed into Tobruk. Lexie was tense with anticipation and she could feel the nervous energy amongst all on board. In the distance, they could hear gunfire, continuous gunfire and even on the ship's deck, Lexie imagined she could feel the vibrations of battle at her feet, like the earth and ocean were wounded.

'This is the nearest we have come to actual fighting,' she whispered to Kitty.

'You don't have to whisper,' Kitty teased her, 'talking loudly won't give away our position to the enemy.'

'You never know, loose lips sink ships and all that,' Lexie said as another round of shelling could be heard in the distance.

Kitty shuddered. 'Imagine being in it. I don't know how our men do it.'

*****

The sea was littered with sunken vessels with only their masts showing. The remains of others lurking just under the surface made navigation difficult. Their hospital ship came into the harbour under the protection of the night shadows and they began to unload their cargo onto a beach alongside a jetty and evacuate the injured. Around them, activity in the harbour was constant; German aircraft droned overhead as the crew and injured repeatedly took cover only to resurface later when the all-clear was given.

Along with all the medical crew, Kitty and Lexie made countless trips back and forth loading and unloading where they could help; staying out of the way when they couldn't. Eventually they stopped and watched the ship being loaded; a parade of injured soldiers being carried on board on stretchers, hobbling on with crutches or walking as fast as their wounds would allow.

Lexie shook her head, dumbfounded; neither she nor Kitty had ever seen so many casualties at one time. Gerald, Liz and the crew that had been on board for some time, seemed to take it in their stride. Hundreds of injured men were being carried on board using everything from stretchers to cargo nets.

They saw Adam as he came up the gangway and walked towards them. 'We're sailing shortly ladies. Will you be all right?' he frowned at Kitty.

'Of course she will.' Lexie patted Kitty's arm.

'My sea legs are getting better every day,' she told him with a smile.

Adam gave her an affectionate look and continued on his way.

'Are they really?' Lexie asked.

'No,' Kitty admitted. 'I hate being at sea. I don't know how much longer I can do it.'

Lexie nodded and they prepared for the long haul ahead.

*****

'It'll get worse than this,' Liz told Lexie as they walked around the lower deck helping patients settle. 'We've been packed like sardines before.'

'Trying to keep them all comfortable and treat them all at once is going to be a major challenge,' Lexie said.

'Especially when they can't get up. Ever delivered five hundred bed pans in one night?' Liz asked and laughed at Lexie's look of shock realisation.

Liz sobered and came closer to Lexie, whispering in her ear, 'we've already lost one, can you believe it? He's been taken back off the ship before we sail.'

Lexie sighed, knowing the pain that news would deliver. The captain walked by, startling them with his loud voice.

'We'll be sailing shortly. When you go to the upper deck, keep your helmets on and try not to stand around like targets,' he instructed the nurses.

Adam passed the girls, as he and other medics made their way around the injured soldiers, reading their field cards which detailed their wounds and treatment. Several nurses followed closely behind taking instructions. For the next few hours, as the ship sailed away from Tobruk and the patients were settled, Lexie barely set eyes on Liz or Kitty. She moved between patients, administrating help as needed, supporting the doctors and nurses, trying to get soldiers settled, dressing wounds, setting up traction or bringing water and bed pans on request.

Later that night, lying in bed exhausted, she heard Liz mutter something.

'What was that?' Lexie lifted her head off the bed.

'I said, don't tell Kitty, but we've been under way for hours.'

'I heard that,' Kitty assured her from the bunk beneath Lexie, 'but I've been too busy to be sick.'

Lexie could feel the slight movement of the ship as it sailed.

'Where are we off to?' Kitty asked.

'We're heading to South Africa, I believe,' Liz informed them.

Lexie brightened. 'I hope we stop in Cape Town. I heard the beaches are stunning.'

'Yeah, we might see some of it from the ship,' Liz teased her.

Lexie chuckled. Still fully clothed, she pulled a rough wool blanket over herself and settled into the humming rhythm of the ship to sleep.

*****

Lexie began early the next day—cleaning the men, removing their infested clothing and feeding them where necessary.

'This sea air should do you wonders,' Lexie heard Gerald saying to one of the patients. He winked at Lexie as he helped the man up the ladder to heal in the sun on the upper deck.

Later that afternoon, when they had stopped work to grab a late lunch, Kitty informed the girls of her plan.

'I'm going to give myself until the return trip to England to decide if I can do this,' she declared. 'I've felt much better the last two days or maybe I've been too busy to notice how terrible I feel.'

'Does Adam know your plan?' Lexie asked.

'It was his idea.'

'And then?' Liz asked. 'What happens if you don't get your permanent sea legs?'

'We'll pick a port I guess.' Kitty shrugged. 'I'm sorry to be such a wet blanket.' She turned to Lexie.

'Don't be silly,' Lexie assured her eating a forkful of stew and watching Kitty attempt to do the same. 'It's all an adventure for me and you can't help it if you're not a mermaid.' She squeezed Kitty's arm.

'You could stay on board, Lex,' Liz announced. 'Gerald and I will look after you. Then if Kitty and Adam decide to serve at some exotic European location, we'll probably sail there and have stopovers regularly anyway.'

Lexie noticed Kitty's face drop at the thought of the separation.

'You're right, three might be a crowd and I should leave the lovebirds to it,' she teased.

'No,' Kitty protested.

Lexie continued. 'Thanks for the babysitting offer, Liz, but one step at a time. We'll see how the landlubber copes with the rest of the trip.'

Adam appeared and dropped down beside them. Kitty fetched him a cup of tea, placing it in front of him. He thanked her with a quick kiss on the cheek, waving off the offer of the ship's stew.

'Keep it to yourselves at this stage, but we're being followed,' he said.

Lexie looked up at him. 'By sea? How? Where?'

'Something's on the sonar,' he said. 'Might be a German sub.'

Kitty shuddered. 'But we're in the middle of the ocean. If we're torpedoed here, there's nothing around for miles and miles, and all those injured men.'

Adam shushed her. 'I know. And our escort ship is nearby. If we're a target for a torpedo, so are they.'

Liz shook her head. 'Can't they see the red crosses? It's a disgrace.'

'I agree,' Adam said, 'but it's war.'

Liz snorted. 'Every one of these hospital ships needs to be armed,' she said.

As Liz finished speaking, the drone of an engine became audible—a plane.

'Not from the air too,' Kitty pleaded.

They sat waiting and listening, straining to hear or know what their future and that of the men on board might be.

'Back to it,' Liz said and the small group rose, wearing looks of positivity that wasn't fooling anyone.

Chapter 35

Lexie's heart was drumming a thousand beats a minute. *What will we do with all these men if we are bombed at sea? Men in traction, men incapable of walking let alone swimming and all those too injured to be moved.* She tried to look calm and smile as she walked among the crew and patients, but panic made her feel as sick as Kitty.

Men began to ask about the sound of aircraft and those who sensed that everything wasn't going to be okay, fell into a brooding silence like the lull before a storm.

Forget about the aircraft, Lexie stressed. *What's below us?*

Lexie and Liz climbed the ladder to the upper deck. There were men lying everywhere on the deck, recovering in the warmth of the sun.

Lexie looked skyward; the plane was louder now and coming out of the sun towards them.

'Get down, German plane,' someone yelled. The plane came down the port side, machine gunning the decks. Men scrambled for cover, half of the deck was shot to pieces and bodies lay motionless. Then with a roar that frightened Lexie to her core, the ship shuddered. The plane was forgotten.

Torpedo! She knew it. It had to be. She felt it invading the ship's exterior, forcing her down onto the deck with the impact. The ship began to list heavily. Lexie struggled to her feet as people ran around her and voices were raised in fright. The ship continued to list and groan.

She heard a cry from the deck behind the bridge; the ship's fuel had been ignited on impact, and the ship was on fire from the bridge. Lexie saw two nurses in front of her running toward the ladder and followed their lead, but within seconds there was another explosion and then another. She could see the smoke now and the smell filled her nostrils. She followed the nurses down the ladder to the lower deck leaping from the rungs as others desperately clawed their way up. Another enormous shudder threw her to the ground again and around her, soldiers fell from their beds, yelling in pain on impact. The ship began to list even more severely and the lights went out, plunging them into darkness.

Lexie felt along the bed frames, feeling hands grabbing at her, hearing choking and coughing, and cries for help. She helped an injured soldier out of his bunk, allowing him to put his weight on her. They swayed towards the exit. As she passed, other soldiers called to her, begged her to come back; so many hands reaching for help. She got her patient to the ladder where more hands helped pull him up and she ran back to the next closest patient, helping the soldier to his feet. He was a head taller and a decade older and had seen more than his fair share of the war by the look of his injuries.

Around Lexie, other soldiers hobbled without assistance towards the ladder, some leaned on nurses, others who were unable to move continued to beg for help. Lexie felt caught up in the pandemonium; it was everyone for themselves as they bumped into each other, shuffling to get clear and through the hatch, like a packed train carriage all pushing towards the door at once. Someone yelled out that the oil tanks were on fire. She heard the order to abandon ship, over the tannoy system. Immobile patients were trying to get to the ladder any way they could, pulling themselves along by their hands, clinging to the nurses and crew, dragging saline drips tangled to their bodies and the bed frames. Lexie struggled with another patient, young and wounded in both legs; she pushed him up the ladder as best she could manage while he used his arms to lift the weight of his body to try and get to the upper deck. He was pulled up by someone above, strong arms gripping his shoulders. She ran back to help yet another patient. Gerald passed her with a soldier over his shoulders; he was straining with the effort.

'Go,' he yelled to Lexie, 'the ship's taking on water fast, get up on deck now and get in a lifeboat.'

Lexie looked around. 'I'll take someone with me,' she called and helped another soldier who was crawling along the floor. He rose, leaning on her, stumbling to the ladder. Gerald had passed his patient up and pushed Lexie up before the soldier she was helping. She turned back to see him helping the soldier after her.

She stumbled onto the upper deck, falling with the shuddering and listing of the ship. The flames and smoke were overwhelming, the screaming deafening, she stepped over bodies and felt a hand clinging to her skirt. She had to pull away.

The ship was sinking now, sinking fast and preventing some of the lifeboats from being deployed. One was on fire, but Lexie couldn't make out if that was … no, it was a man. She turned away in horror.

She couldn't see more than a few feet in front of her now; the smoke was thick and the sounds of destruction and panic were everywhere. People were clinging to each other, to anything and anyone. Lexie saw the hazy outline of a lifeboat pulling away from the ship but it was dragged with the flow back towards the bow, and the next second it went up in flames. People dived into the water, others lay floating on the debris. Lexie saw the captain, he was trying to fight the fire and Adam was with him. Where was Kitty? Liz?

Everything seemed to happen in slow motion but it had been only a matter of minutes since the vessel was hit. The ship rocked again; groaning as if it were human. Everything was a blur; a blur of people and movement, of noise and panic, people bumping into her, shouts of abandon ship, shouts from the soldiers below trapped in their beds. Lexie could only move as fast as the stream of people in front of her, trying to get onto a lifeboat or overboard, but soon the water would come up and meet them. She watched as people jumped, several of the nursing staff crying as they helped to drag patients to the lifeboats. Lexie realised the roaring in her ears was the sound of the ship sinking.

She felt someone's hand on her arm and she saw Gerald again. He dragged her to the edge trying to find a lifeboat. She looked back; the decks were tilting dangerously and thick smoke was coming up through the hatches. No one could be alive below now. She allowed Gerald to steer her towards a lifeboat before realising that she had no great desire to live; she was acting purely on her instinct of self-preservation. She thought she heard Kitty scream her name. *Where was Kitty?*

Within moments Lexie found herself in the water—she gasped—the impact of the cold on her body was like a knife. Around her hundreds of men and nurses were trying to stay afloat. More nurses and soldiers were leaping from the deck as the ship began to disappear below the surface. Some patients floated, some disappeared from sight beneath the waves.

The bodies in the water were like target practice for the Germans as the aircraft returned and shells spat into the water around them. It was all so quick, so frantic. Lexie looked around but couldn't make out faces, just bodies and arms flailing. Bits of furniture floated like rafts on the surface with hands grabbing for a piece of salvation. She couldn't hear or see Kitty or Liz or Gerald or Adam. She hoped they were in a lifeboat. The convoy ship was nowhere to be seen; sunk or fighting back?

Lexie choked on water and tried to breathe. She swam, large awkward strokes and tried to think about James, but she couldn't find him in her memory. He was gone. She thought of her family; her mother, Carrie, her father, but they were part of another life and another time. Inside her, something had died. She bumped against something and saw it was a soldier—a man she had bathed only that morning—bobbing dead in the water. She immersed her head into the icy ocean and into the silence. So peaceful. Instinctively gasping for air, she surfaced again to the noise; the whistle of bullets, rancid smoke, the crunch of the ship, the yelling, screaming and splashing all around her. She yearned for the quiet below the surface. She could go to James. Around her, panicked voices continued to cry for help but the cold had numbed her body and she was so very tired.

Soon, she too floated lifelessly on the water's surface.

Chapter 36

Today ...

Rachael used her reporter status to her advantage. If her grandmother, Carrie, didn't know who owned that dilapidated old place, Rachael would find out one way or the other.

She pulled her car into the curb and parked around the corner from Autumn Manor. She didn't want to raise suspicion. Dressed in dark colours, Rachael grabbed her camera off the seat and locked the car. In her handbag she had a torch and a phone just in case she got into any trouble. She glanced around—it was close to noon on a week day—most people were either at work or at school with the exception of a few elderly folks who peeked out from behind their curtains or walked by with their shopping or dog on their daily walk.

I'll show you the pics, Gran, next Sunday. Rachael knew she would be scolded for sneaking into the house but also knew her grandmother would be fascinated. She intended to pitch the story to her editor—an editorial piece on the history of some of the town's oldest residences and their purposes today. Clearly Autumn Manor didn't have much of a purpose at the moment, but someone owned it and they weren't doing a thing with it.

Rachael stared at the front and snapped a couple of photos.

Imagine if I bought it, she thought. How ironic would that be? Not that I could afford it but … interesting idea.

She stood looking at the house with her head tilted to the side.

Imagine if I renovated it and Gran got to live here after all, before she died. The wheel would have gone full circle. But I could probably only afford to buy it with my inheritance from Gran …

Rachael thought about her grandfather, Anson. *He may not have been Gran's first love but he was good at looking after her, and ultimately me too. Or I could sell the house that Mum and Dad left me to make an offer on Autumn Manor.* Rachael sighed at the thought.

She strode to the side of the house, glanced around and when she was satisfied that the coast was clear, Rachael slipped through the gap in the wire fencing and entered the yard. She circled around to the back of the property. The deck continued all the way around the house. There was nothing of significance in the backyard except a recently added high timber fence on the far end of the property, a good half-acre away and those glorious bluebells.

At least there was still enough land left to give the property space and avoid the mansion on a handkerchief syndrome, she thought.

Rachael tested her weight on the back steps and finding them sturdy enough to stand on, she walked onto the deck. She didn't expect to find squatters present during the day and the security patrol signs on the fence might have deterred a few from setting up home.

Rachael tested the back door. It wasn't locked, just stuck. The timber frame had moved over the years and the door would not budge. She stood back; she never expected it would be easy to enter. The windows were closed and some were sealed with tape. She could peel back the paper and masking tape on a broken one and reseal it later, but that was a last resort.

She made her way around to the side and found another entrance door. Probably the laundry. She tried that door but it felt firmly locked. Rachael slammed her shoulder against the timber. The door moved a few inches, scraping on the frame. Enough to give her hope. She stood away, took a deep breath and pushed in again. This time it gave way quickly and she stumbled into the room unexpectedly.

It was as though she had allowed the house to breathe as warm, musty air wafted past her. Rachael looked around; the room was a large pantry, nothing worthy of a photo. Timber shelves lined the walls from floor to ceiling. Maybe this was the cook's larder, she thought. Rachael felt for the torch in her handbag, and then secured the door so it looked closed from the street, but stayed slightly ajar in case she needed a quick exit. She had seen too many horror movies not to be prepared.

With the windows boarded up or covered with newspaper, very little light entered the house. She turned on her torch and moved through the larder room, finding herself in a hallway. She opted to go right and then to the left, walking into a huge dining room. Rachael let out a low whistle in astonishment and turned around in a circle. The room was enormous with two broken chandeliers hanging limply from the ceiling and large wall to floor windows that showed glimpses of the front porch and street.

Gran was right—the detail, even though the house was deteriorating was still stunning. A carved timber frieze featuring little birds and flowers followed the ceiling line around the room. The ceiling itself was covered in decorative plaster moulds and paintings. She wandered through the room, through an ornate arch to another equally grand room with a fireplace.

This is your fireplace, Gran. There's the two angels, the little cherubs on either side. Rachael leant forward to look at the angels. She looked into the fireplace; there was no evidence that it had been used anytime recently. It was every bit as ornate as Gran had described except that bits of marble had been chipped away.

Rachael let out her breath; she realised she had been holding it until now. She steadied herself and tried to breathe normally. The house seemed to breathe with her—sounds of movement: scurrying, branches scraping, windows rattling and the occasional moan of the wind through the cracks in the window frames—but Rachael refused to let her imagination scare her. She snapped some photos and turned.

'Oh my God,' she gasped and stepped back. Her eyes were drawn up a staircase, an enormous staircase that branched out to rooms on both sides and at the top of the staircase, was a man, still intact and perfectly preserved in a huge, life-sized portrait. Rachael took a photo and stepped back to capture the grandeur of the staircase in more photos.

This place must have been something in its day when it was surrounded by acreage and filled with life and laughter, she sighed.

Rachael tested the stairs. *Best to hold onto the banister just in case.* She gripped a rail that moved slightly and ran her hand over the mahogany timber, still smooth to this day.

'How I would love to restore you to your former glory,' she told the house. She heard a noise and stopped.

Nothing. Was the noise from outside?

Rachael moved away from the stairs back to the front windows. She glanced through some peep-holes made by torn newspaper to the outside. No one was there; no one had spotted her entry. She turned and began to ascend the staircase again.

At the top, she read the inscription on the enormous frame

of the painting—'James Theroux, son of Frances and Audrey Theroux, 1939.'

'Frances … Frank,' Rachael whispered. 'Frank who hanged himself.' She stood back and looked at James. He was a handsome man; tall, with dark hair. His blue eyes were portrayed with a hint of compassion and mischief. He was probably about twenty or twenty-one at the time of the portrait sitting.

'So you are the great love of Aunt Lexie's life.' Rachael studied him. 'Hello James, I'm Rachael, Carrie's granddaughter,' she introduced herself and snapped some photos of James before turning back to look down the staircase. She imagined her grandmother wandering around in a ball gown.

She looked left, then right and decided to go right first. Along the hallway were a number of large rooms; bedrooms, powder rooms, wardrobes, what looked like a study from the remaining shelving on the wall. She made her way back to the staircase, stopped and listened, but again heard nothing untoward, although every little noise unsettled her slightly.

On the left, she found more large rooms with ornate ceilings, broken light fittings and faded wallpaper. She rubbed the rose wallpaper in one of the rooms and found the roses to be made of velvet. 'Must have cost a bit,' she said to no one.

At the end of the hallway on the left hand side of the stairs, there was another small staircase, of just five narrow stairs leading to a small door. She looked around, shrugged and went up.

Might as well see it all, she told herself.

She pushed open the door and found herself in a large room with a low ceiling. Rachael took a few photos. *Maybe the maid's quarters*, she closed the door on retreat.

Rachael returned to the staircase and made her way down, keeping a grip on the rail and imagining a crowd below. She went past the fireplace and into the front room to the right. Rachael took a few more photos. She stood back and studied the room; the windows could be seen from the front as you walked up the path. This room would get the morning sun. She looked up at the ceiling. And a noose could easily be placed through the exposed beams. She shuddered, snapped a shot and vowed not to show that shot to her grandmother.

*****

Rachael dropped into the front seat of her car and instinctively locked the door. She looked at the digital shots she had captured; they were good. Tomorrow, she would show her editor and grandmother and get some paid work time to research Autumn Manor.

She returned her gaze to the house.

Why was it still standing? Who owned it now? Why was it neglected? What photos of it still exist from its glory days? What was the sad history of the Theroux family? Rachael admonished herself for showing so little interest in her family history up until now. The two photo albums she had at home featured very little of her past. Her mother—the only child of Carrie and Anson—had died in a car accident when Rachael was five years of age. Her father lived another ten years before dying of a lung-related illness which smoking a pack of cigarettes a day hadn't helped. She had no siblings. Her great aunt Lexie had no children. Her grandfather, Anson, had died five years ago on New Year's Day. A terrible start to the year for her grandmother then.

Rachael thought of her grandmother. *It really is just you and me left in the world, Gran.* The thought unhinged Rachael. *Oh but I do have aunt Anna,* she thought of her grandfather's sister,

283

a rich divorcee on her second husband and umpteenth European cruise. Rachael barely knew her but had heard she was once a very glamorous woman and despite her age, was still regarded as such. Anna also had three sons, but Rachael had never met them. Aunt Anna had sent a Christmas card to Anson every year without fail when he was alive, accompanied by a generic typed letter that went to everyone, telling of her marvellous exploits over the past year and those of her wonderful sons, Huey, Duey and Luey. Rachael smiled at the thought.

I guess I'm not really alone in the world then. I could look up the cousins if I was desperate.

Rachael couldn't wait to begin her research and first of all, she would visit the archives at the library.

There must be some pre-war photos and even some press clippings about the goings-on at Autumn Manor.

She checked her phone for messages and finding herself commitment-free, turned her car towards the State Library.

Chapter 37

'I'd love to help. That's my area of specialty.' The library historian smiled at Rachael. 'I'll show you.' He rose from his desk, towering a good foot over her and headed to the centre of the floor where rows of microfiche machines sat, waiting to be brought to life.

Cute, Rachael checked him out from behind. *About my age, no ring on his finger. Hmm, this research might just pay off.*

He pulled out a chair in front of a microfiche reader and gestured for Rachael to sit down. 'I'm Aidan by the way. Aidan Murray.'

'Rachael.' She offered her hand. *Nice shake, not limp or sweaty.*

'Are you a student?' he asked.

'No, a reporter,' she said and saw him stiffen. 'But this is a personal project.'

'Oh good.' He smiled. 'Not that we don't like reporters, we get lots of journalists doing research here.'

'It's just that you have to be on your guard?' Rachael asked.

'We are a cautious lot; we don't want negative press. Our funding relies on goodwill.' Aidan shrugged. 'So you're looking for newspapers for this region around the time of the Second World War. Anything in particular?'

'Yes.' Rachael reached for her pad. 'I'm researching an old house on Main Avenue.'

'The haunted house where that poor man hanged himself during the war?' Aidan asked enthusiastically.

'Yes, that's the one! It belonged to a friend of my grandmother's.'

'Really? Uh, sorry about the hanging comment.'

Rachael smiled at him. 'No apology necessary, that's how I think of it too. Doesn't everyone? But it was called Autumn Manor in its heyday.'

'Autumn Manor,' Aidan repeated after her. 'I've watched that house for years. I hate seeing it so run down, it makes me quite angry. I even did a search on it once to see if I could find the owner and make an offer.'

'And?' Rachael leaned forward with renewed interest. *Fancy a librarian able to afford such a house.*

'It's owned by a trust. I wrote to them but got a curt reply saying the property was not for sale and thanking me for my interest.' Aidan shrugged. 'I don't get it—why would the owner let it get run down, it only depreciates more.'

'I don't get it either.' Rachael shook her head.

'Excuse me, just a sec.' He motioned he had to attend to a waiting patron. 'I'll be right back.'

'Of course.' Rachael was sure she was getting special attention. She hurriedly drew out her compact, powered her nose and checked her teeth. *All good.* She turned the microfiche reader on and looked at the screen, not sure where to start. Her eyes explored the rest of the library; modern and stark, all glass and white walls.

'Sorry about that.' He dropped down in a seat beside her. Rachael noticed his eyes were a dark brown and sparkled. 'And who does your grandmother think owns Autumn Manor now?'

'She doesn't know. She said she had a vague memory that her father said it was left to a charity, but it was so many years ago, the war was on, she had lost her sister, you know how it was—women didn't get involved much in money affairs then.'

Aidan nodded. 'True.'

Rachael continued. 'All she could tell me was that Frank—that's the man who hanged himself—and his wife, Autumn, uh Audrey, and their son, James, are all dead. My Aunt Lexie was married to James but died before ever having the chance to live in the house or be included in any updated Will, anyway that's Gran's take on it. There's no one left in that clan,' Rachael said. 'I've been driving past the house for years without a thought but now that I've found out Gran has a connection to it, I want to know everything.'

Aidan smiled. 'I'd want to know too; the house is in your blood, so to speak.'

'I have to confess that while it is personal, it's work for me too,' Rachael continued. 'I thought I might pitch a feature to my editor on some of the historic houses around the area and their backgrounds. That way, he pays me for some of my time on the project.'

'That sounds great. I'd love to do up an old character home.'

'So would I. To restore it to its former glory ...' Rachael almost let the cat out of the bag by mentioning the fireplace, but checked herself. She wasn't supposed to have been inside the house.

They exchanged looks and Rachael looked away, embarrassed.

A mutual interest and an attraction.

'Well, the best thing to do,' Aidan turned his attention to the microfiche, 'is to select a date or you'll find yourself reading everything and forgetting what you came in here for. You scroll through the pages like this.' He showed Rachael how to move the slides along, 'and if you find anything you like, you can print it out.'

'Fantastic, thank you.'

'So, put the date in here.' He showed her, 'and I'm over there if you need any help. Any help at all,' he said again.

'Thank you, Aidan.' Rachael looked up at him.

'My pleasure.' He smiled and walked back to his desk with Rachael staring after him.

*****

'Rachael what were you thinking? I can't believe you went into the house,' Carrie gasped as Rachael broke the news of her adventure to her grandmother.

'It was your idea! Besides it wasn't dangerous at all, Gran, honestly.' Rachael bit into a scone at the tea house that they visited every Sunday.

'You could have fallen through the floorboards or the roof might have collapsed on you or …' Carrie fanned herself with her handkerchief as if shocked. She pressed it to her face before folding it back into the lilac sleeve of her dress.

'I could have had an accident on the way to pick you up.' Rachael finished her sentence. 'You were the one who dragged me there last week, remember?'

'That's different. I don't mind if the house falls on me. I'm old and on borrowed time,' Carrie declared. 'So, what did you find?' she asked, enthusiastically.

Rachael grinned. 'Oh Gran, it was just like you said.' She reached into her bag and pulled out an envelope. 'I took photos.'

Carrie clapped her hands together. 'Oh my goodness, I haven't been inside Autumn Manor for … why it must be nearly seventy years … no … yes … that long, good grief!'

Rachael pulled the photos from the envelope. She sat them in her lap and looked at her grandmother.

288

'Do you want to see them?' she hesitated.

'Of course,' Carrie insisted.

'You won't be upset because of its state of disrepair or memories that might come back?'

'Of course I will,' Carrie smiled, 'isn't that what history is all about?'

'I guess.' Rachael hesitated and then handed the first photo to Carrie; the one of the staircase leading to the top floor.

'Oh my,' Carrie sighed, 'look at it now.' She touched the photo as though expecting to feel the texture of the banister rail. 'How it has deteriorated,' she sighed.

Slowly, Rachael handed over each photo, gathering the pile to hide the front room beam photo at the bottom.

Her grandmother paused with each shot, reliving her memories; her hand moved from her throat to her face and back to her lap.

'Ah the fireplace,' she smiled. 'I can't believe the little cherubs are still there! But they have been chipped away, haven't they?'

'Yes, it's a shame. How I would love to restore it, Gran. Wouldn't that be a project that would give you purpose? I know I renovated the house Mum and Dad left me, but this, this is something else,' she looked at each photo with her grandmother. Imagine breathing life back into her and living there surrounded by all the history. It would be like having roots.' Rachael passed another photo to her grandmother and Carrie gasped.

'James! The portrait, it's still there?' she looked up at Rachael.

'Yes.' Rachael looked at the photo of James' portrait at the top of the stairs—faded and in disrepair—but still there. 'It gave me an awful fright. I thought there was a man at the top of the stairs. How old was he when it was done, Gran, do you know?'

'It was his twentieth birthday, I remember it like it was yesterday.'

'He was very handsome.' Rachael studied the photo upside down.

'Wasn't he just?' Carrie agreed. 'He took my breath away until I fell in love with your grandfather.'

Carrie looked at the next photo, the inscription on the portrait. She reached for her handkerchief and dabbed her eyes.

'I'm sorry if I've upset you, Gran.' Carrie placed her hand on her grandmother's arm.

'No.' Carrie exclaimed, 'you have made my day. It's like all these memories were yesterday but yet a lifetime ago, it's a strange feeling.'

'Can I ask you some questions? About the family history?' Rachael asked not wanting to upset Carrie more.

'Yes dear, anything.'

'Where are Aunty Lexie and James buried?'

Carrie looked surprised. 'Well Lexie was buried at sea, in the Red Sea, where she drowned. James died in a prisoner of war camp. He's buried in Slovenia. Only his identity discs came home.' She gazed out of the window.

'I wish we could visit them,' Rachael continued.

'Why this sudden interest in history?' Carrie asked.

'Autumn Manor; taking me there last week ignited my interest,' Rachael said. 'And I guess I'm old enough now to be interested in my family history—it's nice to have something, a family connection ... with Mum and Dad gone, it's just you and me, Gran.'

'You have your Aunty Anna and her boys of course. Anna loved her brother, Anson, but all she ever wanted was to be kept in the manner to which she had become accustomed and to travel, and she succeeded at both. Her boys must be old men by now. They likely have sons or daughters about your age.'

'Cousins whom I wouldn't know if I fell over them, shame really.' Rachael sighed. 'But back to immediate family, why wasn't a headstone erected for Lexie or James?' Rachael persisted.

'I suppose that does seem odd now, but after the war it was just a different time. We were dealing with so much grief and many people never got their loved ones' bodies back. It was accepted. We had a mass of course, but no burial. Both of their names will be recorded on honour rolls. We could check ... somehow,' Carrie offered.

'I will,' Rachael brightened. 'There'll be records online now.'

Carrie handed back one of the photos. 'You know, your grandfather forbade me to go Autumn Manor once James and Lexie passed away. It was leased out anyway ... but it's amazing to see inside again.'

'But why?' Rachael asked.

'Why what, dear?'

'Why would he ban you, and, more importantly, why did you do what your husband told you to do?'

Carrie frowned. 'I rarely did what I was told; that was my problem, but this time it suited me. I knew Anson was protecting me, he was like that. He tried to keep problems from me, quite traditional in his ways and that suited me. Plus I never had much of a mind for business or finance,' she said. 'My memories of Lexie and James are still painful. They say time heals but Rachael, it doesn't heal, it just makes the pain a little duller. I didn't want to go to the house, I wanted to move forward and put the War behind us. Besides, your grandfather was a little jealous of Lexie and James, which didn't help. He loved Lexie once, did you know that?'

'You mean you were his second choice?' Rachael returned to her scone.

'I don't know that I was his second choice in the love stakes, but I don't mind being second to Lexie nowadays. It's an honour, she was a wonderful girl. But no, Lexie and Anson were supposed to marry, it was arranged. The two families wanted it, but Lexie didn't so she rebelled and accepted James's proposal. She really did love James. It would have been a marriage of convenience if she had married Anson … it was just for the family's sake not for love.'

'I'm glad people marry for love nowadays, well most of the time. But I guess to some degree, you marry within your own social network or education network most times.' Rachael thought about it.

'Yes, it's not dissimilar perhaps,' Carrie agreed. 'But I don't know that your grandfather ever loved Lexie. He never said anything to me that made me think it was anything other than duty. But he would have married her if she had said yes.'

'Did you love Grandfather? Or is that too rude to ask?' Rachael looked at her grandmother.

Carrie chuckled. 'As if that has ever stopped you, young lady.'

'True.' Rachael laughed.

'I didn't love him in my early years. I was in love with James. I knew James first, we were friends. I don't know whether I continued to love James because I couldn't have him or if I really ever did. I never thought much about Anson, he was always Lexie's so I suppose I always thought of him as a big brother. But one day—this was during the war—he arrived when I was working as a volunteer at the canteen. He was at the station seeing off a business friend and I bumped into him. He offered my mother and me a lift home and he was charming and warm and funny. I had never known him to be like that. I was a bit taken.'

Rachael touched her heart. 'That's romantic, Gran. So how long until he asked you out?'

'Well I heard he asked Father's permission first and of course that was granted. Father loved Anson. Within days a dozen cream long-stemmed roses arrived. You don't know how hard it was to get flowers during the war or how frivolous it was to spend money on them. They were beautiful and within a week, he was picking me up regularly in his grand car, with his dashing ways. He really did spoil me terribly and I was charmed by him.'

'Lexie must have been shocked, was she?' Rachael asked.

'She was, but she was happy too. She didn't like to think she had hurt me stealing James away and she thought we made a good pair, Anson and I. It was never love at first sight, but I did fall in love with him. There is no doubt that when I married your grandfather, I was in love with him and I loved him for all the years we spent together.'

Rachael refilled her grandmother's tea cup. 'That's so comforting to know, Gran. It gives me hope.'

'Yes, I live in hope too, dear, that you meet someone soon.' Carrie sighed. 'I can't live forever, and if I could just get you settled and maybe see a great-grandchild into the world!'

'Good grief,' Rachael exclaimed.

Her grandmother frowned.

'Oh alright, I'll see what I can do.' Rachael grinned. 'In fact, I've just met someone special … do you believe in love at first sight?'

Chapter 38

Rachael took a deep breath; butterflies, crazy at my age! It had been a long time since she had felt the rush of excitement she felt about Aidan or any man for that matter. She hadn't slept for thinking about him. He had a warmth and energy, he was conservative—she liked them conservative—and he seemed unpretentious. Plus he seemed to be genuinely interested in her project. This could be big, she told herself, but he might be married—he's not wearing a ring—he's probably got a girlfriend.

She looked herself over one more time. The blue blouse was a good choice for complementing her blue eyes and auburn hair and she was wearing her most flattering jeans with her favourite shoes; she could wear heels with Aidan given how he towered above her.

'Good as it's going to get,' she said, then smiled. *But pretty good!* She liked to be positive. Rachael grabbed her folder, bag, phone and keys. They had agreed to do some independent research each on Autumn Manor and come back together again in a few days to compare notes. *It was a safe way to ask me for a date, if that's what he's doing,* Rachael smiled. She breathed into her hand; *yep smells like mouthwash. Just go,* she scolded herself and raced out of the front door, locking it behind her.

Twenty minutes later, just on midday, she arrived outside the coffee shop on the lower level of the State Library and then she saw him. He was walking down the stairs from the library floor above and on looking up he saw her instantly. She could tell from his look that this was more than a research mission to him as well.

hat's your history I wonder? You must be early thirties or so and surely collected some baggage along the way. Married, divorced, gay, single, kids? Please be uncomplicated and available!

'Hello,' he said coming to her side. He extended his hand, changed his mind and leaned in to kiss her on the cheek. They entered the coffee shop exchanging small talk about the weather. He indicated a table. 'This do?'

'Perfect.' Rachael dropped into a chair and looked around her. 'Great view.' She glanced out through the open glass doors to the river. 'How have you been since I saw you … um, two days and three text messages-a-go?'

Aidan laughed. 'Fantastic. I've been on a mission.'

Rachael felt a wave of disappointment. *Perhaps he really was just excited about the project.*

'I haven't been the best investigative journalist,' she said. 'My boss had another project for me so I've only been able to do some internet research.' Her voice was somewhat more guarded now that she realised the attraction might be one way.

'I've hit the jackpot,' he said enthusiastically and then stopped. 'Sorry, I always get carried away when I'm on a research mission … my ex-wife used to complain that she was a library widow. I'll order first, then we can chill out and talk. He waved to the waitress and they both ordered coffee.'

Rachael's heart had momentarily stopped beating at the mention of his wife, but kicked into gear again on hearing she was officially the 'ex'. *Straight and divorced.* Her eyes surreptitiously searched his face. He was as good as she remembered and invented in his absence. *Concentrate, this is not the research mission that you are on.*

'So,' he fished, 'is your boyfriend interested in this house too or is he just seeing potential work ahead of him if you make an offer on it?'

'I think the prospect of renovating a house as run down as Autumn Manor would pretty much scare off any guy.' Rachael frowned. 'But at the moment, this week,' she teased, 'I'm not seeing anyone. I did break up with a guy about four months ago, so I've been reconnecting with my girlfriends and catching up on chick flicks.'

'Ah, yes, best to get as many of those in before the next round of dates. I've been doing the same thing in a more masculine way.'

Rachael laughed.

'I'm divorced, about three years ago now and I've dated a bit. Nothing much else to report.' He shrugged.

Rachael nodded. *Glad we got that sorted,* she thought happily. 'So, come on, tell me, I know you are dying to.'

'Am I that transparent?' Aidan smiled. 'Okay, I am. I found out who owns Autumn Manor.'

Rachael gasped in surprise. She clapped her hands together almost knocking the coffee from the waitress's hand as she set it down in front of them.

Aidan started. 'My boss, the chief librarian's brother works for the national trust. One call and I got a report.' He picked up a manila folder. Aidan flipped it open. 'This house has had an interesting history.'

'Really? Go on.' Rachael encouraged.

'Well, it belonged to the Theroux family for several generations. The original owner was Thomas Theroux. He bought the land and built the house in the early 1880s. Then, he married, and had one son and five daughters; two of those daughters surviving into adulthood.'

'I'm guessing his son survived if the house stayed in the Theroux family, because women couldn't own land in those days could they?' Rachael asked.

'Well, before 1870, if a woman was single or widowed she was allowed to own land, but if she married, then it became the property of her husband. But the Theroux daughters were lucky because in 1870 the Married Women's Property Act came in which allowed women to be legally the rightful owners of the money they earned and to inherit property. But it was irrelevant anyway ...'

'Why?' Rachael asked.

'Because when Thomas died aged fifty-seven,' he checked the notes, 'yep fifty-seven, the house went to his only son, Frances, who was the eldest anyway.'

'That would be Frank, the man who hanged himself,' Rachael mused.

'Yes. He lived in it all his life. He married a woman named Audrey.'

Rachael nodded. 'Gran said her nickname was Autumn and Frank named the house after her.'

'Ah, Autumn Manor.' Aidan put the pieces together. He sipped his coffee. 'How's your coffee?'

Rachael hit his arm. 'Stop teasing me ... come on ...'

Aidan grinned. 'Okay, okay. Frank died, as we all know, by hanging himself. That was in 1940. I found the newspaper clippings ...'

'So did I!' Rachael jumped in. 'He received a telegram saying his son was killed in action—World War II—his only child.'

'Yes, but he wasn't.' Aidan continued, 'I mean, he was the only child, but he wasn't killed in action, at least not then. It was a mistake.'

'Really?' Rachael stopped sipping and looked up at him. 'I didn't find that.'

'I searched for Frank's name and found a reference in a later clipping which said that his son, James, presumed dead, was found alive and had returned home.'

Rachael shook her head. 'How horrendous. Funny Gran didn't tell me that.'

'James did die eventually … but it was in a POW camp in Slovenia about a year later. Anyway, the house was supposed to go to James of course, but then James died and he was an only child.'

Rachael frowned. 'But there must have been distant relatives if Frank had two living sisters.'

Aidan shrugged. 'Maybe, but James married when he was on leave.' Aidan pulled out a copy of a marriage certificate.

'Wow, you really have given this some time,' Rachael said.

'I just downloaded it.' Aidan grinned, pleased with her praise. He handed the copy to her. The names of James Frances Theroux and Alexandra Mary Taylor were there with their signatures and that of the witnesses, Katherine Jane Mills and Frances Eileen Smedley. Rachael repeated the names.

'Alexandra … Lexie …' Rachael whispered. It was strange to see her name written—Gran's sister—it seemed so impersonal.

'You know of her?' Aidan asked.

'Yes, I do,' Rachael answered, keeping her history close to her chest.

Aidan continued. 'Then, about ten months after they were married, James died in that prisoner of war camp and since his wife, Alexandra, outlived him, she inherited the house, because women could own property by then. But Alexandra also died in the war, about four months after James. She was on a hospital ship. They often went down, torpedoed, even though they had huge red crosses all over them. So, by law, her family inherited the house and her closest living relative was …' Aidan stopped again and turned a page.

Samuel Taylor! Rachael thought, but did not interrupt him.

'Alexandra's father, Samuel Taylor,' Aidan confirmed. 'I found a press clipping about some local petition collecting signatures to preserve the area and Taylor was very much in favour because he refused to sell the manor's estate for subdivision. There was a lot of contention at that time about the large properties being sold off for subdivision with new housing estates springing up everywhere. Anyway, according to the records, he refused to sell it and instead, he leased it out.'

'Imagine running a business in that grand old mansion,' Rachael said.

'Amazing,' Aidan agreed and continued. 'It was leased out until about the late sixties to various businesses and then for another ten years it was used as a women's refuge centre. Probably because it has so many rooms. Then in the late seventies, it was boarded up. Don't know why, maybe it took too much work to maintain or maybe he had plans but never put them into effect. So nothing was done but the lawn cut and rates paid.'

Rachael couldn't speak. Her mind was processing the name. *Samuel Taylor … her paternal great grandfather, her grandmother's father who didn't like James because he married his daughter, but ended up inheriting James' house! Gran thought it was left to a charity as dictated by the Theroux's Will or was she just told that?*

'Shall I go on?' Aidan continued. 'Keeping up?'

Rachael nodded.

'You're not sorry you began this now are you?' He frowned at her.

'No, definitely not, I'm just absorbing it all,' Rachael assured him. 'I've been walking, or running actually, past that house since childhood, so I'm a bit blown away now to hear about its history.'

Aidan continued. 'Quite sad isn't it? Makes it more real when you think of the lives that have come and gone and been cut short. Anyway, it seems Samuel Taylor owned it all that time. When he died in 1985, according to this file, he left it to his son-in-law, Anson Howell.'

Anson! Grandfather owned it … and he never told Gran. Why wasn't she told at the reading of the Will? Rachael's eyes had become huge.

Oblivious, Aidan continued. 'Then, for a number of years there was a bit of wrangling,' Aidan referred to his file again. 'I'm a bit short on detail here, but it looks like after Samuel Taylor died, a few of Frank Theroux's relatives came out of the woodwork and tried to make a claim on it.'

Rachael nodded. 'That must have been his two remaining sisters or their descendants.'

'Mm, not sure because the names are not Theroux, but if they are sisters or nieces of Frank, they may have married and have different names,' Aidan shrugged and reeled off the name of the claimants.

Rachael shook her head. 'I don't know those names either.'

'But,' Aidan said, 'the original transfer to Alexandra via marriage was legal and after close to ten years of tying up the courts, while the house sat boarded up and continuing to deteriorate, the contenders lost and ownership was retained by

Anson Howell as decreed in Samuel Taylor's Will. It was about 1995 when all that was finalised.'

'So the last rightful owner of the house was Anson Howell,' Rachael whispered, thinking out aloud.

'So you know this Anson person?' Aidan asked.

'I sure do … but keep going, I'll explain what I know when you finish.' Rachael's stomach churned, worried that there was a twist to come and someone else had since taken possession.

'That's it. Since the property challenge got dropped in about 1995, it has been in Anson Howell's hands, just managed by a family trust through an accountancy firm that keeps paying the rates and for lawn maintenance! No house maintenance obviously.' Aidan closed the file. 'I don't get it! Why would they let it go to ruin?'

Rachael shook her head, trying to process her thoughts. 'Wow, Aidan, you have really excelled on this one.'

He grinned and shrugged. 'I love a research challenge, I love the dig. When I was a kid I wanted to be a palaeontologist and dig up prehistoric fossils, but I loved books so much that I thought I'd dig there instead—much cleaner.' He sat back and pushed the folder away. 'Another coffee?' he asked.

'Tea please.' She stopped to notice the other people around her for the first time in the last half hour. Aidan ordered tea and coffee; Rachael turned to watch the river and the people walking along the path.

'So what do you know?' Aidan's voice brought her back to the present.

Rachael exhaled, 'well I know for a fact that Anson Howell died in 2001. So for the past nine years since his death, that firm, the accounting firm, has continued to uphold the estate in the same manner as before … why?'

'Seems weird that whoever has inherited Autumn Manor now doesn't sell it or do it up,' Aidan agreed.

'Maybe they don't know they own it,' Rachael thought out loud. 'Maybe they just know there's a parcel of wealth and the accountants are managing it.'

Aidan scoffed. 'Seriously? If you scored an inheritance wouldn't you want to know everything it consisted of?'

Rachael studied him. 'Not if you were nearly ninety and your husband, Anson, had always looked after your affairs. Then when he passed, the financial side of your life too was always managed for you, and you thought the house had been left to a charity group. Why would you get involved now when your husband had appointed a firm to do it on your behalf?' She continued assembling her thoughts as she went. 'What if you never knew you owned the house … maybe if your husband was worried that you might want to restore it to its former glory and your love for him might wane while you rekindled feelings for someone else … even if it was a lifetime ago … or if he thought it might bring back the pain of war and too many unhappy memories of your sister and brother-in-law.'

Aidan frowned. 'What am I not getting here?'

Rachael smiled at him. 'You know my surname is Price, don't you?' she asked.

Aidan nodded. 'It was on your card.'

'My parents were both killed in a car accident when I was twelve …'

'God, that's terrible.'

Rachael continued. 'My mum was Margaret Howell and she married my father, Lawrence Price.'

'Margaret Howell …' Aidan repeated and leaned forward in his seat with interest.

'After the accident, my grandmother and grandfather raised me. My gran is Carrie Howell.'

Aidan's eyes narrowed as he played the name back in his head. 'Howell. So your grandfather was Anson Howell?'

'And my great grandfather was Samuel Taylor.'

Aidan let out a low whistle and fell back in his seat.

Rachael continued. 'Gran said her father, Samuel Taylor, hated James and Frank Theroux, but loved Anson like a son. I bet when he inherited the Theroux house he kept it out of spite. I bet that my great grandmother Moira, and Gran, never knew it was in the family or they would have insisted on looking after it.'

'But do you really think your grandfather, Anson, was protecting your gran by not telling her about Autumn Manor?'

Rachael shrugged. 'Gran was probably never involved in the finances and I think Grandad knew she once loved James and knew she loved that house. I suspect he was just going to let it pass to the beneficiary of their Wills and not ever tell her. Spare her the decision of what to do.'

Aidan leaned forward, locking his hands on the table and staring intently at Rachael as he asked, 'and who is the beneficiary of Anson and Carrie's Wills?'

Rachael smiled. 'I am, Aidan. My Gran owns Autumn Manor and one day, I will.'

Chapter 39

Rachel called up the website, following the instructions from the Commonwealth War Grave's Commission. She spooled through the names in the 'Debt of Honour' list of Britain's fallen.

'So many,' Rachael sighed.

'Yes,' Carrie agreed, sitting beside her. 'So many.'

'Here it is!' Rachael stopped at a name.

'Alexandra Theroux,' Carrie said aloud. She touched the name on the screen.

'Doesn't seem enough … just one line amongst all these others, does it, Gran?'

Carrie straightened up. 'No, but they live on in the memory of their loved ones and of course, in your freedom, my girl. But you know that. Go to the 'M' section, dear.'

Rachael scrolled down. Carrie pointed to another name.

'And here is Kathryn Mills. Kitty, your Aunt Lexie's best friend. What an amusing girl Kitty was, always high spirited.'

Rachael studied the name. 'So how did Kitty die?'

'She was a VAD, a volunteer nurses' aid, the same as Lexie. They were together on the hospital ship when it was sunk by the Germans.'

'At least they died together,' Rachael said.

'Hmm, they died in the same attack but I don't know that they were together.' Carrie leaned back in her chair. 'Kitty was engaged to a doctor whose name escapes me now—a nice fellow. Anyway, he survived the torpedoing. After the war, he came to pay his respects and he told us that they couldn't find Lexie in the final moments of the ship's sinking. You have to realise there were hundreds of injured soldiers, nurses and crew aboard and of course with the noise and I imagine panic and fire, well they got separated. The doctor said he and Kitty called out for Lexie but then they were separated when he went to help the captain fight the fire on deck. He never saw Lexie or Kitty again. You can imagine his devastation; he was engaged to marry Kitty.'

'Dreadful.' Rachael shook her head. 'They were so brave. It must have been terrifying.'

'I can't imagine it.' Carrie shook her head. 'I've tried too many a time so I could feel closer to Lexie and understand her last hours on this earth, but I never found anyone who survived who could tell me about her death. One soldier remembered her helping him to the rail, but he was the only survivor I could find who recalled her.'

They sat in silence for a while. Eventually Rachael said, 'I'll see if I can find James' name.' She entered his name and located the record. 'Here it is. Apparently he's commemorated at the British and Commonwealth War Cemetery at Suda Bay. It's on the northern coast of Crete. I'm glad we did this,' she added.

'Me too.' Carrie took her hand. 'Now, I believe we have an accountant to visit!'

*****

Rachael opened the door to the accountant's reception foyer for Carrie and followed her in. Carrie was dressed for business, in a dark blue suit, stockings, medium heeled shoes and a blue and white matching hat.

'Thank you, dear.' Carrie smiled entering the room.

The offices of Bertram, Barnett & Guner Accountants were in a restored terrace house on the outskirts of the city in an area that had recently been gentrified. No doubt it was unrecognisable to anyone who previously knew it. The outside of the building was pristine white with charcoal trim, while the inside was contemporary with white tiles and modern art. Along the walls were black and white head shots of the founding partners through to the modern photos of the latest Bertram, Barnett and Guner in office.

Rachael announced their arrival to the receptionist and they took a seat and waited.

Today, the senior partner was to meet with them, a Mr. Bernard Bertram, Chartered Accountant, who had worked in the practice for just over fifty years, having started his articles as a fifteen-year-old. He proudly told Rachael on the phone that he had had the pleasure of knowing her father prior to his early and unfortunate demise and also her grandfather, Anson. He had even met Samuel Taylor, her great grandfather, whom he had found very forbidding when he was a young accountant still wet behind the ears. Rachael liked him.

They had barely sat down when the door of one of the offices opened and Mr. Bernard Bertram stepped out. He was dressed immaculately in a very expensive grey suit with a crisp white shirt and blue tie and greeted them with a welcoming smile.

'Mrs. Howell and Ms Price, how delightful to see you.' Mr. Bertram, reached for both of their hands in turn, shaking them briefly before showing the ladies through to his office.

He offered tea but they declined.

'So,' he settled into the large bottle green dimpled leather chair behind his desk, 'can I just say it has been our privilege to manage your family's business for almost the past century. We are very proud of that,' he gushed.

Rachael turned to Gran who smiled warmly at him.

'And, may I say, Mr. Bertram, how grateful I am that you have done so and done so admirably. Please understand I am not here to change that arrangement. It has been a great comfort, especially since my husband's departure.'

'Thank you, that's very kind. As you can imagine, Mr. Howell was very particular in his instructions and we are committed to safeguarding your future financial security.'

Carrie laughed. 'I imagine he was particular. But today, I wanted to speak with you concerning a matter of the heart, a bit of history you might say. History which will change the future, hence my dear granddaughter, Rachael, my only living blood relative, is here with me.'

Mr. Bertram acknowledged Rachael with a smile and nod.

'May I be forthright?' Carrie asked as she placed her hands on her lap.

'Of course,' Mr. Bertram encouraged.

'The house and land at 1 Arcadia Lane—am I correct in understanding that this property was inherited by my sister, Alexandra, through marriage, then by my father, Samuel and in turn by my husband, Anson? I believe it is now mine, is that correct?'

'Ah, Arcadia Lane.' Mr. Bertram opened the Howell file. 'I have instructions from Mr. Howell on that property.' He found the page. 'Yes.'

'Yes? Yes I own it? Yes I was not to be told about it?' Carrie enquired.

'It was always part of the estate ... it may not have been specified ...' he began to stumble.

'Mr. Bertram, you are doing a wonderful job for me. But on Anson's death, when we went through the assets, you never mentioned this house ...'

Mr. Bertram began to interrupt but Carrie talked on.

'Now I know I am old, but I would remember if you told me I had inherited Autumn Manor. In fact, I wish I had known that it passed to my family on Lex ... uh, Alexandra's death.'

She leaned forward as though conveying a confidence. 'My father told me that James' Will had not been changed in time to make Alexandra the beneficiary and that the house was left to a charity. Naturally, I believed this. I was a young girl, I didn't know any better, and over the years I saw the house leased out to businesses and later to a charity group.'

Mr. Bertram cleared his throat and adjusted his tie. He began to speak but Carrie continued.

'Mr. Bertram, my father did a great injustice to me. I loved that house and he knew that it meant a lot to me. But Anson?'

'Mrs. Howell, I apologise,' Mr. Bertram continued. 'But your husband was very strict in his instructions about this property. He said the house would cause you grief and bring back unhappy memories. He didn't want it sold in case it drew your attention, but we were to continue its basic maintenance and it was to be inherited in due course according to the provisions of your own Will.'

Carrie nodded. 'I see. I'm sure he meant to protect me and I take some responsibility, I never asked after it again of course, I suppose I couldn't bear to see it occupied by strangers and businesses when it was once part of our family ... such a strong memory and link to my sister and James.'

'Yes, I see,' Mr. Bertram said, 'but your husband was most adamant about it, he said you had suffered enough.'

Carrie sighed. 'Mr. Bertram, I am a very wealthy woman am I not?'

Mr. Bertram took a sip of water. 'I think it would be fair to say that you would not easily be able to spend your wealth even if you lived to be a hundred and worked very hard at spending it.'

Carrie smiled. 'Heaven forbid I should live until I'm one hundred, Mr. Bertram, but I have new instructions for you.'

Rachael noticed his eyes widen. He sat up straighter and reached for his pen.

Carrie continued. 'Effective immediately, I want the property title for 1 Arcadia Lane transferred to my granddaughter, Rachael Price.'

Rachael gasped. 'Gran, you don't have to do that. Think about it …'

Carrie patted Rachael's hand. 'I have thought about it, my dear. I am old, you are of an age where you can restore that home to its former glory and then if you choose not to enjoy it for yourself, you can sell it and profit … but I suspect you will want to enjoy it.'

'Oh Gran, I've dreamt of living in that grand old manor!'

'Mr. Bertram,' Carrie returned her attention to her accountant. 'I would also like a significant proportion of my wealth placed in an account for Rachael with access available on her signature only. This is so she has the funds to undertake the renovation. I have a figure in mind.' Carrie opened her purse and pulled out a piece of paper. She looked at Rachael apologetically. 'In my day, women didn't talk of money, dear.' She handed the piece of paper to Mr. Bertram. 'Can you transfer that amount please?'

'Of course, Mrs. Howell, but I must caution you that it might not be in your best interest to give away fifty percent of your estate at this point in time,' he stammered.

Rachael gasped again. 'Gran, no, that's too much, way too generous …'

Carrie raised her hand in protest. 'Mr. Bertram said himself, I wouldn't live long enough to spend my wealth. What's the fun in having it stashed away and you not inheriting it until you are well into your middle years? No, Mr. Bertram, I will still have more than ample to live on won't I, even if I live to one hundred?'

Mr. Bertram smiled and nodded. 'Yes, Mrs. Howell, you will indeed have more than you'll ever need even under this new arrangement. Even should you live to the age of two hundred, you won't be found wanting. You could easily have stayed in the Howell family home and hired staff …'

'No, no, I didn't want to rattle around there by myself. I have friends at Hope Town.'

'Then consider it done, Mrs. Howell,' Mr. Bertram announced.

Carrie nodded at Rachael, 'it is done, my dear.'

Rachael shrieked in delight. 'Oh, my God, Gran, I don't believe it. We own Autumn Manor. We are going to restore it to how it used to look. You can guide and direct me on all the finer details. It will be mind-blowing … we can make it exactly like it once was, it will be our project.'

Carrie laughed and turned to Mr. Bertram and nodded. 'See, everyone's happy. I can't wait to see the old house loved again, but you must put your own mark on it, Rachael dear, for a new generation. It will be a great tribute to James and Frank and my Lexie.'

Mr. Bertram smiled. 'I'll have the papers drawn up and get back to you next week.'

'Next week?' Carrie said alarmed. 'I could be dead by then. How about tomorrow?'

Mr. Bertram looked at Carrie and Rachael and at his diary. 'Well it's very short notice and there's quite a bit of work to do ...'

'Come, come, Mr. Bertram, these are standard contracts are they not? And as you said, we are long-time clients.'

'Of course.' He glanced at his diary. 'Two-thirty tomorrow for the signing?'

Carrie looked at Rachael. 'Will that suit us my dear?'

'Yes, please!' Rachael practically squealed.

Carrie rose. 'Thank you, Mr. Bertram. Two-thirty it is. And we want to access the property immediately afterwards please.' Carrie turned to Rachael, 'perhaps you might want to bring your researcher friend and ask him to bring a torch.'

Rachael threw her arms around her grandmother.

'I can't believe it ... Autumn Manor ... come on, Gran. We have a lot of planning to do! Thank you Mr. Bertram, thank you!' She rushed to the door and opened it for Carrie who, still chuckling, passed through it with a wave and a nod to the receptionist.

Chapter 40

Twelve months later …

Carrie Howell and her granddaughter, Rachael Price, stood on the terrace, looking out over Autumn Manor's manicured grounds. Soon, nearly a hundred guests would be arriving for the house warming party, traipsing across the gardens, dancing by the fountain and sipping champagne on the terrace. But for now, it was peaceful. Carrie closed her eyes and breathed in deeply—the air offered a heady mix of freshly cut grass and pungent roses, carried by the slightest breeze—it was promising to be a perfect evening. The only sound that could be heard was the occasional stray musical note floating across the grounds as a jazz band set up their instruments in the gazebo.

The house was restored in all its glory; it had taken twelve intense months of full-time project management by Rachael and a lot of input from Carrie and Aidan. The fireplaces, the furnishings, the chandeliers, the staircase—all as Carrie remembered. The house glowed from top to bottom; the smell of fresh paint and polished floors gave it a new feeling. Champagne flutes sparkled on tables adorned with well-pressed white tablecloths and small lights decorated the pillars and trees, ready to sparkle as night encroached. Inside, through the French doors and across the waxed floors, the kitchen was quiet. All the food had been delivered and hospitality students from the local technical college were being briefed by their teacher on their various roles tonight as waiters and waitresses.

At the top of the stairs, James' portrait held court over a wall of family photographs, finally merging the Theroux, Taylor and Howell families.

Carrie opened her eyes. She turned to Rachael and took her hand.

'How happy James and Lexie would be to see the house like this. It's marvellous what you have done my dear, breathtakingly marvellous.'

Rachael leaned into her grandmother and kissed her cheek.

'You made it possible Gran, isn't it amazing to see it come alive? Isn't she a grand old girl?' Rachael spoke as though she knew the house personally. 'I hated seeing her run down, I think everyone who passed it thought that.'

'You made it happen, dear, you and Aidan,' Carrie said. 'I just financed it but you breathed life back into this home with a passion. Your passion and your future.'

'Hello there,' a voice called and both ladies turned to look across the lawn.

Carrie smiled and waved seeing the delight in her granddaughter's face as Aidan Murray walked across the lawn towards them, smiling. He was striking in his black-tie suit with his dark unkempt hair falling over his eyes. His arms were laden with an enormous bunch of long-stemmed white roses.

Carrie heard Rachael sigh, struck by his handsomeness. At the bottom of the terrace steps, he stopped and bowed. Both ladies laughed.

'Mrs. Howell, Ms. Price, may I say how delightful you both look.'

'Well, thank you young man, you are most kind,' Carrie chuckled.

'And you look good enough to eat,' Rachael added. 'Those roses are stunning.'

'Yes, they are,' he said and mounting the steps, he unexpectantly stopped in front of Rachael's grandmother and presented Carrie the bouquet. 'Mrs. Howell, welcome back. I imagine it must be like a reunion or homecoming.'

Carrie gasped and tears filled her eyes.

'Oh Aidan, how very, very, thoughtful,' she said, surprised. 'Why, you've made me cry.' She reached into her sleeve withdrawing a dainty white handkerchief and dabbed her eyes. She looked around. 'Yes, it is a bit like coming back after a long absence to find all your memories intact.'

Rachael blinked back tears.

Aidan stepped up onto the terrace beside Rachael. He kissed her and put his arm around her shoulders as they looked out over the lawn and the party preparations.

'I can't believe we've finally got to this day,' he sighed. 'After all the labouring, tears and take-aways.'

'I know.' Rachael laughed. 'There were a few times there when I thought if I painted one more inch of timber, or pulled out one more weed, or one more tradesman didn't come when he promised, I would scream. But look at it now.'

Carrie smiled at Aidan and he winked back.

'I saw that!' Rachael exclaimed. 'What are you two up to?'

'Nothing, nothing,' Carrie assured her. 'I have to go inside to get a vase for these lovely roses, please excuse me.' She sighed again as she entered the house with its sprawling staircase inviting her to climb to the upper level and the little cherubs shining on the fireplace.

*****

'Come for a walk with me?' Aidan took Rachael's hand and led her down the front steps.

'But the guests will be arriving soon.' She looked back at the house.

'We've got time. Besides your gran's there. Just a quick walk, around the garden.'

'Okay,' she frowned allowing herself to be led away.

They walked down the path, past the statue-surrounded fountain where birds flew in and out nipping at the water and where soon, guests would wade in various stages of dress and undress as the night rolled on. They passed the restored gazebo where the jazz band warmed up with *I've Got You Under My Skin*.

'Did I mention that you look stunning tonight?' Aidan cast a glance over Rachael's silver ankle-length gown that hugged her figure and showed it off to her best advantage.

'I can't recall whether you said that to me or Gran,' Rachael teased.

'Two generations of beauty.' Aidan smiled. 'I'm glad we made it a black-tie night, it gives it that edge of importance so befitting this house.'

'And glamour,' Rachael agreed.

He led Rachael off the path to a timber bench. Once, the bench had been turned the other way and had overlooked the lake behind them, but that part of the property had been sold off some time ago. Now it was positioned perfectly to be able to sit and fully appreciate the grandeur of the house.

'This is nice.' Rachael said sitting next to Aidan.

'A moment of peace before we spend the rest of the night circulating and being hospitable.' Aidan turned slightly and dropped to one knee in front of Rachael.

He heard her gasp with surprise. Aidan smiled and taking a strand of her auburn hair between his fingers, moved the lock from her face. He touched her cheek and then cupped her small face in his hands.

'Rach, the last eighteen months have been the happiest days of my life. You captivated me from the moment you walked into the library. There was a connection. I've made one mistake before in the love stakes but it has taught me about giving and committing. I'm not afraid to commit to you and I hope you feel the same way about me. I love you, Rachael Price.'

His face was level with hers now and he moved closer to kiss her. He could hear her short, sharp breath as he closed his eyes waiting to feel the touch of her lips on his own. He inhaled her scent and felt the returned press of her lips on his.

Aidan pulled away, opening his eyes to look into hers. 'Rachael, will you marry me?'

Rachael smiled as tears ran down her face.

'Yes,' she whispered, 'definitely, definitely, yes!'

Aidan laughed and stood with a groan, dropping beside her onto the bench. 'Thank God, I might not have been able to get up again if I had to convince you.'

He held her close and kissed her, then pulled away.

'I almost forgot.' He reached into his coat pocket, pulled out a small black jewellery box and turning it to face Rachael, he opened it.

She gasped, 'Oh Aidan, it's stunning.'

He took out the ring and returning the empty box to his jacket pocket, he took Rachael's left hand and slipped it onto her engagement finger.

'I know it's risky buying a ring and not taking you with me,' he said, 'but this is a special ring.'

'It's Gran's engagement ring, I remember now, I've only ever seen it once before because she prefers just to wear the wedding band.' Rachael traced her finger along the deep blue sapphire stones around the enormous solitaire diamond.

'Yes, she's been in on the secret. This was her mother's engagement ring too. It would have gone to your gran's sister, being the eldest, but when she died, Carrie was next in line. When I spoke to her about proposing to you, she offered it and hoped you would accept it. I'm happy to buy you a ring though, don't get me wrong, if you want something else …'

Rachael hushed him. 'It's perfect. I couldn't think of anything more perfect.'

'I had it cleaned and fitted. I snuck one of your rings into the jewellers so he could cut it to the right size.'

Rachael looked away from her diamond-studded finger and smiled at him. 'I love you.'

'I love you too.' He leaned in to kiss her.

'Do you think you'll take my name? Be Mrs. Rachael Murray?' he asked.

'No.'

'Oh.' His face fell. 'I understand … I guess people know you as Price … especially after this high profile project,' he nodded at the house, 'plus there's your work and friends to think of …'

'I will be Ms. Rachael Murray, not Mrs.,' she said.

A grin spread over Aidan's face. 'Got me again,' he put his hand over his heart.

'I've got the perfect house for us to begin our life in,' she smiled at him.

*****

Carrie saw them coming back across the lawn, holding hands.

From afar, he looked like James; dark, tall and handsome. She watched as her beloved granddaughter stared at him in adoration, raising her hand to look at the engagement ring promising her future happiness. Rachael looked up and seeing Carrie on the terrace, waved, turning her bejewelled hand to show her grandmother.

Carrie clapped her hands together and sighed with happiness.

'It is your time now, Rachael and Aidan,' she whispered. 'Welcome home.'

Epilogue

After Lexie's and Kitty's deaths at sea, the war raged for another three years, until the final battles and the German surrenders took place in late April and early May 1945.

Nothing could or would ever be the same even though families were eventually reunited or heard news of their loved ones. Here is what we know of the men and women who feature in this tale.

Sandy—Corporal Shaun Gibson survived the camp and returned home after the war. He tried to return to teaching, but he was dismissed after arriving at work drunk and being unable to perform his duties on numerous occasions. He fatally shot himself the Christmas after his return.

Misty—Private Alastair Mistoff returned home and resumed work as a baker in his father's bakery. He married a local girl and had three sons.

Private Daniel Briton—was shot for stealing food in the camp, three months after James Theroux's death. Seven other men were shot with him to make an example of young Briton.

The Stooges—the four young men whom the platoon nicknamed the Stooges—twins, George and Will Leadbetter, Jim Davies and Matthew Pearce—were separated at Dunkirk. George and Will were injured but survived, returning to battle once declared fit and able. They survived the war. Jim Davies lost both legs and was honourably discharged, Matthew Pearce was fatally wounded.

Liz and Gerald both survived the hospital ship's sinking. They were rescued and returned to Alexandria where they joined another hospital ship two months later. They were married after the war in a civil ceremony. Gerald continued to work in the hospital environment and Liz went into training. She trained hundreds of nurses over the years and was a much-loved teacher. Gerald died at the age of seventy-one. Liz outlived him by ten years. They had no children.

Esther (Esther Anne Johnston) who nursed with Lexie and Kitty in London, was reunited with her husband after the war. Her husband began a milk run and they had four children, twin boys, a girl and another son. Esther did not return to nursing.

Franny (Frances Eileen Smedley) attracted many men and received some wonderful gifts during the time that the girls shared a room at the London hospital, but there was only ever one man for her. After the war, she took her vows and became a Catholic nun. Franny took the name of Saint Frances in the Good Samaritan Order and taught religion and mathematics at a private girls' school until her retirement. She died at the age of eighty-two.

Anna Howell divorced her first husband after a year of marriage and remarried within two years. She had three sons with her second husband. She died of heart failure at the ripe old age of 95, but never returned home to be introduced to her great neice, Rachael or to see Carrie, her sister-in-law, again.

Jonathan and Mrs. Atkinson were dismissed once Samuel Taylor took charge of Autumn Manor. Mrs. Atkinson remained in the same town as her sister until the end of her days. She went to mass on the anniversary of Frank Theroux's death every year for the rest of her life. Jonathan retired after his dismissal from Autumn Manor. He lived with his daughter until he met another lady in the town and remarried at 65 years of age. They lived to a ripe age.

Doctor Adam Gardam searched for Kitty for the remaining three years he spent in service aboard the various hospital ships hoping she may have somehow survived. Her body was never found. He returned to England after the war and worked in the London General Hospital until retirement. While on duty, he met another nurse and married within six months of meeting her. They had a daughter who died at birth and a son who went on to play professional cricket for England.

THE END

Resources:

This novel is a work of fiction, however I have tried to be historically accurate with dates and circumstances. The characters and events are fictional.

I am indebted to those who shared their stories and historians who captured the information for public record. I acknowledge the exceptional BBC World War II People's War website which archived WW2 memories from the public. Of great assistance were the resources such as World War 2 troop ships site:
- http://www.bbc.co.uk/ww2peopleswar/
- http://www.ww2troopships.com/

Editorial support:

Thank you to journalist, Chris Adams, for his assistance with research throughout the writing of this novel.

Thank you also to the Atlas Productions support network: Sally Odgers for proofreading and valuable insight; Editor, Michael whose insider knowledge was highly valued; Merle Goltz for an additional set of eyes; and, my writing partner Atlas, for companionship and support.

About the author:

After studying English Literature and Communications at universities in Queensland, Australia, Helen Goltz has worked as a journalist and marketer in print, TV, radio and public relations. She was born in Toowoomba and has made her home in Brisbane.

Visit the website and blog at: www.helengoltz.com
Or Facebook at: www.facebook.com/HelenGoltz.Author
Follow on Twitter at: @helengoltz

Also by Helen Goltz: Historical mystery with a dash of romance – the *Miss Hayward & the Detective* series:

Murder at the Freak Show

Matilda Hayward is determined to have a career, after all, it is 1888! While reporting for the Women's Journal newspaper, Matilda is sent to cover the visiting 'Freak Show' and to interview Mrs Anna Tufton, a giantess. During the interview, the giantess slips a note to Matilda begging for her help to escape from the show she is forced to do by her husband. But when the giantess's husband is found murdered, the giantess is a likely suspect.

Matilda enlists her lawyer brother, Amos, to help prove the giantess is no killer and to free her from a life of exploitation. But a close family friend, Detective Thomas Ashdown – who has feelings for Matilda having known her since childhood – would prefer Matilda was nowhere near his murder case. There is mystery, danger, and love afoot!

The Artist's Missing Muse

Beautiful muse, Miss Sapphire Reubens, the inspiration for her lover's latest art exhibition, is missing – items of her clothing found in the river. Worryingly, Miss Matilda Hayward and her fellow writer for the Women's Journal, Miss Alice Doran, enjoyed a preview of the inspired work featuring Miss Reubens immersed in water. Was it a death portrait?

When another two artists are found murdered and posed in the manner of their paintings, Matilda and her new beau, Detective Thomas Ashdown, fear the artist's inspiration may have come from ill means. There is mystery, passion and love afoot!

Mystery at the Asylum

Miss Matilda Hayward has a nose for a story which serves her well as a writer for the Women's Journal newspaper. Her beau, Detective Thomas Ashdown, is not quite as enthusiastic about her role. Nevertheless, as suggested by her editor, Mrs Lawson, Matilda intends to extend herself and seek more life experience to improve her writing. So when her brother, Elijah, takes up a doctor's position at the Asylum for the Insane, Matilda takes the opportunity to volunteer.

Joined by her illustrator friend, Miss Georgina Urry, the two ladies are thrust into the mystery of a number of strange asylum deaths as patients believe they can fly. When Thomas is sent to investigate the death of a former asylum patient who threw herself from the city hall clocktower, their worlds collide. Now the race is on to find the sinister threat dwelling inside the dark and gloomy walls of the asylum.

There is secrecy, danger, and love afoot!

The Mortician's Clue

Miss Matilda Hayward has been assigned her first book review for the Women's Journal newspaper and she is very much enjoying Mr Linton Turner's novel, The Pyjama Girl Mystery, until it comes to life. When a young lady is found murdered and left on the church steps dressed only in blue satin pyjamas – just like in the plot of the novel – the author immediately comes under suspicion. But no one can identify the victim.

Matilda's beau, Detective Thomas Ashdown, is on the case, and with his partner, Detective Harry Dart, they hire a talented mortician, Miss Phoebe Astin, to illustrate the deceased lady for identification purposes. After Matilda and her friend, Miss Georgina Urry, make Phoebe's acquaintance, the three ladies find themselves unwillingly caught in a battle of words and hearts between an author and a poet with deadly intent. There is secrecy, danger, and love afoot!

The Jesse Clarke Series – cosy mysteries:

Death by Sugar

Private investigator, Jesse Clarke, thought sugar was such a friendly substance, until it appears in two of her cases for all the wrong reasons. Traces of sugar were connected to a bomb that blew up her client's Mercedes and could sugar have duped the immune system of a client's mother over thirty years ago, resulting in death? Juggling the two cases—one in the present and one in the past—Jesse finds herself talking to the living and the dead to get results.

Death by Disguise

Private investigator Jesse Clarke knew it wasn't going to be a normal week when Spiderman steals a collection of costumes made for the next Comic Con, Batman drops in to warn her that all is not as it seems and two dead people are spotted alive but their death certificates say otherwise. Jesse finds herself talking to witches, superheroes and morticians to solve her two cases!